Maxwell Street Blues

by

Marc Krulewitch

(Originally Published by Alibi/Penguin Random House.
All Rights Reverted to the Author on September 12, 2018)

I0592723

1

"I feared you wouldn't know me."

His ashen face did not remind me of the quaint grifter or winsome confidence trickster. Nor did I see an aging racketeer broken by prison. But I knew Bernie Landau—my father. He found me through "contacts" who specialized in making sure people were found. He wore dingy gray slacks with an argyle cardigan sweater that draped his eighty-year-old frame as though slung over a wire hanger. His pasty cheeks sagged like someone had disfigured a clay face. In his hand he gripped part of a rolled-up newspaper as if his sixteen-year absence had fostered an intense desire to smack me.

"It took you a week to find me?" I said. "Did your people try the phone book?"

Dad shrugged. "I only got sprung ten days ago. And I wasn't sure finding you was such a good idea. I thought maybe you're still mad at me."

I didn't buy his weak attempt at regret. Either way, I had more anger for the Fed bastards who took our house, our cars, my ten-speed Peugeot, and, for fun, tore down the basketball hoop and backboard from the garage roof. As a freshman in high school, I came home one day to find it mangled on the driveway where I'd spent many hours winning championships on last-second shots.

"Interesting line of work you've chosen, Jules," Dad said and fell back into an old overstuffed leather recliner, failing to notice the black-and-white cat whose privilege it was to sleep there. He regarded Punim's screech and subsequent catapult off his shoulder as one might notice a wandering gnat. He settled in and fingered the stuffing that bulged from a large tear on the armrest. Then he searched the bare white walls of my apartment while his face morphed into a familiar scowl. I watched his eyeballs follow my favorite scratch zig-zagging down from the crown molding and dead-ending at the baseboard. "Hound-dog business been good to you!"

"I'm thrifty. And don't worry about the cat."

Dad fidgeted in the chair and took a breath. Then he started tapping the rolled-up newspaper against his knee. "Is this what life looks like without the curse?"

The curse referred to our family history, starting with Great-Granddad, who made a fortune among his immigrant brethren of pushcart peddlers working the open-air market of Chicago's Maxwell Street. From this miserable residue, Great-Granddad guaranteed a dependable stream of extorted money and earned the monikers of iron-fisted ward boss, political dictator, city hall chieftain—and scoundrel. In addition to ward committeeman, he also held offices with fancifully arcane titles such as City Collector and City Sealer of Weights and Measures. Some of my relatives called him the smartest man they ever knew and pointed to his chauffeur-driven limousine on a municipal salary as proof. Others pointed to the same thing and called him a gangster. Regardless, those who knew him or knew of him understood why the scandal of Great-Granddad's remembrance inspired passion sixty or more years after the man died in my father's childhood bed. Where better to assign the blame for a family's perpetually bad attitude?

Dad leaned forward and stared into the hardwood floor. "That college you went to have a president?"

"Of course, why?"

"We got a college president here in the city, President Tate. You know he's tearing up Maxwell Street?"

If it were possible to nod one's head sarcastically, that's what I did. "The poor getting screwed again. What a surprise. And wasn't it our family who first made their money by shafting the poor down there?"

Dad gave me his angry glare. "Times were different. That's where we got our start—but now it's part of history. And we're part of this history, whether you like it or not. You can't run away from your family, you know. It'll follow you wherever you go. And I'm not ashamed of it and neither should you be. Anyway, one of those preservation groups tried to get Maxwell Street designated as a historical site. But the son-of-a-bitch Tate beat them down, and now he's gonna crap all over it!"

Despite his cadaverous appearance, Dad was still full of piss and vinegar. "I never claimed to be ashamed," I said. "And you can't just blame Tate. There are trustees and legislators to hate, too."

Dad tried and failed to look disappointed in me—who had just gotten out of prison? He said,

"How can you live like this?" and then added, "What kind of work have you been getting?"

At age thirty-one, I had dozens of contacts and a neat apartment in a two-flat building on North Halsted Street. Husbands and wives behaving badly paid my rent and kept raspberry sorbet in the freezer. An observer might conclude my frequent naps and lack of close friends signified unhappiness. But I didn't give a damn what others thought and had long ago reconciled with my undiagnosed sleep disorder. Friends? They always disappointed you. Besides, I'd kept plenty busy since expanding into the realms of background investigations, surveillance, and skip traces. Living the dream.

Dad really was asking why my suburban nurturing had not begotten a career that included retirement accounts, paid vacations, and health care that didn't rely on places called The People's Clinic or the emergency room.

"You find out yet what a bullet can do to a man's head?" he asked.

"Give me time."

"You act reckless in your line of work, and it could be a short career. After you've felt the end of a muzzle pushing into your skull, then you can be a smart ass."

I looked forward to that day just to say I knew what it felt like, assuming I survived. "So what do you want?"

Dad winced as he pushed himself up from the chair and walked to my Wall of Blame, a collection of psychotic-looking adulterous faces I had proudly captured. He seemed older than his eighty years. Then he walked to the window that overlooked the street. "Remind me: for this you went to college?"

"You went to college, too."

I thought I got to him, but he countered with a smile and a nod. Then he took a folded piece of paper from his pocket. "You're a sharp little prick," he said and handed me a check for two thousand dollars.

I hadn't seen a dime from the man since he went away. "What the hell is this?"

"When's the last time you saw Snooky?"

"What's the check for?"

"Just answer the question."

Snook was a CPA and a close friend of the family. Snooky's father, Henry, was my dad's original business partner. As a manufacturer's representative of ladies coats, Dad would go on the road selling the lines while Henry stayed in the showroom. Together they had built a profitable numbers racket among the shop owners of apparel stores in the little towns downstate. Dad called it an "untapped niche market." Acute leukemia killed Henry when Snooky was a young teenager. Dad treated him like a second son and Snooky let me adopt him as my big brother. He jokingly called me "the little brother I always never wanted."

Snooky introduced me to folk music when my parents didn't know Bob Dylan from Bob Hope. He showed me how to roll my first joint and gave me a bong for my fifteenth birthday. For my sixteenth, he introduced me to Bunny, who took my virginity. Snooky later told me she owed him a favor for advice on hiding cash from the Feds. Dad could've cut his prison time in half had he given up Snooky and his pals.

"I don't know," I said. "I think we had lunch a few weeks ago."

"Do you know what he was up to? Like who he was working with?"

"The only legit client he talks about is Audrey, who owns a tattoo shop. I think he's got a hard-on for her. All the hoods he calls Guido."

How many upper-middle-class suburban boys hung out with gangsters' bookkeepers while smoking pot and laughing their asses off at descriptions of Guido showing off his earlobe collection or Fat Mackerel shitting his pants after a phony no-knock raid? Snooky loved to laugh and we did a whole lot of laughing.

"I guess you don't read the paper much," Dad said, then tossed the metro section at my feet. "This one is three days old." Above the fold, a headline screamed about the alarming number of unidentified meth-heads full of bullet holes found on the streets. Below the fold, a smaller headline introduced a murder victim with a name. "Snooky took two bullets in the head," Dad said.

First the room swayed, then I saw flashing white spots. I closed my eyes for several seconds, then opened them to a wave of nausea washing over me. Somehow, I found the couch before my knees buckled.

A year after Dad got busted, Mom was diagnosed with pancreatic cancer and died six months later. My father's associates invited me to move in with them, since Dad already shared a much bigger house with hundreds of guys wearing orange jumpsuits. As a child I had spent many summer afternoons at one or another of these uncles' houses, learning the art of opening the door without letting someone in unless they answered the right question. I also became proficient at stuffing piles of cash into shoeboxes and stacking them in the hollow space under the stairway. "You'll grow up to be a good earner," they liked to say. But I wanted to live with Snooky.

I'd probably be dead or in prison if not for Snooky. He talked me into going to college, even drove me down to Champaign every fall to make sure I got settled in. Snooky wasn't thrilled I chose investigations as a career, but that didn't stop him from setting me up with Sid Frownstein, a kind of legendary hard-boiled snoop from the old school who had deftly walked that equivocal line between investigation and manipulation until he retired to a lakefront condo and a hobby of restoring antique cars. It was Frownie who first told me stories of my family's infamous past. When Frownie became my mentor, Dad wrote me his last letter, the one in which he threatened to break out of prison and beat my ass if I followed in Frownie's footsteps. From that point on, I had no doubt what my career would be.

"They found his body on a pile of construction debris," I said, reading from the article. I noticed a small photograph of the heap next to an advertisement for cosmetics. "Three hundred and fifty dollars in his wallet. Credit cards untouched.

And what the hell was he doing on Maxwell Street? Snooky had no dealings on the South Side."

Looking out the window Dad said, "I thought you never talked business."

I answered through a lump in my throat. "Payback for setting me up with Frownie? You want to buy my silence for two grand?" I didn't know if I meant it.

Dad turned and stared at me as if reading the words off my forehead. "I don't believe my ears. Is this really how you turned out?"

"Snooky liked how I turned out."

"Snooky was like a son to me—you know that! You think I'd kill him? Your father's a killer—that's what you think?"

I didn't answer. If Dad killed people, I wouldn't have minded that much—although his killing Snook would've pissed me off.

"Sixteen years later you show up to tell me Snooky's dead. What else you got?"

Dad sat back down in the recliner and started rubbing his forehead. "I want you to find out who killed him and why."

Tears spilled out of my eyes. "Suddenly you trust me with this?"

"Snooky was family. You can only trust family with finding the truth. You may hate my guts, you may hate where you came from, but I think you'll be honest."

"I never said I hated where I came from—whatever that means."

"Well, we'll see. Once you start investigating murders, history has a habit of getting in the way."

"We were a family of petty criminals. Who gives a shit?"

Dad gave me a savage look. He wanted to address my comment directly but instead said, "Christ, what you don't know. What you don't see. But like I said, I think you'll be honest. And if I'm paying you, that's the least I expect."

I had always imagined my first murder case would arrive via bereaved widow or suspicious life insurance company. But in that moment, everything seemed appropriate, if not logical.

* * *

The next morning, before heading to Sheridan Road, the passageway into the land of leafy communities dotting Lake Michigan's beaches, I wasted twenty minutes in the muggy July heat trying to remember where I parked my 1983 Honda Civic. I was a son of the North Shore, but the territory neither held a special place in my heart nor evoked pangs of nostalgia. Having gained entrance through the ill-gotten dividends of my father, I considered myself an ersatz alumnus.

Frownie lived in a five-bedroom penthouse with spectacular views of the shoreline. After Frownie cut me loose, he said his door would always be open. He had that broad, uneducated Chicago accent straight out of central casting. "Come here, ya little schmuck," he said when I appeared at his door. He grabbed the back of my neck and pulled me into his chest. His vise-like grip defied the appearance of a skinny geezer old enough to remember Prohibition. He power-walked five miles a day up and down the beach—in any crappy Chicago weather. His scrawny arms were made of rebar. "C'mon, I wanna show you somethin'."

I followed him from his apartment into the underground garage to a row of perfectly restored antique cars. "This is my latest baby," he said. "Lincoln KB Convertible Coupe, 1933 . . ."

When he finished describing how he copped his first bare breast in the rumble seat of the same car, I said, "Nice, Frownie. Can we go upstairs and talk?"

You'd think a man whose career earned him the trust of drug dealers, killers, pimps, and police chiefs wouldn't be so sensitive. "I'm just an old fart, is that it?" Frownie said. "I got nothin' better to do than bore young pricks like you?"

"I need to talk business."

Frownie smiled. "I know. Let's go."

As we walked to the elevator I thought of our first meeting, how he demanded I explain why a North Shore college boy wanted to become a private investigator. A final exam had never been so mentally exhausting. I would say something like, "I want to help people get peace of mind," and he would snarl, "Don't give me that helping people crap! Be a nurse if you want to help people." This went on for what seemed like hours. Not until I lost my temper and shouted, "I want to be out in the dirty stinking city full of scumbags, and be my own boss, looking for whatever, telling someone to go fuck themselves," did Frownie begin to take me seriously.

Everything in his condo looked gloriously vintage; nothing looked old. The maple draw-leaf dining table, the mahogany console, the Art Deco couch and chair. Even the square wooden "High Fidelity" box looked as if it had just been purchased new. I fingered through the vinyl record collection. The sleeves were hardly worn, the corners barely frayed. Glenn Miller and the like were well dusted and in their prime.

I sank into the leather couch while Frownie stood with his back to me and poured a drink from his custom walnut and granite bar. "You started drinking yet?" Frownie said. When I hesitated, he said, "Ya gotta start drinkin', Julie. You can't go into a saloon and order ginger ale. Nobody's gonna take you seriously."

"Relax, I'm a drinker," I lied.

Frownie handed me a tulip-shaped glass half-filled with an amber-colored liquid and sat across from me in a high-back parlor chair. I watched his nose hover a couple inches from the rim before he carefully swished the fluid around and sipped. I imitated his routine, pleasantly surprised by the warm smoky flavor.

"Ever had single malt?" Frownie said.

"Many times," I said, and Frownie laughed because we both knew I had lied again. "And another thing, I cuss a lot more than I used to."

Frownie wasn't impressed. We sat in silence for a few moments before he said, "You never worked a murder case with me. I didn't train you for that—and for a reason!" Frownie's words provoked an unexpected ache of sadness. A quivering lip gave me away. "And it ain't ever a good idea to get all emotional on a case. You spent a few years following me around, asking questions. And you asked the right questions, good questions. That's how I know you can do this job. But murder is a whole different game."

"You and Dad are talking now?"

"I still read newspapers. It's a coincidence you show up a few days after Snooky gets two in the head?" Frownie took another sip. "Too bad. He was a good man."

"He was a lot more than just a good man to me," I said.

Frownie shrugged. "You swim with sharks long enough, you know what can happen. He got a lot of cash pushed his way. You give them a reason to suspect something, and you're finished."

Snooky may have been a pot-smoking money launderer who learned to play the role of the criminal's bean counter, but at heart he wasn't a wise guy who in his spare time hung out at titty bars and played poker with greasy hoods. He started with my dad's earnings and from there gained a reputation. His bread and butter was always the North Side retailers who didn't have the time to worry about estimated quarterly taxes. Bookstores, dress shops, cafes, comic-book sellers—those were his people.

"I've been asked to take his case."

"Investigatin' murder is a hell of a lot different than lookin' for lost kittens. Your name—"

"Dad already warned me."

"Maybe changin' your name—"

"Forget about it."

"That's what I thought." Frownie took a long sip and gulped hard. "Even if I wanted you to start investigatin' murders, this ain't a good one to get your feet wet on."

"I should wait for a good murder?"

"Don't give me this good-and-bad shit. Sometimes it's obvious; it's cut-and-dried. A guy was screwing his neighbor's seventeen-year-old daughter, and then one day his battered body is found propped against a pillar on Lower Wacker Drive. The moral to the story: sniffin' around the wrong sandbox might get you buried."

Frownie walked to the bar and poured himself another drink. "Snook handled money," he continued. "Lots of it. There ain't no bigger sandbox in the world than the one full of cash. That's one serious goddamn sandbox."

"Why don't you tell me what you know—as a favor," I said. "Gimme a push in the right direction."

"I don't know shit, Julie, I'm retired. It doesn't take a private investigator to know Snook was too nice. He trusted too many people. Why the hell a mild-mannered nice-lookin' guy like that didn't just stay legit and settle for a good livin' is beyond me."

Silence again. Then I took my largest sip of the single malt, waited for the fumes to finish meandering through my nasal cavities, and said, "He got a thrill from being around sketchy people. I remember being home from school during the summer, and we would hang out in his basement smoking pot. It was nice and cool down there. Snooky would tell me he worked only for interesting people. He had a natural gift with numbers, but it was the personalities that made the job interesting. The fringy ones he liked best. Gaining the trust of thugs turned him on."

Frownie drained his whiskey, smacked his lips, and gently placed the glass on the coffee table between us. "Walk away from this," he said, sounding a touch irritated.

"We know for sure who clipped him?"

"If your old man was speaking to me, I'd tell him to nail your ass back to the high chair. Snook handled money. Money puts the single malt in these glasses, but one day you take a sip and realize you just drank poison. Snook knew that."

"Snooky wasn't a thief."

"How do you know? You think a man handlin' millions of dollars year after year don't get cocky? It only takes one time, Julie, one time stickin' your hand where it don't belong and you're done. There's no big mystery here. Snooky fucked up and he paid the price."

I would receive no blessing from Frownie this day. But after another round of dead air, he said, "You better start carrying, you know."

"I still have the Colt I found in the trunk of Dad's car all those years ago."

Frownie sighed. "That gun's older than you. Make sure you know how to use it."

2

My investigation would start with Audrey, who owned a tattoo shop on Armitage called Taudrey Tats, a cozy storefront operation devoted to the cheap and gaudy. On the front door it said, "Sole Proprietor and Mistress of Poor Taste, L. Audrey Moreau." When I walked in, she was standing in the rear with her arms crossed, staring at sheets of black and gray drawings hanging from a rack. A sign that read "The Kitschen" hung from a crossbeam. Photos of her work covered the walls. A well-muscled shoulder adorned with a golden retriever carrying a giant crucifix in its mouth caught my eye, as did a buttock decorated with Jack Frost roasting on a spit operated by a humanized chestnut.

As I approached the work space, she glanced at me and said, "Yes?"

Of medium height and slender like a dancer, Audrey wore her silky black hair in a long ponytail. Her forehead was hidden by bangs that accentuated large black eyes. She exuded loveliness. A sleeveless black dress reaching mid-thigh iced this lovely cake. Even her fancy ballerina slippers were black. She had the wondrous expression of a little girl. I guessed twenty-two, although I would've believed sixteen. On her skin I saw a single tattoo depicting moon phases across her right shoulder, beginning with a full black circle and progressing to an almost full waxing gibbous.

"I'm Jules Landau, a private investigator. I'd like to ask you about Charles Snook."

"You mean Snooky," she said and giggled before returning her attention to the rack.

"I mean Snooky."

She removed one of the drawings and placed it on a light box. "Uh-oh, what did he do?" she said.

"When was the last time you saw him?"

16

She gave me her full attention. "You're a private investigator?"

I showed her a copy of my license. She mouthed my name. "I've never met a private investigator. Do you have neat spying gadgets like a cuff link that takes pictures or something?"

I played along. "No, but I've got a pen that can record conversations. And I've never met a tattoo artist."

"What did you expect?

"Someone covered in tattoos. What did you expect?"

Audrey thought for a moment. "Definitely not anyone tall and thin like you. Older. Uglier. Heavier. Wearing a hat. You've got such a baby face. How long have you been doing this?"

"Eight years. Five as an apprentice, three on my own—but this is my first murder case."

That was shockingly unfair. Audrey stared at me, and, if possible, turned paler. She sat down in what looked like an antique hydraulic dentist's chair.

"When?" she whispered.

"I'm sorry. I should have given you a little warning."

"When?"

"Four days ago."

"How?"

"Shot twice."

She ran into a tiny bathroom that doubled as a cleaning supply closet. After the initial retching gave way to heaving sobs, it occurred to me Snooky may have been banging this young thing. I stepped

17

back into the gallery and waited for her to get her act together. I looked around. Not much to the place except four walls and a couple of closets, although in the back a cinder-block wall protruded about two-thirds into the room. Against one of the walls stood a long, narrow utility table. A black skirt hung from the edge. I guessed she used the space under the table for extra storage. The irreverent pictures on the walls defied the vulnerable figure she now presented. But observing Mother Goose selling her dog to a Chinese restaurant made me wonder why disturbing images should bounce around such a pretty head.

For some reason, it made sense Audrey would like Snooky, a man handsome in a pretty kind of way who loved expensive suits and had delicate features, including the kind of long eyelashes women dreamed of having. It used to annoy me how Dad occasionally stared at Snooky with a puzzled expression. When I finally told him to cut it out, Dad said, "I wonder if he's queer?" Actually, whenever Snooky took me to any North Side club, younger women like Audrey always gravitated to him. He liked to tell reassuring stories when asked for advice on a career path or when one had reached a romantic crossroad. As the night would wear on, the conversation typically degenerated into hilarious tales of frustrated love or misguided fashion.

Suggestions that he would make a successful gay man infuriated Snooky. He loved women, but the ones he desired most did not sense in him the spicy recklessness required to take him seriously as a potential mate. When he did find companionship, she would be pretty enough for the moment but intellectually inferior. She would find him initially charming, while he focused on the possibility of getting laid regularly—"a short-term novelty that would soon be eclipsed by the emptiness of the rest of the day," he said.

Audrey emerged from the closet keeping her gaze toward the floor. She smoothed her dress tightly around her legs as she lowered herself into the hydraulic chair. "I'm sorry," she said dabbing a cloth at her mouth. "He was a male character I really liked."

"That's a strange way to describe someone."

"Not if you understood our relationship. We are all just characters in a drama. We both had that view, which is probably why we got along so well."

"You're right about that. He was quite the storyteller. When did you last see him? Did he appear stressed?"

"Not stressed. Last Thursday we went through my weekly expenses like we always did. As usual he teased me about not keeping track of receipts, and I gave him grief about his wardrobe. Then we had lunch and chatted."

"What time did he leave on Thursday?"

"About two-thirty."

"He was found early Saturday morning. Did he mention anything new? Anything you hadn't heard before, like a new client he'd taken on or an investment opportunity he was thinking about?"

Audrey sat up and crossed her legs. That she offered me an intimate glimpse along her inner thigh seemed of no consequence. "I can't think of anything—" She stopped and brought a hand to her mouth and then blinked away a tear.

"Did Snooky ever discuss his clients?"

Audrey thought for a few seconds. "He talked in code about people, and then I would make up stories about them. I didn't know who they were, but their names came right out of comic books. Big Moe, Panda Puss, Tuna Fish. Then we started making things up together. It was really silly, but he had this absurd way of talking about people that made me laugh."

"What about context? Were these associates, middlemen? Was he taking care of their money?"

"I don't know who they were. He would just say, 'I work with this guy named Fuzzy,' and then I would talk about how Fuzzy dressed and that his hair was flammable or that he lived in his mother's basement."

A young teenager walked through the door, and Audrey excused herself to speak quietly to him. She put her hand on his shoulder and steered him out of the shop. Then she locked the door and flipped over the "Closed" sign.

When she returned to the chair, she crossed her arms and let her head fall forward so her chin rested against her chest. She sighed deeply. Then she lifted her head and said, "Milly. Milly was our newest nickname for one of his clients. She was really nervous, so I called her Milly Mouse."

"What was she nervous about?"

Audrey frowned. "He didn't tell me those things. He just imitated the way she talked, and I made up stories and we laughed. She was probably nervous about money. I mean that's what he did, right? He worked with people's money?"

"He did," I said noting her sudden change of demeanor.

Audrey giggled. "I never understood all the different aspects of his job. He was so cryptic. 'I help people avoid future negotiations,' or 'I'm an obfuscation manager.' One day I asked him if he worked with crooks, and he said, 'I have a rule. Every relationship is allowed either one secret or one lie.' He never explained what he meant, but I didn't care."

She sat silently, apparently lost in thought. Before leaving, I put one of my business cards on the arm of the chair and said, "If something comes to mind, I hope you'll call."

Audrey didn't look at me, but I think she nodded.

3

I could see the bottom of my front door as I walked up the staircase to the landing on the second floor. As a murder investigator, I wondered if I should put a piece of tape across the door jamb. Frownie always said that crap was for movies.

I entered my apartment unprepared for a confrontation with a domestic short-haired cat unhappy I had run out of fresh livers, kidneys, hearts, and gizzards—her usual breakfast. She walked lazy circles around me while yowling and whipping her tail back and forth. A gift of regurgitated kibble on the kitchen table served as a reminder to visit a carniceria soon.

Punim had found me not long after I moved in, strolling through the kitchen door that opened onto the porch connected to the back stairway. I assumed she would come and go as she pleased during the warm months, but not until she chose to put down stakes in my apartment did I feel truly honored. I never saw a flyer posted anywhere nearby mourning a lost cat with a black dot of a nose inside a white mask. I officially belonged to her.

I opened the drawer where I kept emergency treats and gave Punim a pile of Kitty Krank, which she ate grudgingly, having become spoiled by raw organs. For myself, I put a slice of raw tofu on toast and topped it with sliced tomatoes, fake mayo, and toasted ground sesame seeds. I ate and thought about Snooky and Audrey. At first the age difference made it painful to picture them other than as business friends, but after considering the irreverence of Audrey's artwork, I thought maybe she needed to play out some kind of freaky subconscious daddy complex. I guess anyone is capable of creating disturbing images.

I would have to visit Snooky's house. I had known this since Dad's arrival. I probably should have gone there first, but my veneer was not yet calloused enough to look the sentimental beast in the eye, and I knew the cops would never find where he hid his book. I also knew it would serve me well to become tougher. I attached my shoulder holster, dropped in the Colt, and put on a linen sport jacket I had found at a thrift store. The coat looked good with jeans, and I couldn't deny I felt pretty damn cool carrying a gun.

Snooky had bought his Bucktown bungalow before the Latin and Polish working-class families and their "artist" neighbors had been replaced by the moneyed swarm that would follow. He had ignored my father's advice not to buy in that "trashy neighborhood" and watched his investment grow tenfold. I assumed the extra key would still be hidden in the same place, but as it turned out, I didn't need it.

* * *

A black and white had parked in front of the house. The uniform behind the wheel was reading the paper. It looked like the yellow crime scene tape had been tossed down as if nobody gave a damn who crossed it. I had just closed the door to my Civic when I noticed a man sitting on the front stoop watching me. He leaned back on his elbows looking very comfortable. I took my time crossing the grassy parkway to the walk that led to the front door. When I reached the first step, the man said, "Did you know the deceased?"

I recognized Detective Jimmy Kalijero because he had run the sting operation that busted my father's illegal gambling enterprise. For several months, hidden cameras and undercover agents had observed Dad's gaming tables. The local media reported tens of thousands of dollars were exchanged nightly, although Dad insisted his house was strictly low stakes—a little fun for regular Joes who couldn't afford to go to Vegas—and that the police had exaggerated their big score to make themselves look good. Either way, Dad was charged with illegal gambling and received extra time since he had already been caught running a numbers racket a few years before I was born.

I had grown sick of my peers tiptoeing around my family's misfortune, so I decided to embrace the shame as a badge of honor and hung the framed newspaper article on my dorm wall. Kalijero smiled proudly in the accompanying photo as he led my father and several other cuffed suspects to jail. A son of Greek immigrants, Kalijero stood about six feet tall with dark, closely cropped hair and a chest like the front end of a Mack truck. His prominent nose and brown skin gave him a rather heroic look. He wore a tight blue polo shirt with tan slacks. Around his thick neck hung a gold pendant of the Parthenon.

"Charles Snook was like family," I said.

Kalijero stared at me a few seconds, and as if reading my mind said, "You look older, but you haven't changed much, either."

"You know me from somewhere?"

"There are pictures of you and your dad on the wall inside." Kalijero stepped down and offered his hand. "Nothing personal. I was just doing my job."

I shook his hand and said, "I would've preferred keeping my ten-speed Peugeot."

Kalijero looked confused and then a lightbulb went off. "That was the Feds. They'd yank a Popsicle out of a kid's mouth if they thought it was bought with dirty money."

I nodded as if letting him off the hook, and said, "Are you investigating the murder or just in the habit of hanging around a dead man's house?"

24

Kalijero shrugged. "We all go fishing sometimes—just to see what we'll catch. I saw the pictures on the wall and thought, 'What the hell. I get paid either way.'"

"So you caught me."

"Downtown they want a half-assed attempt before chalking it up to a mob flunky getting clipped." Kalijero fished a cigarette out of his breast pocket, lit up, and took a long drag. "I don't know. This guy was pretty clean. Even our informants are puzzled. You here to get some personal things?"

"I'm here to investigate a murder."

Kalijero laughed. "So it's true?"

"What does that mean?"

"Bernie Landau's kid's a private eye. C'mon, it sounds funny."

"No, it sounds ironic. Anyway, there's no way in hell Snooky would've been stupid enough to steal from the mob. He cleaned their money, that's all. And you knew that! You guys were kind of like friends."

"Friends? I wouldn't go that far. I mean, yeah, he was a likable guy and all. But we were still hoping to get a wire on him one day."

"Never would've happened."

Kalijero gave me one of those you don't know shit looks, dropped his cigarette, and rubbed it out with his toe. "Do me a favor," he said. "Go in there and find something. I need a real lead or Snooky's case is gonna be shit-canned real soon."

Kalijero's cooperative attitude concerned me, and when he didn't follow me into the house, I became curious. In fact, everything about his being there made me suspicious as hell. I entered the foyer and almost fell into a pile of Snooky's beloved Scandinavian furniture smashed into kindling and covered with chunks of his cherished Steuben glass animal collection. The air had a sweet antiseptic odor. The scene repeated itself throughout the house, including the kitchen, where chunks of the granite countertop shared the floor with splintered cherry cabinets. Also scattered about was the odd vial or glass pipe, something I had never before seen in the house. I left this pathetic scene for the basement, hoping to find some vestige of my childhood, but even that sacred room had been defiled. The saddest part of this whole mess was that the bastards who had tossed the place weren't even lukewarm in finding what they wanted. I walked back to the front porch and saw Kalijero looking at me from the walk, smoking another cigarette. He took it out of his mouth and said, "I think someone was looking for something."

"And you thought I'd get it for you."

"You want to find a killer?"

"He showed me how to cook bowls, not books."

"Are you sure that's all he was cooking?" He took a glass pipe out of his pocket to show me.

"My whole life, all I ever saw was pot in his house. Something's not right."

Kalijero frowned and flicked his cigarette into a juniper bush. "I'm on your side, Jules. I don't like seeing civilians blown away for no good reason. If he was skimming or playing around with the wrong money, then we'll know why he got hit. And if we can follow where the money's going, it could lead to a lot of bad guys going to prison."

"Let me ask you something, Jimmy. If your closest friend had information written down somewhere that would send a lot of bad guys to prison, would he tell you where it was? Would he put a big fucking target on your forehead?"

Suddenly, the Greek god turned into a little boy who got underwear for Christmas. His face darkened and he said, "I didn't realize you knew everything already. You're so goddamn smart, you've got it all figured out. Do me a favor, private investigator, and pretend I might be as smart as you." Then Zorba flung one of his business cards at my feet and stomped back to the police car. How presumptuous to assume I would pick it up.

4

On the way home I stopped at a Mexican restaurant on Lincoln where I was always welcomed as Señor Gato. In the back they ran a small carniceria where animal parts gringos never thought of eating were sold. For five bucks I could take home enough carnage to keep a certain domestic short-haired content for a month along with a bag of tortilla chips right out of the oven. These were bootleg quality chips, so thick and crunchy they had to have been illegal.

When I returned to my apartment, Punim was sleeping in the recliner. I started dividing her food into daily portions to be frozen and thought about my meeting with Kalijero. For a city with no shortage of murders, he seemed awfully interested in this one. Maybe he saw an opportunity to be a hero. Maybe he saw his picture in the paper for nailing crooks who had signed up for Snooky's cleaning service. I tossed a chicken heart into Punim's bowl and lay on the couch.

I awoke a few hours later in the murkiness of early evening. After throwing cold water on my face, I headed my car back to Bucktown. Of the numerous cars parked on Snooky's street, the one with a human silhouette in the passenger seat caught my eye. I passed the house, drove a few blocks, and then circled back. I parked where the alley met the sidewalk. I turned off the lights, left the car running, and walked down the alley, trying to stay in the shadows. Old bungalow neighborhoods meant window air-conditioning units, each with varying degrees of humming and buzzing. This would work to my advantage. When I reached the backyard of the house next to Snooky's, I opened the gate in the chain-link fence, stepped into the shadow of the neighbor's garage, and waited. Within minutes, a figure briefly appeared from the side of Snooky's house and then retreated back into the darkness. Sloppy. I got the feeling they didn't want to be there. They hadn't thought about the streetlamps giving away the guys in the house whenever they moved. I figured two inside, one in front, and one on each side of the house. They probably owed Kalijero favors.

About three feet of lighted yard lay between the garage shadow and the enormous oak tree said to be one of the oldest in Bucktown. It forked about ten feet up where a large hollow had formed. From a distance, you wouldn't notice the opening because Snooky had glued together chunks of tree fungus to fashion a covering that fit snugly over the hole. The wooden bench next to the tree balanced precariously on twisted roots. I had to be careful. I figured the odds were in my favor that I could jump into the tree's shadow without being noticed. If Kalijero's goons saw me, I'd proceed to the front of the house and hope the old lady who lived next to Snooky remembered when he introduced us, and that she appreciated my stopping by to remember her neighbor.

I jumped across and waited. Nothing happened. No quick movements or whispers. I carefully stepped onto the bench and pushed on the fungus door. It seemed stuck, so I shoved it with the heel of my hand and it popped off, bounced against my forearm, and fell to the ground. I braced for commotion but still nothing. A flame flickered from the side of the house. One of them had lit a cigarette. I'd have to tell Kalijero to stop using short-timer cops dedicated only to padding their pensions. As expected, Snooky's notebook was double-wrapped in plastic bags. I looked around thinking this had been too easy, that somewhere along the line I would be challenged. But there would be no tests that evening. I stepped off the bench, walked through the gate, and within minutes I was on my way home.

5

I flipped the switch that controlled two gooseneck floor lamps, one next to the couch and the other next to the recliner. The warm glow transformed my space into a cozy oasis in a dark city. I was thinking I needed to get some pictures on the walls when the specter of an old man caught the corner of my eye, and in that suspended moment before my heart flipped, I heard the words, "You're dead!" and stumbled backward onto the couch.

"You see how easy it is to get dead?" Dad said.

"Goddamn it!" I wanted to push the son of a bitch through the wall. "What the hell are you doing?"

"Why don't you have that door rigged?"

"Don't do that again. How'd you get in?"

"I use this to spread jelly." Dad showed me a butter knife and then tossed it on the wood coffee table.

"What do you want?"

"What've you got?"

"It's been one day!"

"I'm your client who's paying you. What's that? You just get back from the library?"

I let my head fall back. I tried to calm down, tossing the book on the table and monitoring my heartbeat. "If you're so smart, why don't you tell me what I've got?" I said.

Dad picked up the book and sat next to me. After tossing the plastic wrap on the floor, he took out his reading glasses. He turned a few pages, and a smile crept across his mouth. He mumbled for a few minutes until he looked at me grinning. "I referred a lot of these guys to Snooky."

I walked into the kitchen and returned with a pen and legal pad. "Write down which names you

30

know and which you don't. You know anyone called Milly?"

"Don't know Milly," Dad said and took the pad and drew a line down the middle of the page. He seemed pleased that I had asked for his help. On one side he started listing the alias "Guidos" he already knew about—J.J., Big A, Jackass.

"Jackass?"

"He worked for Borseti collecting coins from cigarette machines and jukeboxes. He had big pointy ears like a donkey."

"Borseti owned the North Side machines?"

"Borseti owned bartenders. See this?" Dad pointed at a payment to Pulaski Vending. "This was a small operation. Borseti set up Pulaski as a company that collected for the bartenders. Bartender calls for dirty laundry pick up. Jackass gives bartender his cut and brings the rest to Snooky. Snooky gives Jackass a check to give to Pulaski for his services. Pulaski gives Jackass an envelope full of clean paper laundry."

Dad licked his index finger and began turning pages. Occasionally, he would stop and write down some names and then resume. At the end of the book, he said, "Snooky had a more complicated system going on with your Milly, and with four other guys called Devil, Chance, Franky, and Butch, I don't know these guys. The others I remember. Small-time stuff. Most of those guys were pussycats, regular Joes who had cash operations on the side that needed cleaning."

"Any drug dealers?"

Dad sized me up as if about to tear out my throat.

"Don't get ticked off. I can't assume anything."

From what we could tell, beginning in March, Devil had started giving Snooky two separate monthly payments of fifteen grand, which were then cleaned through Franky. I knew that meant Swanky Franky's, a hugely successful hot dog joint and a long-time client of Snooky's. From Franky's, the money was split between several bank accounts, later to be wired back into Franky's account before it was paid out to Franky's "investors," Milly, Chance, and Butch.

"All these account numbers," Dad said. "That's what they'll want. The book should no longer exist—unless you get an emergency."

"Tomorrow I'll go see what Swanky Franky knows," I said.

Dad appeared lost in thought until he said, "You see that picture of that college president Tate tossing the first shovel full of dirt? It was like he threw it on my coffin."

I didn't respond. What do you say to someone mourning the world of his grandfather? Then he said, "I'm sorry for scaring the crap out of you. But for chrissake, you gotta think of these things! If you're gonna investigate murders, you don't know what kind of bastards you'll meet. There's nothing people won't do for money, Jules."

Of course, he was right. I had been too cocky about this business. But for some reason, I didn't care.

6

I awoke the next morning thinking about Audrey. Something about the combination of a beautiful woman and violently disturbing artwork I found hard to resist. And as I watched my oatmeal cook in the microwave, I thought our conversation should be resumed—over lunch, perhaps. But first I had to visit Frank to see what he didn't know.

On the way to my car, I noticed a black Crown Victoria illegally parked across the street. At ten I arrived at Swanky Franky's Clark and Halsted location and was surprised to find the door open. A Mexican kid mopping the floor told me in broken English they were not open yet, and I told him in broken Spanish I wanted to see el jefe. I sat at a table and watched the steady flow of pedestrian traffic pass Frank's front door. You couldn't find a more perfect place to hide fifteen grand each month. A short, pudgy, gray-haired man emerged from the back wiping his hands on a white apron covered in the pastels of fast food. I recognized Frank from his newspaper ads boasting foie gras hot dogs and fries cooked in duck fat. I could tell by his expression he was going to be a lot of fun. About ten feet from me, he shouted, "We open at eleven o'clock."

I introduced myself and said I wanted to talk about Snooky. "He's a dead fuck and I'm gonna have a line out the door in an hour. That's all there is to talk about."

I guess when you net six figures from liver sandwiches you can talk that way to strangers. "Did you ever examine or question his accounting methods?" Even I knew what a stupid question that was for a guy like Frank.

"Why the fuck would I? That's what I paid him for."

"So you had no idea he laundered money through all those dead pigs you sell?"

Frank's eyes widened, and he looked as if he were choking. "What do you mean?" he whispered.

"I mean he took someone else's money and blended it with yours so nobody would notice." Frank sat down, red-faced and panting. I almost felt sorry for him. "You're not in trouble, Frank. I'm just trying to find out whose money he was hiding."

"Did he take my money?"

"He was hiding someone else's money—to avoid taxes."

"Who are you again?"

I took out my license and handed it to him. He stared at it and gave it back. "I don't know shit. Snooky would show up every month, I would give him my financial stuff, and that was it. A few times a year, we went over taxes and profits and payroll and that kind of stuff. But I swear to Christ we never talked about hiding money—he wasn't stealing from me, was he?"

I thought of all the suffering that went into producing the sandwiches that were making Frank a rich man. I said, "Who can say for sure?" Then I gave him one of my cards and suggested he consult a tax attorney in case the IRS came knocking. Even Swanky Franky had to suffer sometimes.

* * *

July is the season when Chicago's grime hangs in the air, clogging your pores, rendering antiperspirants useless. I could feel my face morphing into a giant blackhead as I approached Taudrey Tats. Once inside, I saw Audrey drawing a broken heart on the left pectoral of a brawny client lying flat on his back in The Kitschen chair. She wore a black T-shirt and black jeans. A bald-headed kid with a lightning bolt meandering across his skull sat on a bench paging through Skin & Ink. On his shoulder was the unfinished face of an owl. Both the owl and the kid looked pissed off.

I watched while sitting in the loveseat that bordered the waiting area and her work space. She was still coloring when she said, "A little busy right now."

"I'm interested in a tattoo," I said.

Audrey said nothing and continued working. A few minutes later she told Brawny to take five and motioned for me to follow her. She led me to another closet-sized room that had a small wood table with a tiny lamp on it and a folded-up massage table.

"I can't just drop everything at a moment's notice."

Her anger was unconvincing. "I apologize. I was in the area so I thought I'd stop by and see if we could meet for lunch."

Audrey stared at me for a moment and said, "If you're looking for a girlfriend, I doubt I'm your type."

"I'm looking for a murderer, and you have no idea what type I prefer."

"Of course," she said. "The pain over Snooky is still very close to the surface for me, and when I saw you walk in, it bubbled up."

That sounded rehearsed, but I played along. "I've heard the fastest route through pain is straight ahead." Definitely rehearsed, but I saw the beginnings of a smile. "Just give me one last conversation to wrap things up, and I promise to leave you alone."

She sighed. "Come back at one," she said and walked away.

7

When I got home I saw the Crown Vic still illegally parked. I had enough time to clean up, offer a liver to Punim, and check messages. "May I suggest, private investigator, you acquaint yourself with cell phone technology . . ." Kalijero was checking in, as if we were partners. He had called an hour earlier, wanting to compare notes. He implied he had information. My technological investments consisted of a 26x optical zoom digital camera and a digital pen recorder. Although I did own a cell phone, I had yet to give myself over to it. I had control issues to work out. I erased the message and watched Punim devour a liver. I thought about Kalijero's attention. It was not flattering. I'd get back to him eventually, but for now I'd play hard to get.

I returned to Taudrey Tats freshly showered and stubble free. Audrey was working on Lightning Bolt's owl, now remarkably detailed and lifelike. Her ponytail hung over one shoulder, which

36

allowed me to study the curve of her neck. Her T-shirt was short and untucked, offering a landscape of the small of her back. Minutes later, the tattoo machine stopped buzzing.

"There you go," she said and held a mirror about six inches from Lightning Bolt's shoulder. He seemed pleased with what he saw, and she escorted him out the front door without taking any money. She adjusted the clock on the "Be Right Back" sign to return in forty minutes then began dragging a heavy blackout drape across the front wall, eclipsing even the front door.

"You pull that across every time you leave?"

"You think all that expensive equipment was just waiting for me when I showed up? No point in tempting any window shoppers with thieving on their minds. Also, I have clients who have to feel secure when I'm working on certain areas of the body."

"I noticed that guy you were working on didn't pay you," I said.

"Touch-ups are free," she said.

I suggested a place down the street that made pita pocket sandwiches. Audrey put an enormous purple bag over her shoulder.

"So how do we get out of here?"

Audrey lifted the drape from the floor and looked at me as if I was an idiot. I took it from her and held it above my head while she walked under it. Once outside, I asked if she used her shoulder bag to deliver newspapers in her spare time, but she appeared too distracted to acknowledge my joke or give me more than a one-word response to any other attempts at small talk. Her energy seemed to change while I picked out the ingredients for my sandwich. After we sat, she said, "You got something against meat?" She took a bite of her chicken sandwich.

"Only when it's cooked," I said, and she surprised the hell out of me with a spasm of laughter that brought her close to spitting out her food. When I was sure she didn't need the Heimlich maneuver, I laughed with her.

"That Milly you mentioned was getting payments from Snooky," I said.

"She worked for him?"

"I doubt it."

"What was the money for?"

"That's what I'm trying to find out, which brings me to ask one more time: can you remember anything specific he said about why Milly was nervous?"

"I have nothing for you," Audrey said and the tone of her voice told me she meant it. She took another bite of her sandwich and stared at a point in space above my head. Then she said, "Are you happy, Jules?"

"I'm ecstatic."

"Why did you pick this career?"

"Why do you care?"

"If you're going to keep popping up in my life, you'll become a character in my story, and I need to learn about you. Why did you pick this career?"

"Just make something up."

"That question ticks you off."

It did for some reason. "I like puzzles, mysteries, figuring things out—being my own boss. And I guess I wanted a different kind of life."

"Different from what?"

"Different from what was expected."

Audrey returned her gaze back into space then said, "But can't this kind of work be dangerous?"

"I suppose. How did you meet Snooky?"

"My father got his name from a financial consultant who likes to work with professors."

"Your father's a professor?" I wondered what Daddy thought of his little girl's career.

"Yeah, but he doesn't teach anymore. He became disillusioned with my generation, and now he's just an administrator at the University of Illinois at Chicago, giving him more time to dabble in real estate."

"What kind of real estate?"

"I don't know."

This was news. I thought Snooky's legit clients were all shop owners. "Can you get this consultant's phone number for me?"

Audrey reached into her shoulder bag and handed me a business card for Susan Conway, Personal Financial Consultant. I thought it strange that her office was in a university building. "My father got a vacant office for her to use in exchange for being a guest lecturer at the business school."

I put the card in my pocket and wondered what the tax-paying public would think of this arrangement. We ate in silence until she said, "I have to get back," and wrapped what was left of her sandwich in a couple of napkins and stuffed it in her bag. When we stepped outside, I reiterated my promise not to bother her again and told her I was parked in the opposite direction. She gave me half of a goodbye wave, and we both turned to leave. A few steps down the sidewalk, she called my name. I turned and she said, "I wanted a different kind of life, too."

8

Outside my apartment, the Crown Vic was still a scofflaw. I stood in front of the car waving my arms at the tinted windshield. This action elicited no response so I moved to the driver's side window and tapped on the blackened glass. When that didn't work, I climbed onto the hood and lay across the windshield while pounding my fists on the roof.

This time the door opened and a short bald guy stepped out. "Get off, you stupid fuck!"

I jumped down and yelled back, "Did you know you're parked illegally? Did you know that windshield tint is only allowed on the top six inches? Did you know tint on the driver's side window is illegal?"

His looked like his head would explode. "You skinny shit, I could tear you in half!"

"You want me to call the cops and report a rent-a-Guido harassment in progress?"

He took a step toward me and then retreated. "Why don't you call the cops and see what happens, dumb ass?" he said and got back into the car. As I suspected, a Kalijero stooge.

I walked up the stairs to my apartment unconcerned with Guido but satisfied I had found a potential lead, and perhaps a connection with a beautiful woman. I expressed my gratitude by offering up a fresh kidney to the domestic short-haired goddess who shook the organ violently before swallowing it.

Once again the light was blinking on my answering machine. Once again Kalijero's voice spoke. ". . . I'm not the bad guy, Jules. There's no reason we can't work together . . ." Two messages in three hours. I might have to get a restraining order.

* * *

I called Susan Conway and told her I was investigating the murder of Charles Snook, and I hoped she wouldn't mind if I asked her a few questions regarding the last time she saw him.

"Yes, of course," Conway said and then asked, "Are you a professional private investigator?"

"I'm not a cop and, yes, I get paid to investigate."

"I'll be in my office for another two hours, you're welcome to stop by."

I drove south toward the university feeling cockier than ever. As I approached the huge concrete slabs that made up the university's original buildings, I wondered how many people recognized the irony of an architectural style called Brutalism in a neighborhood where Snooky's body was found on a debris pile of what used to be cheap apartments for poor Maxwell Street peddlers. The area surrounding the campus was a frenzied construction zone. Let's hide the crime as quickly as possible.

Susan Conway's office was in the Jordan wing of the graduate business school next to the finance library. When I arrived, the door was open and she was working at her desk. I knocked lightly and introduced myself. She hurried over to shake my hand before inviting me to sit on one of the two chairs in front of her desk.

Curious as to what she would reveal of her connection to the university, I asked for an overview of her job, and she said she counseled impoverished graduate students not to give up on achieving financial independence. "You can start with saving a dollar a week," she said. "If you believe you're worthy of wealth, you will achieve it." Tall and attractive, she spoke with the kind of confident saleswoman's optimism I imagined made it difficult for people to leave without writing a check. Her walls were covered with eight by ten photographs of her posing alongside well-known Christian conservatives, several of whom had made fortunes with their television and radio shows.

"I see you have celebrity clients."

Conway smiled. "Those are teachers, not clients."

"Not exactly the role models one expects to see in a financial advisor's office."

"Oh, but you're wrong! You see, God rewards those who seek the right path."

I didn't see. "I'm investigating the murder of Charles Snook, and I was told he had done some work for you."

Suddenly, the beaming face of confidence turned pale. She closed her eyes and took several deep breaths. "When I heard the news and saw his name—I assumed there could only be one Snooky." Her voice wavered, "He helped me with my tax return. That was last February. How did you know?"

"Audrey, the daughter of a professor—"

"Jerry's daughter. I didn't know she was in town."

"Just curious. Why would you need Snooky's help?"

"I'm not a tax expert."

"Had you seen Snooky since February?"

"We had breakfast Friday morning."

"Did you talk about taxes or was this a social call?"

"He was very personable and intelligent, so it was hard not to talk about other things."

We took turns glancing at each other and then looking away until I said, "You knew why I was coming over, right?"

"You told me on the phone. Why are you asking?"

"When I first walked in, you were businesswoman of the year. I mention Snooky and you're shell-shocked."

"I have to put aside personal emotions when explaining my occupation. Everyone has the potential to need financial counseling."

"You thought I was an impoverished graduate student?"

"Well, no," she said and started rubbing the back of her neck. "I don't limit myself to students. I'm glad to talk to anyone."

"I'm glad I left my checkbook at home." She didn't laugh. "Were you and Snooky more than friends?"

Susan Conway stood and walked to the window overlooking a construction site for new graduate housing. "Charles—I mean Snooky—was a wonderful person. He had a tremendous curiosity about spiritual prosperity. Long after my taxes were finished, he continued stopping by. We'd go out to lunch or to the opera. We felt great intimacy toward each other."

"What time did Friday morning's breakfast end?"

"About nine-thirty. I was to be a guest speaker at a graduate seminar at ten."

"Did he give you a reason for being down here other than to see you?"

"He always said he was here on business. I just assumed he had clients in this area."

"What about Friday morning? Did he mention anybody he was seeing that morning?"

Conway walked back to her desk but didn't sit. She began arranging paper clips with her index finger. Without looking up, she said, "He never mentioned names. He just made references— someone involved with city government or something to do with real estate. He had his briefcase with him on Friday, so I assumed he was in the area on business. But these were asides. Our time together was of a more personal nature."

"Did he confide in you?"

"What do you mean?"

"People who feel great intimacy often confide in each other."

She looked away and said, "I told you he didn't use names. We didn't betray confidences. It was much too risky—"

"So you knew he laundered money?"

"I knew no such thing!"

"Then what was risky?"

"We both worked with other people's money, Mr. Landau. Money is confidential by nature. And I don't appreciate what you're implying."

"Snooky watched me grow up. He helped me become a man."

Conway sat back down. "His loss must bring you great pain."

"I need to know as much as possible about the people he associated with."

Conway hesitated and then said, "But we must find space to be thankful for the time we did have with him. I even thanked Jerry for recommending Snooky, thus bringing him into my life—"

"Audrey's dad recommended Snooky to you?"

"This surprises you?"

I dialed it back down. "I just thought it was the other way around. Are you sure he introduced you?"

"Of course. I had inherited some rental property and needed tax advice. Jerry and I served on a steering committee together for a local nonprofit, and that's when he recommended him. In fact, Jerry had some business to discuss with Snooky and invited me along to meet him and ask

45

my real estate questions. I decided to just hire him to do my taxes."

"Snooky knew about your arrangement with Audrey's father?"

Conway gave me a puzzled look. "What arrangement?"

"Running a for-profit business from a public university office, and, perhaps, evangelizing while you're at it."

"The university treats me as if I was an adjunct professor. Adjunct professors are allowed to work outside the academic scope. You should check the bylaws, Mr. Landau. And my job is to counsel people. I resent the suggestion I proselytize." I'd hit a nerve.

"Checking the bylaws is a good idea," I said. "I hope you don't mind if I stop by again should I have more questions."

"As you said, it's a public university. Whether I mind or not is irrelevant."

* * *

Because I was still dissecting my conversation with Conway as I walked back to my apartment, I didn't notice the Crown Vic still parked in front of my building until an angry voice interrupted my thoughts. I turned and saw Kalijero's face looking out the passenger side window.

"What do I gotta do to get a call back?" he said.

"You're being too needy, Jimmy. It's a turnoff." I resumed walking and heard the car door slam.

"What the fuck, Jules," Kalijero said, running over. "We're on the same team here. Let's look over what we got."

I stopped and faced him. "Okay, you start. Whaddya got?"

Kalijero frowned. "There's a rumor someone was messing around Snooky's neighbor's backyard."

"What else you got?"

"You're starting to piss me off. Was that you? You got some evidence you want to show me?"

"I'll tell you what, Jimmy, you come clean with me, and I'll do the same. Why do you care so much about his murder?"

"Like I said, I don't like seeing civilians get hurt—"

"Why not just tell me why you care so much—"

"Because I don't have to!" Kalijero shouted. "I'm the police, remember? It's you who has to talk, and if you don't start soon, I'll have you arrested for obstruction!" Kalijero took a step back and wiped the spittle off his mouth. He looked pathetic standing there taking deep breaths, trying to calm himself. I resumed walking toward my building. "You're too cocky, Landau," Kalijero shouted. "That might get you into trouble." Once again, I knew he was right.

9

I lay down on the couch and tried to collect my thoughts. The apartment's one window air conditioner struggled to keep pace with the July

47

heat, but the white noise helped me drift into one of those late afternoon slumbers where the events of the past two days ricocheted around my subconscious. Audrey, Kalijero, and Susan Conway took turns demanding my attention while I became increasingly aware of pressure on my abdomen with intermittent pinpricks. Consciousness returned with the phone ringing. Punim lay on my pelvis kneading with her front paws.

"A cop just stopped by," the female voice said, and it took a moment for the dust to settle in my brain before I recognized Audrey's voice.

"Detective Kalijero. He's been tracking me."

"He wanted to know what we talked about. He freaked me out."

"Just tell him what you know. He's the police."

"I said we talked about my friendship with Snooky and that I told you someone named Milly was nervous. Then he asked if you had a book of Snooky's clients, and I said I didn't know."

"There is no book."

"He scared me. He really wanted that book. It almost felt like he was threatening me. Are you sure you don't have a book? I don't want him coming back here."

I reassured Audrey she had nothing to fear or hide and told her to always cooperate with the cops, and then I said, "I'm sorry for all the hassle. Was it possible Snooky knew your father before he was hired as his accountant?"

"No."

"And you're absolutely sure about that?"

A pause and then, "Well, Snooky never mentioned knowing my dad. I don't see why he would. Dad did his own taxes and didn't run a business on the side."

"But you said something about real estate."

"Sure, but I don't think it's anything too complicated. Collecting rent on a couple of condos or something."

"That's right," I said.

"Someone just walked in." She hung up.

10

The unmistakable smell of fried lunch meat. "You want some?" Frownie said.

I declined and watched a man in his eighties place strips of American cheese on bologna slices, spread mayo over white toast, and then slap together dinner. I bet his LDL cholesterol was less than one hundred. We sat down at the fancy dining room table in his high-rise apartment.

"So whaddya got?" Frownie said and took a bite of his sandwich.

"I've got a man lying to his daughter about knowing Snooky. I got a police detective who's got a hard-on for me."

Without looking up from his plate Frownie said, "The liar—what does he do?"

"College administrator."

"Who's his kid?"

"One of Snooky's favorite clients."

"Who's the cop?"

"Kalijero."

49

Frownie stopped chewing and looked at me. "The guy who put your dad away?"

"Yeah. Why's he so hot for me?"

Frownie started chewing again. "Lots of reasons," Frownie said. "You think Kalijero hired Snooky for his cleaning service?"

"No idea. Does a lying professor and a horny cop mean they know each other?"

"It doesn't mean anything. Could be a million reasons why the college man knew Snooky. But Kalijero surprises me. He was clean when I knew him. The daughter—what does she know?"

"Nothing."

"You gettin' into her britches?"

"You're a sick bastard."

Frownie wiped the grease off his mouth with a cloth napkin and took a deep breath. "From the start I didn't like it, Julie. Mob scum is bad enough, now maybe a dirty cop?"

I waited a few seconds and said, "You know I'm not dropping it."

Frownie rubbed his eyes and sighed. "You gonna talk to the kid's father?"

"That was my plan," I said.

Frownie gave me his favorite expression, make sure you give him enough rope to hang himself, and then said, "If you find out Kalijero is dirty, you go to the Feds."

We walked to the door. I could tell he was upset. Frownie said, "The best investigators are the ones who don't get emotional—but I told you that already. They stay detached and let things play out before reachin' conclusions. They don't show what they're thinkin' or feelin'. Can you do that?"

"It's in my bloodline," I said.

"I'll never forgive myself if I outlive you. Do me a favor and let me die first."

* * *

That Frownie's somber words failed to penetrate my consciousness I attributed to the family curse. That is, the genetic code responsible for my family's propensity toward graft also explained why I drove home thinking only of cold pomegranate juice and Cubs baseball. With luck, Punim would stretch out on my lap and allow me to stroke her belly. My goal for the evening was to think of a way to question Audrey's father, the college man.

Walking from my car to my apartment, I was feeling good. I caught a glimpse of myself acting in the movie of life as a private eye in a big city investigating a murder. In two days I had found two liars, I thought, and then Frownie's words hit me hard in the face.

11

"Proud of yourself?" His voice competed with the pulsating pain from my right cheekbone. "What're you doing in this goddamn business?" was the next sound from my father's mouth and my left eye opened to see his big snoot standing over me.

"What happened?" I said.

"You're in the emergency room. You got clubbed in the face. Ten stitches and a fractured cheekbone. I found you leaning against the door to your apartment."

Dad put an ice pack in my hand and moved both to my eye. The cold felt good. "You should've told me Kalijero was on your ass. This ain't worth dying over, you know."

"How did you know about Kalijero?"

"It's a coincidence I'm here? He called my parole officer and got my number. I tried calling, but you don't answer. So I stopped by and there you were."

"So he's on my ass. So what?"

"So what? This was a message, Jules. You probably only got hit once. A few more with whatever they used, and you wouldn't be waking up."

"I'll be more careful next time."

"I'd be responsible for my own son's death—"

"You're the second old man today who wants to be responsible for my death! I'll be responsible for my own death, okay?" A nurse walked over and asked if everything was all right. My head throbbed. Dad looked as if he didn't recognize me. He sat down in the chair and stared into space.

"Oh, c'mon," I said. "I would've found out about Snooky anyway, and I'd be in the same situation whether you knocked on my door two days ago or not. So what did Kalijero say?"

Dad turned to me. "He thought he could threaten me. He said he could nail you for obstruction, and I would be your accomplice. He'd

52

make sure I spent my last days in prison. You've got him shitting his pants."

"He wants that book I showed you."

Dad nodded. "Maybe Kalijero got in too deep. Maybe he killed Snooky. Or maybe he just knows who did and why."

"The book doesn't mean shit."

"He doesn't know that. He's desperate."

"I'm fine," I said. "Try not to worry."

"It's my fault you got into this. I was a shitty father. It was your mother's weakness that she accepted me for who I was. I didn't deserve her. She loved me no matter what." Dad pushed himself up from the chair. "Your mother got sick just a year after I went away. It's my fault she died so young."

"Oh, c'mon, Dad. You can't blame yourself for that. And Mom just wanted me to be happy. She wouldn't have cared what I did for a living."

"I don't know. She was first generation, remember. I think she would've wanted more for you."

"Blame Great-Granddad, not yourself." Dad didn't respond. "Listen," I said. "I like my life. I like doing what I'm doing. I don't mind taking a beating. And if I get killed, that's the price I'll pay, but this is exactly the way I want it." Dad gave me the all is lost look. "And you're not doing me any favors by turning into a guilt-ridden old man. I want your help, but not if you're going to get all sentimental and repentant." He departed with a faint smile, failing to hide his resignation.

12

I awoke the next morning with my right eye engulfed in hideous shades of purple, yellow, and green. In the middle of it all were ten dissolvable stitches under a bandage. It hurt to blink. A horrified middle-aged woman at the health and beauty aids store applied beige foundation to my face as I stood in the aisle. She offered to pay for the bottle. Then I drove to the university's administration building, a massive concrete monolith serving as the symbolic tombstone for the dying neighborhood surrounding it. I pulled in behind a row of illegally parked pickup trucks and asked a nearby construction worker holding a "Slow" sign if anyone paid attention to parking ordinances during construction hours. He pointed out that the trucks all had special construction permits. I took out twenty dollars and asked if he could secure a permit for my Honda. The man took the money and assured me I had no worries.

The lobby was cold enough to hang meat. I stared at the directory for several moments but could not find a Professor Moreau. My first murder case required my first cell phone call.

Audrey picked up on the third ring. She sounded stressed.

"Look for Dr. Tate," she said.

"Your father is President Tate?"

"No. My father is Chancellor Tate."

How logical that every previous instant of my life had occurred so I would hear Audrey's words in that moment. It almost seemed unfair that it could have been this easy, as if I should have worked harder before having "Chance" from Snooky's notebook fall into my lap. Would Milly, Devil, and Butch be as accommodating?

* * *

Chancellor Tate's photo hung prominently in the lobby. He was handsome in the silver-haired corporate style, a chiseled-featured CEO who still had a thirty-four-inch waist and probably modeled for GQ in his spare time. Alongside the chancellor hung photos of the president, provost, and regents. Their somber expressions reflected disapproval of the mobs crisscrossing the marble floor in their torn jeans and facial piercings.

I just wanted a few minutes with Tate, just enough time to put his brain in overdrive. I took the elevator to the tenth floor and asked to see the chancellor. His secretary looked about fifty and wore a white sweater with a large red and blue GO Flames! button pinned below the shoulder. She looked like a retired cheerleader. She asked if I was a graduate student, and when I said no, she said I would have to make an appointment.

"What time does he eat lunch?"

"Sir, you will have to make an appointment. Next Monday would be the earliest opening."

I wrote "Snooky" on one of my business cards and asked if she would hand it to him. She said she would put it in his in-box. I asked if I could just quickly hand it to him and leave. She said I'd have to make an appointment.

The door behind her was closed, which didn't necessarily mean Tate was in, but I thought, What the hell, and bypassed Ms. Flame to crash the party. Stretched out on a leather couch, the silver-haired chancellor napped with an ice pack across his forehead.

"Jerry, he just barged in—"

Tate swung his legs off the couch and sat up. His eyes moved back and forth between Ms. Flame and me like a Betty Boop wall clock.

"Is something wrong?" Tate said.

"He just barged in, Jerry—"

"I'm sorry to bother you, sir. I'm a private investigator looking into an important matter." I handed him my card.

Tate squinted at the card. Ms. Flame grabbed reading glasses off his desk and handed them to him. "I said he had to make an appointment—"

Tate waved her off. "That's fine, Barb." Barb gave boss-man a helpless look before walking out.

Tate picked up the ice pack from the floor and put it in a small fridge against the wall. Then he sat behind his desk and stared at the card a few more seconds. "You're not the police?" He stared at my eye.

"I fell off my skateboard. No, I'm not the police."

"Someone is paying you to be here?"

I wondered if all chancellors were this sharp. "Tell me what you know about Charles Snook."

Tate looked around. "I believe he did some work for an associate of mine—and of course I heard about his tragic death. How did you get my name?"

"The usual record checks."

"Records? I had no business with this man. I never even met him."

The power was intoxicating. "Ah, you know, these bean-counter guys write everything down. Maybe that associate you mentioned gave him your name as a potential client. You're one of a long list of names I have to track down. It's all really routine, boring work."

"I wish I had something for you, but like I said, I never met the man."

"What about your associate? Did he ever talk to you about him?"

"No, she didn't—or maybe she mentioned his unusual name, which is why I remember it. And then the paper running the story and finding his body just a block from here."

"Maybe I could talk to this associate?"

"Perhaps. Uh, Susan something. She was in the assembly with me. We were acquaintances, really . . ."

"No problem," I said. "If you think of her name, give me a call." I could feel Tate's relief. Even the lights brightened. I thanked the chancellor for his time and made a move toward the door and stopped. "You know anything about real estate?" I said. "I was thinking about investment property— no pensions in my business."

"Well, I have a mortgage," he said and laughed. "Honestly, Mr. Landau, my experience is higher education. The university offers adult education courses on real estate."

I thanked him again, and as I walked out, I also thanked Ms. Flame for her time.

13

At the lobby's Starbucks, I grabbed a Tribune and ordered a tall iced mocha. The girl behind the counter kept staring at my eye. "Covering a nasty bruise," I said. "You should see what the other guy looks like." She smiled quickly and looked away.

Iced coffee in hand, I stepped into the midday heat and was sweating by the time I had crossed the street to my car. The construction worker hadn't moved. I waved, and he saluted. Capitalist pig. My gut told me that about now Tate's mind was racing, and the worst-case scenarios were winning the day. Tate knew a dead man had been funneling him laundered money. Tate lied about knowing this dead man. He would need a shoulder to cry on.

I was either lucky or good because less than an hour later the chancellor walked out of the building. I turned the key and my Civic jumped right in as expected. I loved my little machine. Despite the domination of fuel injection, a clean carburetor and unsullied oil still gave you a devoted friend. I turned on my hazards and pretended to peer for an address as I followed Tate for two blocks, pissing off anyone behind me. When he walked into the office of a garage, I drove around the block and saw the garage's exit located on a less busy one-way street, which made it easier for me to pull over and wait with the newspaper partially obscuring my face. Moments later Tate emerged driving a Cadillac de Ville convertible, license plate LJI1158. I repeated, "Leslie-Jane-Irving 1158," until the plate was in the vault.

I knew the chancellor wasn't driving to a restaurant since the neighborhood had every type of food within walking distance, and when you're freaking out, appetite is often the first casualty. He struck me as a North Side snobby type, and I expected him to head back that way, which he did when he turned on Halsted. But then he surprised the hell out of me and turned onto the Eisenhower Expressway. West Side?

Traffic was fairly light, and we were soon outside the city limits. Ten minutes later, he exited onto Ridgeland Avenue, which took us into the suburb of Oak Park. I followed from a safe distance as he led me through a neighborhood of magnificent old mansions on quiet, shady streets lined with enormous trees. He slowed to a stop in front of a white Victorian with a wraparound porch. I parked a block behind him.

Tate held a cell phone to his ear with one hand while gesticulating wildly with the other. From the house, a bearded man in his sixties appeared. He wore a yellow polo shirt with tan slacks. He walked casually, as if it were a routine meeting. As the man reached for the car door, I focused my SLR Ultra Zoom through the windshield and squeezed off a ten-frame burst as he entered the vehicle. Tate put the phone down. If the two were talking, they were doing it while looking straight ahead. The bearded man's head fell back, as if trying to catch a few Zs. A few minutes later a black Escalade turned onto the street from the opposite direction and parked across from them. A fat, smartly dressed man with a butterball face emerged from the car and walked quickly to the powwow. I squeezed off another ten frames, including the Escalade's license plate. As soon as the man climbed into the backseat, Tate started giving him an earful. For fun I triggered ten more frames to see if I could catch a maniacal expression to add to my collection. With luck I would catch a few bubbles of airborne saliva. When the chancellor finished his tirade, the meeting adjourned. I started the Civic and headed back to the expressway with a chancellor, two license plates, an address, and two new faces—all part of some kind of equation. Time to call in a favor.

14

Punim sat on my lap and stared at me. As I dialed the phone, she blinked.

"I love you, too," I said, and as if on cue, she dug her rear claws into my thigh and leaped off. Our love was complicated.

A female voice answered, "Johnny Bonds."

"Jules for Johnny," I said.

On hold for two seconds, then, "Don't tell me, Jules needs bail?"

My pal Johnny Duggan found me after taking a pile of business cards from a restaurant's fishbowl, thus depriving someone of a free lunch. A classy guy.

"I need a favor, my friend."

"Whaddya got?"

Johnny credited me with saving his marriage because I proved his wife was not cheating but really meeting her girlfriends at a diner, and that Sean could also be a woman's name. His wife worked for police communications and ran background checks on the side.

"Two plates and an address." I gave him the information and then decided Tate deserved more attention. "Just for fun. LJI1158. See if he's got parking tickets. I need locations, days of the week, times of day."

"Give Sheila an hour," Johnny said.

Before hanging up, I gave Johnny my cell phone number. It was time, I thought. After all, guys like Johnny were the true heroes. Without guys like him, guys like me wouldn't stand a chance. I prepared a sandwich of textured vegetable protein, wheat gluten, lettuce, tomato, red peppers, and Dijon mustard. Punim got a chicken heart and a kidney from an anonymous donor. I ate while relaxing in the recliner and letting the events of the previous days drift around my consciousness. If they could see me now.

15

A young woman sat in The Kitschen chair while Audrey worked on her shoulder. Audrey's black dress stopped at mid-thigh. I wondered how many short black dresses she owned. Lightning Bolt was there again sitting on the waiting bench, this time paging through Guns & Ammo. "Getting the owl touched up?" I said.

He turned to me but said nothing. I'd never seen eyes so bloodshot. Then he said, "You takin' a fuckin' survey or somethin'?" I didn't know what shocked me more, his rotting teeth or putrid breath.

"Be nice, Jason," Audrey said. Jason threw the magazine down and stormed out.

I walked to the edge of the work space. "I don't think he likes me."

"He gets jealous when men come in," Audrey said without looking at me. "He's a great character."

"Your character is a meth-head."

"As long as he's a paying meth-head," Audrey mumbled. "I think this man has a crush on me," she said to the girl in the chair.

"I'm not sure I was supposed to hear that," I said. "I don't think you're my type, but how about having dinner with me anyway? Tomorrow night?"

Audrey looked up at me. "Ooh! What happened to your eye?"

"I fell."

Audrey gave me her as if face then said, "It'll be a late dinner. I'm here until ten."

"The later the better," I said. I had no idea what I meant.

"What do you do?" the girl in the chair said. She was short, cute, with long black hair like Audrey's, and big blue eyes. She wore a denim skirt with a white spaghetti strap T-shirt. Her eyebrows were bright red and stuck out like neon signs. Her voice matched her appearance—that is, small and trusting.

"He's a private investigator," Audrey said and introduced her friend, "L.A."

"What does L.A. stand for?"

"It stands for L.A.," L.A. said. "You don't look like a private investigator."

"And you don't look old enough to be getting a tattoo. And you should tell your tattoo artist to keep a gun handy with clients like Jason."

Audrey stood and swiveled L.A.'s chair toward the mirror. "What do you think?"

A black and white sea turtle flew through the water. On the side of her neck her hair partially covered another tattoo I couldn't identify. "It's perfect," L.A. said. "I'll be the envy of Echo Park."

"Not very kitschy," I said.

"L.A.'s not a client; she's a kindred soul. And she's old enough to manage her own tattoo shop in Los Angeles."

L.A. walked to a stand-up mirror and admired her new reptile while Audrey cleaned up. I felt awkward standing there, but she had yet to question my presence. I saw this as a good sign. Then Audrey said, "I thought you weren't going to bother me anymore, private investigator. I have a business to run, you know."

"I'll buy an hour of your time."

"Sixty bucks an hour. Have a seat."

I did as told. L.A. kissed Audrey warmly on the cheek then walked out the front door. Audrey pulled up a padded folding chair.

"You two are close."

"We're main characters in each other's stories. There's nothing I wouldn't do for her."

"I don't get it. Do you write these stories down?"

"It's an oral tradition."

I stared a moment to make sure she was serious. "Why do you do this?"

She matched my stare with one of her own. "Because we like telling stories."

It took a few rings before I realized someone was calling my cell phone. "Sheila was all over it," Johnny Bonds said. "Ready?"

"Hang on," I said then walked outside of Taudrey Tats. "Go ahead."

Johnny gave me Tate's address in Evanston. The Escalade belonged to a Jacob Mildish who lived on the South Side, and in that moment I recognized my mistake in assuming the "Milly" from Snooky's notebook was female. With Chance and Milly now accounted for, only Devil and Butch remained. In the Oak Park Victorian lived Daniel Baron. The name sounded familiar, but I couldn't place it.

"And the LIJ1158? Your boy would be the scofflaw king if somebody wasn't voiding his tickets."

"Parking tickets are for little people," I said.

"He likes parking in Lakeview."

"Wrigleyville? Really?"

"I said Lakeview. Only yuppie scum call it Wrigleyville."

"Fine. Which streets?"

"Racine and Addison area," Johnny said. "He likes to park in loading zones and in handicapped-parking-only spaces. Jeez, what an asshole."

"Weekdays? Weekends?"

"Mostly weekends. There are a ton of restaurants and bars in that area. They're probably calling in the complaints. Especially Sundays between eight and ten p.m."

"So he parks after eight, which means he leaves his house no earlier than seven-thirty. Johnny, have I told you I love you?"

"I didn't hear that. And you don't remember where you got this info."

"What info?" I said then hung up.

16

My joy wore off an hour later when I saw Kalijero sitting on the stoop to my building.

"Where's Rent-a-Goon?"

"I'm alone. What the fuck happened to your eye?"

"I got slugged."

"With what? A fist wouldn't do that much damage."

"Of course you wouldn't know anything about this."

Kalijero forced himself to speak calmly. "Okay, now let's take a fucking time out. I know you think I'm a scumbag, but you've got it wrong. You would know if I cracked you one. We'd be face-to-face. None of that ambush crap. And why would I? I got nothing against you. Yeah, you piss me off, but only because you won't give me a chance. And if you had put my old man in the joint, I'd probably hate you, too . . ." Kalijero wore front-pleated gray slacks and a black oxford cloth shirt with gray pinstripes. His mahogany shoes had braided detailing and tassels. He was really trying to win my love.

"Did you get all dressed up for me?" I said. Kalijero closed his eyes and took a deep breath.

"You're too easy, Jimmy," I said. "But I'll make a deal. You tell me the real reason you're so interested in this case—and I mean no bullshit—and I'll give you everything I got." Well, maybe not everything.

Kalijero crossed his arms and looked at me. "Upstairs," he said, and I considered making a crack about having to kiss me first but held back.

Punim greeted us at the door, hissed at my guest, then darted away. Kalijero sat in the recliner and looked around. His struggle not to make a smart-ass comment was obvious. He declined my offer of carrot juice.

"All right, then, Jimmy, spill it," I said.

Kalijero hesitated and then said, "I was running a little business on the side. All cash. Snooky was helping me hide the money."

I nodded, waited for more, and when I realized that was it, I said, "Nope. You're holding back."

"That's what I got! I swear that's all there is."

"What was the job? How much were you making? And who else are you protecting?"

"What difference does it make—"

"Goddamn it! Either give me everything or get out."

Kalijero closed his eyes and started rubbing his chin as if enduring excruciating pain. Then he said, "I started moonlighting as a bouncer at a strip club out by the airport. I pulled in an extra 2K a week. Then I had the idea of promoting the place to the high rollers on layovers. I started chauffeuring them from the gate to the club. For one price, they could get all the drinks and tail they wanted in a back

66

room. I got a cut for each trick. One day a deputy superintendent walks in with a few commanders and some other brass—all wearing plainclothes. They're all looking at me with big grins. Asked me about group rates. I figure they better get a good price or I'll be working there full-time. So now they're getting all the ass they want for free in exchange for security. Word gets out there's a safe place for action. Every cop convention starts coming through Chicago. Then firefighters. The money starts rolling in. I'm getting ten to twelve grand a week. What do I do with it? Stick it in the mattress? I get a hold of Snooky, and like magic he's got the whole trail covered. Then Snooky gets clipped. There's talk of diaries, ledgers, whatever record-keeping these guys have. The pressure from the top is killing me."

If Kalijero was acting, he sure had me convinced. I almost felt sorry for the guy.

"There was a book. All nicknames. My dad looked through it and found only four he didn't know. Snooky never mentioned a cop being a client, and he told me everything."

He didn't tell me everything, but so what?

"But you don't know for sure."

I shrugged. "Who knows anything for sure? What's the name of this strip joint?"

With a straight face Kalijero said, "O'Hare's Tailspin. Okay, Landau, your turn. What do you got?"

"I've got Chancellor Tate lying to me—"

"The university chancellor?"

"Yeah, you know him?"

"He was a guest at Tailspin. VIP treatment. I was told to make sure he got the youngest-looking girl."

"He lied to me and he lied to his own daughter about knowing Snooky. And I've got some guy named Jacob Mildish meeting with Tate. Ever heard of him?"

"Have I heard of him? Seventh district rep. Twenty-five years at least. Connected out the ass. A ruthless, power-hungry son of a bitch."

"Tate met with Mildish immediately after he lied to me. And then a guy named Baron also joined the meeting. Any idea—"

"Construction big shot. He got the redevelopment contract for Maxwell Street. Mildish worries me. A conspiracy theorist's wet dream. A real dark-side kind of guy. Who's Tate's daughter?"

"The tattoo girl. The one you questioned."

Kalijero looked as if I had just spoken Swahili. "What tattoo girl? I haven't questioned anybody."

I studied Jimmy's face. "The day you and that goon were following me and you told me I was too cocky. You didn't stop by Taudrey Tats and question Audrey?"

"Who the fuck is Audrey? And what do you mean following you? I hung out and waited till you got back."

We silently processed this new implication until Kalijero said, "What did that cop look like?"

Audrey answered on the first ring.

"You know it's rude to get a phone call in the middle of a conversation and just walk away," she said. "Especially considering you had just asked me to dinner."

I apologized then asked her to describe the cop who visited her shop. Out loud I repeated, "Short, fat face, fleshy lips, creepy voice," and watched the blood drain from Kalijero's face.

17

"Voss," Kalijero said. "Internal Affairs. He's watching you." Kalijero paced back and forth like those tortured tigers at the Lincoln Park Zoo. "He must've seen us at Snooky's house and then followed you to the tattoo girl . . ."

"Jimmy, get a grip. Snooky only used aliases, and Audrey would've told me if he had info on a dirty cop. And I got no use for Internal Affairs assholes."

"Twenty-five years I've been busting my ass as a cop. For what?"

He bordered on pitiful. "Baron gave fifty grand to Snooky between March and July before it was split between the chancellor and the Honorable Mildish. Guess who got a huge contract from the university?"

Kalijero didn't respond, just stared into the middle distance until he said, "Fuck it!" and, "Watch your back, Landau." Then he walked out.

I didn't get it. Internal Affairs wasn't going to find any book fingering Kalijero by name. The guys upstairs were sure as hell going to keep their yaps shut. There was probably more going on than Kalijero was telling me, but at that point I had too much on the plate in front of me to care.

I called Audrey again, ostensibly to make sure she accepted my apology for rude behavior and that our dinner date was still on. I also asked, "Did Snooky ever mention people in construction?"

Audrey thought for a moment. "Is that the same as a developer?"

"Sometimes."

"There was Uncle Bug-Bear the developer," Audrey said. "Snooky used to say, 'Got a check from my Uncle Bug-Bear. I just love my Uncle Bug-Bear.'"

Audrey was a little girl again as she confirmed for me another alias from Snooky's notebook. In the world of Audrey's giggling, Snooky was just a pleasant memory, an old pal who made her laugh, an actor in her favorite show that starred Chancellor Tate as Chance, the Honorable Jacob Mildish as Milly, and Baron Construction as the Devil.

* * *

I drove to the Kennedy Expressway and headed south to the Eisenhower, then back to Oak Park where I stopped in front of Baron's house. I stepped onto the porch carrying a folder of photographs and stared at the stained glass surrounding the massive front door. The doorbell chimed in the stately manner you would expect, and soon I heard the sharp sound of heels on hardwood until the door opened and a girl about sixteen with short hair dyed blue and a metal loop through her nose looked at me. I introduced myself and asked if her dad was home. She turned and shouted that "someone" was here to see him. To my surprise, he shouted back to show me in.

I followed the girl through a couple of large rooms to a short hallway that led to a smaller room set up for viewing the sixty-inch plasma television mounted on the wall. Baron sat in an armchair watching a baseball game. The girl pointed to her father and walked away.

I knocked lightly on the oak paneling. Baron turned to me, hit the mute button on the remote, and told me to have a seat on the small sofa opposite his chair.

I introduced myself and asked if we could discuss Snooky. He looked at me and said, "Would you believe this used to be the butler's room?"

"That's fascinating. Any idea why Snooky was murdered?"

Baron sighed and then shook his head. "He was a good man. I liked him. And he knew his stuff—"

"You gave Snooky tens of thousands over a five-month period. Care to tell me what it was for?"

Baron looked at me squinty-eyed and said, "You're pretty cocky for a young guy. You stroll into my house and start asking personal questions. I'm not surprised you're walking around with that shiner."

"You didn't have to let me in. You always let strangers into your house?" I took out the photographs of Baron meeting with Mildish and Tate and spread them out on the glass table between us. Baron glanced at them.

"So what do you want?" Baron said. "Get to the point and stop the tough guy crap."

"I don't give a damn where you got your money or what you did with it. All I care about is finding Snooky's killer. And at investigator school they teach us to follow the money. Right now I'm thinking someone pulled some strings so Baron Construction got the university expansion contract. And I'm thinking that Snooky laundered money that was then kicked back as payment for the string-pullers."

Baron rose from his chair, walked to a small liquor cabinet and poured himself a drink. I declined his offer. After sitting back down, he took a sip and said, "Ever study fluid mechanics? Money always takes the path of least resistance. In Chicago, that path is especially slimy. And there is no less resistant path than through a politician. As a student of local history, I seem to recall some characters with the name Landau who understood this principle quite well."

"Why is Snooky dead?" I said.

"I don't know," Baron said. "When I said I liked the guy, I meant it. He understood the system. He knew to keep his mouth shut." Baron started shaking his head. "I don't know," he said again. "He didn't deserve this. Somebody fucked up."

"What do Tate and Mildish say?"

"They say they don't know."

"Do you believe them?"

Baron stared at me for a few seconds and said, "Mildish is the boss. Me and Tate don't know shit. Mildish knows more than he'll ever tell either of us."

"What was that little meeting out front about?"

"About an investigator dropping in for a visit. You got those two bent, that's for sure."

Baron seemed awfully relaxed for someone who could be implicated in murder and bribing government officials. But maybe I was being naïve.

"I want you to set up a meeting for me with Tate and Mildish," I said. "Somewhere public." I gave Baron my cell phone number. "And if I find out you've been jerking me around, I'll have the auditor general crawling up your ass."

18

I was tired and my eye socket throbbed. I chopped up some organ meat and dropped it into Punim's bowl, the sound of which brought her running to the bloody scene. Then I popped some acetaminophen and stretched out on the couch with an ice pack over my eye. There was still some lingering daylight at eight-thirty, but my body told me to let the recent events percolate awhile in an unconscious state. And to be perfectly honest, something about the image of myself crashed on the couch after a successful day of sleuthing was irresistible.

When I opened my eyes again, the subtle hues of daylight confirmed that I had spent the entire night on the couch. Punim sat on the coffee table staring at me, and when I sat up, she darted to the kitchen and waited next to her bowl. I showered and then we ate breakfast together. Halfway through my bowl of oatmeal, the cell phone rang. "Noon," Baron said, "In front of the Melrose diner."

"Are they gonna buy lunch?"

Baron hung up.

* * *

It was a busy restaurant on a busy street, about as public as you can get. I arrived ten minutes early and watched from the dry-cleaning joint across the street. Noon came and went without any sign of Tate or Mildish, and it occurred to me that they, too, were watching the front of the restaurant from another location. My inclination was to give in and be the first to show, but before I could act, a foul odor accosted me, and a raspy voice suggested I not turn around. I felt something hard press into my lower spine while a skinny tentacle reached under my jacket and relieved me of my Colt.

"If that's your dick, you're pretty damned tall," I said. It was supposedly a gay neighborhood, after all.

"Look, fucker," the voice said. "I don't want to hurt you, but I'm getting a hundred bucks to walk you to that black limo next to the diner. If I have to shoot you, they'll give me two hundred." The stink was indescribable.

"How about I give you two hundred bucks to walk away? But I'd like my gun back."

I assumed Shit Breath was thinking about it until he said, "I'm gonna put my arm around your shoulder, and we're gonna walk like a happy couple. The whole time this gun will be under my shirt sticking into your side." While crossing the street, it occurred to me that my ghoulish looking eye—complemented by my new pal—made me look like just another junkie.

74

A rear passenger door swung open and waiting for me in the backseat of the refrigerated Cadillac limousine was the Honorable Jacob Mildish—not a bad ride on a rep's salary. Great-Granddad would've been impressed. Shit Breath gave me a shove and closed the door. A tinted partition separated us from the front seat where the driver lowered his window and handed the meth-head a hundred-dollar bill before driving away.

"I apologize for that," Mildish said. "I hope he wasn't too rude."

Mildish had one of those chubby baby faces that looked downright cartoonish on a man I guessed to be around sixty.

"He threatened to kill me, that's all. And he stole my fully licensed handgun."

"Good god, I'm sorry. I offered him a hundred dollars to get you to come over to the car. It's too darn hot to stand outside. It was Tate's idea to meet here." Then Mildish leaned toward me and said, "How's that eye healing? Tate told me about it so I'd be sure to recognize you."

Because the lore behind the Mildish myth included a hardscrabble upbringing as the son of an iron- and steelworker, I found his grandfatherly manner and aristocratic accent puzzling. "Where is Tate?"

"He's too upset. I told him he'll drop dead if he doesn't relax."

"I see, so what're you gonna do, dump my body somewhere?" I was half serious.

Mildish recoiled as if a cobra had shimmied out of my collar. "You've got the wrong idea, Mr. Landau. I'm a businessman."

"You're a politician."

"Politics is just an aspect of business. I'd be surprised if you didn't know this concept inside and out—given your family history. Either way, accept this fact and your chosen profession will be easier to master."

"Terrific. Who killed Snooky and why?"

"We know it doesn't look good—"

"You mean it looks like Snooky was killed to cover the path leading to kickbacks you and Tate got from the developer who won the university expansion contract? What happened, Your Honor, somebody panic?"

"We don't know who killed Mr. Snook or why. He was completely trustworthy, an expert launderer. Why would we want him dead? That would be a terrible business decision."

We sat in silence. Small shivers began racing through me, and I thought I might have entered stage-one hypothermia. If only to take my mind off the cold, I said, "You can't think of any reason someone would want Snooky dead?"

Mildish took a deep breath and rotated his fat body to face me. "Mr. Landau, I have racked my brains over this, and I can't think of a single reason why someone would do this. Could it have just been a random act of violence?"

I laughed. "Two random bullets in his head, three hundred random dollars still in his wallet, his body randomly lying on a pile of construction debris and showing no random signs of struggle."

Silence again until Mildish said, "I feel compelled to ask what your intentions are."

"I'm being paid to find Snooky's killer, nothing else. As long as you're not lying to me, I don't care what you do."

Mildish stared at me and sort of smiled. "That's the attitude I was hoping for. I'm not convinced you can maintain it, but for now I'll give you the benefit of the doubt."

"You don't trust me."

"Do you trust me?"

"It would be bad for business to trust you."

"Touché!" Mildish said and laughed loudly. Then he reached into his breast pocket and produced a billfold. He counted out some cash and handed it to me. "Will this cover the cost of a new gun?" I looked at the seven hundred-dollar bills, handed two of them back to Mildish. "Now we're even," I said.

19

I came home with a Glock .40-caliber and called my father. I told him what was up with Kalijero and about my meetings with Baron and Mildish. He sounded tired but enjoyed hearing about Kalijero's troubles. Mildish troubled him.

"Mildish scares me. While he's shaking your hand, he's picking your pocket."

"Tate's the one that's really squirming," I said. "The others might conveniently forget things, but

Tate's the true liar. It sounds like he panicked, and Snooky ended up dead."

"Who pulled the trigger?"

"I don't know. Guys like Tate don't get their hands dirty."

"You think his kid has anything more to say?"

"I think she does, but I don't know when it will come out. Daddy is a professor after all."

"Don't forget blackmail. I doubt Tate had the final say on a multimillion-dollar contract. You said that yourself when I first came over."

He was right. Trustees would have to give the go-ahead. I felt a renewed appreciation for my father's experience in corruption.

* * *

Tate's house was a three-story brownstone across the street from a large park on a bluff above Lake Michigan. A few decades ago, this building housed three middle-class families. Today you would find couples with seven-figure incomes living their renovated fantasies of stainless steel double sinks, kitchen islands, recessed lighting, and home theaters. I didn't know what I would accomplish by staking out his house on a Saturday afternoon, but the park was well shaded and a nice breeze blew off the lake.

From a picnic table, I sat and focused my camera on the house. I zoomed into the enormous plate glass window and then examined the solid wood door. I put myself in Tate's shoes as a wealthy, educated, middle-aged man running a large public university. An opportunity presented itself for easy money. He got one of the trustees in on it, maybe the comptroller or the treasurer. His Chicago Yacht Club dream was closer than ever.

Then he started to worry, felt vulnerable. Or the trustee started to sweat, started to wonder who knew what and how it could be used against him. The trustee started leaning on Tate to do something. Tate revealed his fears to Mildish and Baron, who both dismissed the neophyte's anxiety. He would get no relief from these two seasoned, well-connected veterans of the game. And how did he know he was not being played for the fool? How did he know Mildish and Baron wouldn't sell him down the river? He lay awake at night thinking his whole life, everything he had worked for, would be destroyed and his name would just be another added to the long list of imprisoned Illinois luminaries.

Tomorrow I would check Tate's trail of parking tickets to see if they led somewhere. Perhaps I would have to look Tate in the eye and present his worst-case scenario until he shit himself. I played with these thoughts awhile longer, only to gradually drift far off-subject to the carefree summer afternoons of my youth. I blamed the cooling lake breeze for casting this nostalgic spell, which ended abruptly with a male voice asking, "Mind if I sit?"

I turned to see a square-headed man with a double chin and one hell of a comb-over sitting on the end of the bench. He wore gray dress slacks and a silk shirt unbuttoned to the top of his protruding belly. A can of root beer could've easily balanced on that shelf. His face lit up as if he recognized an old friend.

"Well, well, well. Run me over with a Cadillac! If it isn't Private Investigator Landau!" His shrill voice sounded like squeaking brakes, the result of being spiked in the voice box while playing football—I would later learn. I imagined he inspired nightmares in young children. "And there you are sitting all by your lonesome."

I remembered Audrey's description of the cop Kalijero called Voss. Short, fat face, fleshy lips, creepy voice—an unmistakable depiction of the man before me. "You must be Detective Voss. Are you following me, Detective Voss?"

"Don't be ridiculous. This just happens to be my favorite place to spend a Saturday afternoon."

"Of course! Coincidence is your middle name."

"Life is full of coincidences, Landau. It's like bloodlines, you know? Who knows how bloodlines intermingled in the deep dark past?"

Voss's eyes appeared unnaturally close together. A rattlesnake would've blushed under his stare. "Then I'm in luck because you're keeping me company today. That's kind of like intermingling, isn't it?"

"Just as you've been keeping company with Kalijero," he said.

"Not to worry. We have an open relationship."

Voss stood and stepped closer. "While playing cops and robbers, I hear you've been sniffing around a lot of stinky tattoo snatch. And at the same time, lickin' Kalijero's ass. Anything you want to share?"

I winced at Voss's raunchy imagery. "What could I possibly share with you?"

"Did you know carrying a concealed weapon is prohibited in Chicago?"

I showed him my FCC card, my PI card, my FOID card, and then invited him to fuck off.

Voss laughed. "Kalijero put your old man away. Why protect him?"

"I'm investigating a murder you and your pals don't care about. I don't give a damn about Kalijero."

"It's not about giving a damn. It's about dirty cops. And if you've got info, you better hand it over. Withholding evidence is a crime, Landau."

"And why would I want to withhold anything from you?"

Voss's face reddened. "You're scum, Landau. And I don't buy your college-boy bullshit. You'll never be more than a two-bit chiseler like your old man and his old man and all the other fathers in your family. I'm more connected in this town than you'll ever be, so if you play games—"

"Arrest me!" I held my arms out straight. "Get out the cuffs and take me!"

Voss put his hands in his pockets and walked a few feet away before turning and retracing his steps. He had acquired the most condescending of smiles. His incisors emerged from his bulbous lips like some kind of hairless rodent.

"Frownie taught you well, Landau," Voss said. "I don't show all my cards, either. I'll take my time, wait, and see where you take me. And when the time's right, I'll show you what I got, and then you'll fold like the cocky little shit you are. And I don't care about your flunky bookkeeper friend.

Since I knew that pretty boy collects pretty things, a few months ago I sent him a glass elephant as a warning. A reminder that I got a good memory. I don't forget who does business with mobsters and how scum like your forefathers can ruin people. They deserve what they get. And, don't you forget, I know more than you think—about all the people you've been talking to—including that little tattoo whore."

Voss flicked one of his business cards on the picnic table and walked away, chuckling and shaking his head. I didn't even try to understand what he meant by his parting comments. But I did know how much his damn smile angered me. And as I drove back to the city, I fantasized what having my fist landing flush against his front teeth might feel like.

20

On the way home, I stopped by a one-story building in an office park where a lab bred mice for snake food. The first birth parents I had ever found as a PI were on a job for a client who worked in the lab. For a discount on my rates, he provided me with the occasional box of frozen babies called "pinkies." Punim loved pinkies.

At four o'clock, I collapsed into the recliner. I closed my eyes and thought of the disingenuous aspect of this date and wanted to admit I would be interested in Audrey had we met under different circumstances. But apart from ordinary lust, I couldn't deny my real motive was to gain more insight into her father through innocent conversation.

When I returned to Taudrey Tats, Audrey was coloring an enormous red rose between the shoulder blades of a woman lying facedown on a massage table. After she wiped off the excess ink and blood, I saw the black widow crawling out from the center.

We walked to an Indian restaurant where I had aloo gobi. Audrey had tandoori chicken and insisted on ordering an entire carafe of Riesling. After drinking the first glass as if it were Kool-Aid, she became at ease, if not playful. I kept the conversation on the light side—soliciting stories of peculiar clients, bizarre tattoo requests—until our food arrived and we had taken our first bites. "How often do you see your father?" I said.

Without looking up she said, "Once in a while."

"Not very close, I guess."

"Not very."

"How come?"

"Why do you care?"

"Can't I just be curious?"

Audrey put down her fork. "Nobody is ever 'just curious.' There has to be an ulterior motive."

"Bullshit. I investigate. Investigators have a natural curiosity about people."

Audrey's face had become pouty. I thought the conversation might be over, but I was wrong. "My father has no respect for women. As a child, he once told me I'd be nothing more than a one-night stand. He thought it was funny. When I got into art school, he told me how disappointed he was and that I was wasting my time. He constantly cheated on my mother."

"Does he live near the campus?"

"No. Somewhere in Evanston."

"You've never been to your dad's house?"

"I know where he lives. That's enough."

"He wanted Snooky to help you with your finances."

"Big deal."

"It wasn't a gesture?"

"He's oblivious. Probably racked with guilt and I'm starting to wonder if maybe he was involved in something."

"What do you mean?"

"He's a snake, you know? A poisonous snake. He'd bite to protect his ass."

"You think he bit Snooky?"

"I don't know, but I wouldn't be surprised if he gets arrested for his murder." Audrey appeared to be searching for words. "You should know I like older men."

I paused. "Duly noted. Do you think your dad is capable of murder?"

"We're all capable of murder, Mr. Private Eye. Maybe I date older men to piss off my father. I haven't decided. But it makes the story interesting. I'm good at making things up as I go along."

"But your father. Do you really think he could kill someone?"

"Are you following what I'm saying?"

"I get it! You like hanging out with daddy types—and I ain't it. Why did your father lie to me about knowing Snooky?"

Audrey smiled and giggled. "Daddy's a liar," she said as she sipped from her fourth glass of wine. I was nursing my first. "But Daddy loved Audrey. Poor, poor Audrey. He loved her so much that he kept telling her this as she tried to sleep. But Daddy wouldn't let her sleep—" Audrey stopped and stared into her wineglass.

Her implication sickened me. "I'm sorry."

Audrey didn't look at me. "He's sorry, too. He's tortured with guilt, or so he says."

I excused myself and paid the bill at the hostess stand. Audrey waited at the door. Outside she said, "Let's go to your place."

She was drunk, vulnerable, psychologically damaged. She was beautiful. "I'm not old enough for you."

She stumbled. "Shut up! Let's just talk and have coffee."

I hated coffee. At my apartment, she sat on the couch. I offered herbal tea. She declined. I sat next to her, but not presumptuously close.

"Where's your gun?" she said.

I laughed, but she didn't get the joke. Then I pointed to my holstered weapon dangling from a hook on the wall. "I check it at the door."

"You put it on when you leave the house?"

"If I'm on a murder case."

"Do you keep it loaded?"

"It's ready to go. Your dad lied to both of us about knowing Snooky."

"He's a liar," Audrey said, then climbed onto my lap and wrapped her arms around my neck. I held her and kissed the side of her face and neck and thought if I squeezed too hard she might break. Eventually our mouths collided, and she pushed me on my back from where I explored the contours of her lovely body. There was no doubt who was in charge of the situation as she opened my pants and guided me into her. By modern standards, my sexual experiences had been few and fleeting, with only one serious relationship under my belt and nothing to match the eroticism of this moment. I wanted only to hang on until she stopped her frenzied gyrations, which she did minutes later before starting up again and continuing until I could hold out no longer.

We laid there sweaty and panting until she climbed off and walked to the bathroom. She returned with neatly combed hair and said, "I'd better go."

As a younger man, I would have given this encounter undeserved significance. As a somewhat older man, I knew better.

21

The next morning, my buddy Santiago waved as I approached his food stand at Diversey and Sheridan. On Sundays he always put aside two specially made breakfast burritos and a weekend Tribune. He called me Señor Ojo Privado. I crossed the street and sat on a park bench near the statue of Goethe and ate while watching a group of teenagers play Hacky Sack. I tried reading the paper but had trouble concentrating. It was day five of my investigation, and while I knew I had uncovered a great deal of information, everything was circumstantial. That is, I had enough evidence to cause a political shit storm but not to convict anyone of Snooky's murder. Two burritos later, my phone rang.

"I don't do that with just anybody," Audrey said.

"I should be flattered?"

"We now have a relationship transcending our common friendship with Snooky. But—"

"You go for older men."

"And you're now a character in my story. That's what I want."

"I have no idea what you're talking about."

"I know," she said and hung up.

It was ten when I got back to my apartment. The potatoes in Santiago's burritos demanded I take a nap. Two hours later my father called and asked if he could come over. He sounded tired but pleased I had welcomed his impending visit. When I saw a limo pull up, it hit me that Dad still appreciated the power of money, regardless of how it was acquired. I waited at the top of the landing. Despite leaning heavily on the railing, he climbed the stairs at an impressive clip. Once inside my apartment, he limped to the recliner and tried to hide the pain as he sat. Then he said, "Tell me where you're at."

"Are you feeling all right?"

He waved me off. "C'mon, talk. What do you got?"

I told him about my conversation with Voss and my plan to shadow Tate that evening.

Voss concerned him. "When Voss said he knew a lot, believe him. He's got one foot in the

police station and another in the street—and he's a
prick on top of it all. When he smells blood, he goes
crazy. He wants Kalijero's ass and usually I'd say
fine, but if he's gonna trample you to get to him,
that's no good. He may even know who killed
Snooky and use it so you give up Kalijero."

"I've got nothing on Kalijero."

Dad didn't respond. I could tell he was
somewhere else. Then he said, "There are some
things you should know. Frownie has this crazy
hatred for Voss. If you mention Voss's name to
Frownie, a valve might pop out of his heart." Dad
leaned back, stared at the ceiling with that faraway
look of distraction.

"Something else you want to tell me?" I said.

"They found prostate cancer a few years ago
but I'm not worried. I'll probably die of something
else before it gets me."

It took a moment to process his statement.
"Why didn't you tell me on Wednesday?"

"Because I told you about Snooky. How much
bad news you want in one day?" He handed me
another check for two thousand. "Now, don't read
anything into this medical crap. You can call my
doc and check with him if you think I'm full of shit.
I got a feeling you don't have much cash in the
bank. Always put money away. You'll never have
any money unless you learn to save it."

"What about you? You got enough money?"

He waved me off again. "You saw the limo,
right? What the hell do you think?"

What did I think? A 1920s Tribune article
compared Great-Granddad Morris Landau's

bleeding of Maxwell Street vendors to a farmer milking a cow. My grandfather told stories of working as the "Market Master," the guy who made sure everything operated legitimately. It was just a coincidence the mayor appointed Morris Landau's son for the job. "I was a first-class grafter," Granddad often said, then cheerfully described the fear he struck in the hearts of hapless immigrants who had escaped czarist Russia only to be screwed by Americans who also spoke Yiddish. "A cut of beef, a nice pair of shoes, it didn't matter. I got it for nothing."

I said to Dad, "I think you would've made Great-Granddad very proud. That's what I think."

Dad smiled and wagged his finger knowingly at me. I knew how to make him happy.

22

Despite the ominous cloud formations hiding the sun, the park across from Tate's house was crowded with early evening Frisbee games and couples on blankets sipping wine. At seven I arrived at the parking lot and waited for Tate's garage door to open, which it did forty-five minutes later.

Since I knew where he was going, I didn't have to follow too close. In the Racine-Addison area, he parked in an alley under a "Loading Zone" sign. Fifteen minutes later, a taxi pulled into the alley and picked up Tate. Now I had to pay attention. The cab headed west on Addison for several miles before turning into a quiet middle-class neighborhood. A few blocks farther, it stopped in front of a nameless corner tavern with a single neon advertisement for

"Half Acre Beer." I watched Tate pay the driver and then shake hands with the bouncer sitting on a bar stool outside the door.

I walked across the street unsure what I felt first: the evening's first raindrop or the bouncer's icy stare. "Hi," I said. He was chomping loudly on gum. His neck was wider than his head. "Is there a cover charge?"

"We're full."

"What do you mean?"

"Fire code says no more can go in."

"I just saw a guy go in."

"He's the last one."

Two young women approached from the sidewalk wearing tight leather skirts barely reaching mid-thigh. The bouncer jumped off the stool and held the door open. Then he sat again and ignored me.

"Sorry, but I gotta ask—?"

"We got room for more girls."

"You sure they're old enough to be in a bar?"

"Mom and Dad are inside."

I held up a stiff hundred-dollar bill and asked if the Franklin pass was valid here. Mr. Neck stared at it a moment and then looked away. I produced two more bills and asked if I could just run in and use the toilet. In one motion, the three bills disappeared into Mr. Neck's fist. Then he jumped down from the stool and disappeared around the corner.

Unlike the building's exterior, the inside boasted panels of stained glass mosaics, a tile floor, upholstered booths, and fancy crystal and brass chandeliers. The room was full of sixty-something men in silk suits sidled up against their dates. It looked like intermission at the annual father-daughter dance. I made my way to the bar and ordered a beer. When the bartender returned with my drink he said, "You wasted a lot of money, my friend. You're too young for this crowd."

"I'm meeting my daughter here," I said and we both laughed.

I saw Tate sitting with a redhead in a skimpy halter dress. They were leaning in to each other while looking at something on the table. I made my way toward them until I was close enough to see several photographs spread across it. They appeared to be of Tate in his younger days wearing a bathing suit. I moved to the opposite side of the table. Tate wore an ear-to-ear grin while his date giggled and played with her hair. I felt sick.

"Excuse me, Dad?" I said, leaning over the table. "Mom would like a word with you outside."

A horrified university chancellor stared at me in disbelief. "Get out of here!" His face had turned crimson. I thought his head might burst.

"Please don't do this to Mom! Her hair will grow back when she's finished the chemo. She doesn't deserve this, Dad . . ." Tate's date vanished into the crowd, leaving only the chancellor and his photographs. I sat next to him and said, "We need to talk. In here or outside—your choice."

"I don't believe this," Tate said.

"Believe it, because I ain't going away until we talk."

Tate stood and led the way outside into a steady drizzle. He was taller than I remembered. As soon as we cleared the door, he yelled, "What are you doing here?" Then he looked at the bouncer. "Goddamn it, why did you let him in?"

The bouncer continued chomping but said nothing. "Let's talk in my car," I said.

"You're harassing me!"

"You want to stand in the rain like an idiot or talk in the car?"

Tate followed me to the Civic and cursed as he squeezed into the passenger seat. "The girls in that bar are all legal age," he said. "I've done nothing wrong."

"You've been lying to me. And you're scared shitless. Why else would you follow me all the way into my car?"

Tate rubbed his eyes. "What do you want?"

"You know what circumstantial evidence is? People are sent away because of it, and I've got a whole bunch. You claimed you had no business with Snooky. That's a lie. You claimed you never met Snooky. That's a lie. You acted as if you barely knew Susan Conway or about her relationship with Snooky. That's a lie. I also know that Snooky was sending you kickbacks from Baron and that Snooky was Audrey's bookkeeper. Those two became pretty close friends, and close friends tend to confide in each other."

Tate glanced out the window. The light rain had turned into a steady downpour. "You think I killed Snooky?" The fear in his voice had disappeared.

"Lying about a dead man will attract suspicion."

Tate closed his eyes for a count and then opened them. "I didn't kill anybody. But I knew if someone started snooping around, it wouldn't look good. Then you showed up, and I didn't know what to do so I denied everything."

"You weren't scared Snooky knew too much about you?"

"Why would I be? Everyone knew him! Everyone said he was the best, completely trustworthy, a goddamn legend. You don't get that way by screwing people."

The chancellor was smarter than I thought. "Why did you tell Audrey that Susan Conway introduced you to Snooky?"

Tate hesitated and said, "I never told her that."

"She says you did."

"Well, she's wrong. And keep her out of this. She's got nothing to do with any of this. Just because she and Snooky were friends doesn't mean she knows anything."

"Baron thinks you and Mildish know more than you're letting on."

"Are you kidding me? I'm the novice here. They approached me just to get access to the trustees—"

I waited for Tate to continue and then said, "Something you want to tell me?"

"Look, I have influence. Lots of people do. I made a case for using Baron Construction, then I just let it go and it turned out for the best."

"You mean Baron got the contract and you got paid off." Tate didn't respond. I said, "When were you approached?"

"In November. The trustees could've told me to go to hell and gone with some other company, and I wouldn't have made an extra dime. We got lucky that Snooky's murder didn't raise any eyebrows regarding the redevelopment contract. Just another dead guy in the big city. If you go explaining to them who exactly that dead man was outside their office windows, they're going to look at me and start asking a lot of questions."

"I understand what you're saying, although I'm having trouble feeling sorry for you."

Tate groaned. "I knew it! You're going to hold this over me until you get whatever it is you want. What do you care if my life is ruined?"

"Relax, Tate, I'm just trying to find the truth. I'll only get mean if I think you or your pals have been holding out on me. Got it?"

He didn't answer but I think he got it.

23

The rain had all but stopped by the time I found a parking place in my neighborhood. I wasn't ready to call it a night, so I decided to take a walk and think about what my next move should be. Water ran through the gutters of Halsted, and a mist hung in the air, forming halos around streetlamps. The sidewalks were full of youthful revelers intoxicated with the boozy urban charm a muggy summer evening in Chicago cast on the young. I walked through crowds lingering outside blues bars and jazz clubs, paused at specialty boutique windows full of scented soybean-wax candles, organic cotton chenille baby blankets, and natural venison dog food. I observed a common man's bar struggling to maintain its seedy image despite its inevitable slide toward de facto Bohemian hangout status.

When I stopped in front of a display of colorfully painted wood-framed mirrors, I caught a whiff of something putrid. I turned back to the crowd but saw only people moving through the night. A few minutes later the odor returned, this time spilling across the back of my neck, and for the second time in a week a blunt object poked me in the ribs.

"Go into the next alley and raise your arms," the voice said. I did as told, thinking a meth-head would just as quickly shoot me on a crowded sidewalk as on a deserted side street. The alley was fairly wide and ran behind several warehouses and a restaurant. Floodlights along the roofs created various shades of darkness. We had walked about thirty yards when the voice ordered me between two semi trailers backed up to a loading dock. I stood in darkness from the waist up, knowing I was in the deepest shit of my life.

"You have a gun," the voice said. "It's on your left side. If you try it, you're dead. Just toss your wallet behind you."

"Why don't you just take my gun so we both can relax?"

Bad suggestion. "Because I'm not that fucking stupid to get that close to you! Now throw me the fucking wallet!"

I pulled the wallet out with my right hand and flicked it backward. I heard him rifle through it and curse.

95

"Forty dollars? Are you kidding? You carry at least a grand. I know you do!"

"Who told you that?"

"I know you do!" he said, and I remembered offering two hundred to the shit breath who escorted me to Mildish's car.

"Dude, I carry a few hundred at most—"

"Bullshit!" he shouted and jammed the gun into my kidney. The barrel bounced around my side as he tried to control his trembling. At any moment I could know the pain of a bullet ripping through my gut. I tried to imagine a quick movement to free myself, but with my body exposed at close range and the brightly illuminated space beneath a trailer the only place to go, my options seemed suicidal. How pathetic to die alone in a dank alley so a junkie who would probably be dead himself in a year could get stoned. I should've stayed on the sidewalk, but then innocent people could've been hurt. Martyrdom was little consolation.

"Okay, you win," I said. "A bunch of cash is wrapped around my ankle." The pressure on my kidney lessened, and for a few seconds I heard only his labored breathing.

"If you're lying, I swear to Christ you're dead," he said then told me to kneel down and get the money.

"Think of what you're saying. The money is on my left ankle. If I bend down, I'm probably gonna go for my gun since I think you're gonna kill me anyway. I might get lucky and kill you first. And even if you shoot first, I might get off a shot and then you'll slowly bleed to death. But if you just take the money yourself, maybe we can both walk away."

I was gambling his brain cell damage would work in my favor. I heard him shuffling around on loose asphalt. When a hand touched my ankle I guessed he held his gun in his right hand near the middle of my left thigh, which meant a bullet's trajectory was more likely to hit my leg muscle or buttock. I dropped my left arm and felt the barrel hit squarely on my palm—I had guessed right. I now had the leverage to keep his barrel immobilized, long enough for me to grab my .40-caliber with my right hand and fire point-blank into his forehead.

I stood frozen in that moment, trying to make sense of the previous minutes, aware of my choke hold on the gun's grip but having no memory of the pistol's report. Gradually, my focus returned to the dead body lying on its back, eyes open, legs folded unnaturally to the side. Despite the gooey mess oozing from the back of his head, there was a surprisingly neat entry wound. I trembled violently and almost stumbled when I stepped over the corpse. A lightning bolt zig-zagged across his bald head: Jason.

I walked out of the alley and merged back into the sidewalk traffic. After a couple of blocks, I stopped to make a call. My shaking hands produced two wrong numbers before Kalijero picked up.

"I just killed a man."

No response, then, "Where is it?"

"West alley off Halsted, before Fullerton."

"Go home and wait."

Why had I called Kalijero? Perhaps because he had just laid bare his own weighty transgression. For some reason, I trusted him.

I didn't remember the walk home, only entering my apartment and sitting down in the recliner. Punim jumped into my lap and started licking the back of my hand. Then she rubbed her head against my chest for a while before rolling over and offering me her white stomach.

An hour later the phone rang. "I'm downstairs," Kalijero said, and I told him the door was unlocked. Kalijero walked in and sat on the couch. "It was a drug deal gone bad," he said. "Just another dead meth-head. Nobody cares."

"You ever kill anyone?" I said.

"You killed a scumbag. We should thank you."

"He thought I walked around with a thousand bucks in my pocket. I wonder how he got that idea?"

"Mayor Daley told him. Their brains are cooked, Jules. The Son of Sam killer took orders from his neighbor's dog. You're a hero. By the way, he had brass knuckles in his pocket."

I waited for more info. "I give up. Why is that important?"

"That cheekbone gash of yours? That's what brass knuckles do."

The first time I saw Lightning Bolt was three days ago at Audrey's shop. Jason looked at a magazine while I waited to ask Audrey out to lunch. That evening he follows me home to smash my face?

"You're telling me the meth-head killed Snooky for drug money?" I said.

"Could be? Although you and Snooky both have that tattoo broad in common."

"You just failed Detective 101. Snooky still had three hundred bucks in his wallet. I had eighty when my dad found me after my encounter with brass knuckles."

Kalijero laughed. "Either way, we'll try to find out where he lived and have a look around."

"You're a shade less burdened than when I last saw you, Detective."

Kalijero shrugged. "I came to a realization. Sometimes a situation is so widespread it works in your favor. Too many got too much to lose. If those guys at the titty club talk, they'll be lucky if only the club burns down. The brass got too many pensions at risk. If you talked, you'd be poison in this town. All Voss's got is whatever that Audrey broad has to say. And you say she's got nothing to show-and-tell."

"She would've told me by now."

"You been chatting with Tate lately?"

"We had a heart-to-heart a couple of hours ago. Why?"

"Just wondering how Tate's business card got into meth-head's pocket."

I stared at Kalijero, unable to attach an emotion to this news. He was at least twenty-five years older than me and had seen most of what a big city had to offer. "You didn't answer my question," I said. "Did you ever kill anyone?"

Kalijero sighed. "One more thing. The junkie's gun wasn't loaded."

I stared at Kalijero waiting for the gag line. "I killed an unarmed man?"

"Don't be a fool! You didn't know it was unloaded. Someone was sending you a message."

"A suicide mission."

"This is getting to you. I know people who specialize in this kind of thing. They can help you figure things out."

The light from the table lamp reflected bright yellow flashes off the gold Parthenon pendant around Kalijero's neck. "I don't need help," I said. "In fact, I never felt better." And it was true.

24

The following morning I felt anxious. I had to explain to Audrey how I lost her a paying customer. If sex with her had made me a character in her story, killing her meth-addicted client had surely enhanced my role. Before I headed to Taudrey Tats, Frownie called, wanting to see how I was holding up after the shooting. "Who told you?" I said.

"It doesn't matter how I know. How're you doing with it?"

"It was the junkie or me. I think I made the right choice."

"How did he get ahold of your Colt?"

Kalijero hadn't told me, but I should've known. "Another junkie took it off me two days ago."

Frownie sighed. "How long until you solve this case?"

"That's a rhetorical question."

100

"Stop with the college words. Now you got this dope business to deal with? Julie, you're killin' me."

"This isn't about dope. Anybody could get robbed by a scumbag."

"Your dad called. He wanted to make amends, but he forgot why he was angry. I told him it was because I taught you to be an investigator. He said there had to be more reason than that. If there was, I don't know about it. Anyway, get enough evidence, give it to the cops, and end this already."

"Does Dad know I blew away a junkie?"

"I didn't say nothin'. Did you hear what I said?" When I promised I would do my best, Frownie hung up without saying goodbye.

* * *

At ten o'clock I walked into Audrey's studio. She was in The Kitschen bent over the light table. As I approached, she held up a tracing of a stork expelling from its ass pointy-headed babies shaped like bombs.

"It's a statement about overpopulation's effect on the planet. What do you think?"

"Your customer with the lightning bolt has violent tendencies."

Audrey lowered the drawing. "His name is Jason and why are you saying this?"

"The cops took one of Tate's business cards off Jason's body."

"His body?"

101

"He tried to rob me last night at gunpoint. Someone told him I had a thousand bucks. I shot him dead."

I saw the Audrey of five days ago who had turned ghostly white with the news of Snooky. "Oh, my god," she said and sat down in the hydraulic chair.

"Where do you think Jason got one of your dad's cards?"

Audrey's sudden look of horror startled me. "You think my father tried to have you killed?"

My laugh was involuntary. "Nobody would give an assassin their business card."

Audrey relaxed a bit. "Of course. He probably found a card here. I never returned Dad's calls, so he would write me letters and stick a card in the envelope. I guess he thought it was funny. In one week, two people I know are dead."

"Having junkies for clients will do that. Let's keep Snooky's death in a different category."

"You look really serious. And I can hear it in your voice."

"I killed someone yesterday."

Audrey looked at me with a little girl's fascination. "Yeah, how was that?"

"I'll never be the same," I deadpanned.

Audrey studied me. "I don't think you will be."

I started for the door. Just before I walked out, Audrey shouted, "Call me?"

25

The combination of Audrey's bizarre personality and learning what a bullet could do to a

102

man's head had cluttered me with conflicting emotions that needed suppressing. But my existential tendencies would have to wait.

I thought I should visit my father soon and also call Kalijero to see if they'd found the dump Jason called home. The sun baked the moisture off the streets, adding to the humidity. I walked in a northeasterly direction, unsure of my destination but gradually succumbing to the call of Diversey Harbor, my favorite place to catch a breeze.

There were closer lakefront beaches, but for some reason the stone amphitheater seats of Diversey Harbor had become my little zone of comfort. I was pretty sweaty by the time I crossed Cannon Drive and passed the Goethe statue. Once at the huge concrete blocks, I sat and tried to assemble my thoughts. From the lake came only the occasional puff of cool air, but the calming effect of the harbor's shimmering beauty made the visit worthwhile.

"Your eye looks better."

The voice came from my right periphery, which accounted for the eye remark. Without turning I said, "I bet you followed me all the way from Halsted, Voss."

"And I'll bet you got a little crush on Miss Tattoo Skank, eh, Landau?"

"Is it really necessary to talk like a sleazy degenerate?"

Voss smiled, stepped down to my row. "Tell me the truth. You think I'm stupid?"

"You care what I think?"

"I bet you know what cliché means, college boy. When I was in uniform, not one cop in a hundred knew what cliché meant. A lot of those guys were walking clichés but would never recognize themselves."

"What the hell are you talking about?"

"What are you doing, Landau? Trying to make up for the sins of your ancestors? Or are you living out some fucked-up Hollywood gumshoe fantasy? Wouldn't you rather be working in an air-conditioned office like your North Shore pals?"

I turned, faced those teeth shining through his fleshy face, and wondered what he gnawed on to keep them from growing into tusks. "What is it with you and my family? Can't you insult me without dragging my forebears into the fray? I mean, what's the point? Do you have a point besides the one on top of your head?"

"Forgive me. I didn't realize how sensitive you were about the Landau legacy. See, my blood is as Chicago blue as yours. Get it? Lots of old trees with roots all tangled up with each other. And trees live a long time. Anyway, falling for Miss Tattoo while investigating a murder. How cliché of you, private investigator."

"It's boy meets girl. Happens all the time with humans." The insult sailed over Voss's head.

"So true. Ever thought how screwed up your judgment gets while strolling in cliché-land? Okay, Landau, I'll show one of my cards: I still have a few friends who work in Homicide. One of them picked up the phone the Monday morning after Snooky's body was found. Turns out the call came from an address on Armitage. Turns out that address has a tattoo shop for a tenant. Now tell me, when was it you first spoke to the tattoo tootsie?" He handed me two pieces of paper: a warrant signed by a district court judge and a phone record from the Armitage address with one line highlighted in yellow.

"Audrey knew Snooky was dead before I spoke to her? Running to the toilet and puking out her guts was all an act? What exactly did the caller say?"

"Show me a card, Landau."

"I got nothing to show on Kalijero."

"I just busted your case wide open, and you still got nothing for me? You sure are an ungrateful bastard. Runs in the family, I guess."

"There you go again—for all I know, you made that phone call from Audrey's shop. Maybe you're trying to blackmail her for some fictional book that exists only in your diseased brain."

Voss shook his head. "Are you really this stupid? Wouldn't she have told you if I was blackmailing her?"

He had a point, but I was done talking. I stood and dropped the documents in Voss's lap. As I walked away he shouted, "My patience is running out, Landau!"

By the time I reached Taudrey Tats, I had a fist-sized knot in my stomach. Audrey was still working at the tracing table; she looked surprised but happy to see me.

"Back so soon?"

I detected no residue of shock or sadness to the news I had given her two hours earlier. "Do people ever come in and ask to use the phone?"

"All the time."

"They use your phone?"

She gave me a puzzled look and said, "My cell phone is for business. They use the shop's phone. Local calls only." She pointed to a cordless unit on a small foyer table beside two phone books. "Go ahead and use it if you want."

Anyone could have made that call, I told myself then dialed Kalijero's number.

"It's Landau."

"Good timing. Meet me at Area B in an hour."

"You want to give me a hint?"

"No," he said and hung up.

* * *

The Area B district station was the picture of drab in an otherwise quaint neighborhood of century-old bungalows, frame houses, and walk-ups. I sat on a backless wooden bench outside the detectives' room and admired the framed photo of the chief of detectives. Against the wall were two vending machines, one for soda, another for delicious sandwiches sealed in plastic. A bulletin board held posters for the "Battle of the Badges" and the "Area B Memorial Motorcycle Ride." There was also a congratulatory letter from the assistant superintendent for Area B's professionalism at the North Side Irish Parade.

Kalijero stuck his head out the door, motioned for me to enter, and closed the door behind us. Deputy Chief Hauser sat with his arms folded, leaning back in a steno chair behind a metal desk. He was a short, round-headed man with a crew cut and matching mustache. He wasn't smiling, and Kalijero didn't bother introducing us.

"Meth-head had a cell phone," Kalijero said. "Your pal Tate is on his call list."

I glanced at Hauser, who stared straight ahead. Kalijero handed me the phone record. "This is the office reception number," I said. "Do we know if he got through?"

Kalijero pointed to another number and said, "That's a landline. Each call was about ten or fifteen seconds long. We traced it to Tate's Evanston address." Then he tossed a GO Flames! button on the desk.

I said, "Tate's business card on meth-head's body? Phone calls on meth-head's cell phone? Tate is smart enough to be a university chancellor but at the same time a complete idiot? Why didn't he just bring meth-head as a guest to the University Club?"

"We're pushing five hundred murders this year," Hauser said. "Schoolkids getting shot left and right. City council doesn't give a damn about some mob ass-kisser getting rubbed out. But if you got a university chancellor dealing meth, that's something else."

"He's being framed for murder," I said. "The meth thing is a distraction."

Hauser leaned forward in his chair and looked at me. "Fine. But if you get information suggesting it's more than a distraction, I want to hear from you. And I don't give a shit if he's your star witness in the flunky's death. You tell us what you know. Got it?"

"Yes, sir."

"We're done. Kalijero, you stay."

I sat on the bench outside the door and listened to the tone of Hauser's voice waver between threatening Kalijero and pleading with him to focus on cases the brass cared about. When Kalijero emerged, he was surprisingly charitable. "He's getting it from all sides—city council, superintendents, the public, the press." As we stepped outside the building, he changed the subject. "You're sure Tate's being framed?"

"I'm not sure of anything."

"Great. What're you going to do about Tattoo Girl?"

"What do you mean?"

"You just said Tate's not the killer."

Kalijero's implication hit me hard. "She thinks he did it," I said. "But she's a piece of work. Would she rat out her own father?"

"If she had a good enough reason," he countered.

"Why should I believe anything she says?"

"She called from her shop—"

"Anyone could've made that call—" I said.

"She said she knew the deceased—"

"When I told her Snooky was dead, she puked her guts out!"

Kalijero glared at me and then spoke slowly like an angry father. "Don't ignore facts just because everything doesn't fit together. And don't let a young piece of ass cloud your judgment."

I conceded his point and said, "Have you found meth-head's flop?"

"An abandoned building. We just cleared out the trash."

By "trash," he meant junkies. "How about letting me have a look around?"

Kalijero wrote an address on the back of a business card and handed it to me. "Show this to one of the uniforms and they'll let you in." Then he walked away, leaving me alone in front of Area B district station.

26

The address was a boarded-up, one-story brick storefront on Ashland near North Avenue. A uniformed officer stood in front. I showed him Kalijero's card, and he stepped aside without saying a word. A urine stench greeted me at the entrance. Graffiti covered the walls. Chunks of broken drywall, syringes, glass pipes, metal spoons, and fast-food containers covered the floor. Filthy mattresses occupied two corners of the room. A building inspector walked around shaking his head. Under his arm, he held several large "Building Condemned" signs.

"You should've seen the two they pulled out of here an hour ago," the inspector said. "It was like one of those zombie horror shows. What are you looking for?"

"I'm not sure," I said and started shoving debris around with my foot. The building inspector walked outside and began hammering the signs into the structure. I kicked a small vial across the floor and for some reason felt compelled to pick it up. A couple of fingerprints were preserved in a dried milky residue. I dropped the vial into my shirt pocket. It wasn't long before the noise and pee odor combined to give me a headache. As I gave the room one last look, my eye caught a sparkle near one of the mattresses. I walked to where I thought I had seen the flash and squatted down, careful not to touch my knees to the filthy floor. I saw, partially covered by a piece of drywall, a glass figurine of an elephant. I picked it up. It seemed miraculous that it had not been chipped or scratched. Voss told me he'd sent a warning to Snooky. Voss had a good memory for who did business with mobsters.

* * *

The debris pile on Maxwell Street looked the same despite Snooky's body no longer lying on top of it. A fifty-five-gallon metal drum overflowed with rubble, as if someone had the idea of keeping the area tidy and then gave up. In cold weather, the drum would've been ablaze and surrounded by bums keeping warm.

Next to the mess, the Juketown Community Bandstand stood relatively unscathed. Perhaps the spirits of the blues performers who had stood on that stage kept the evil developers away. Down the street, crews worked on constructing a chain-link fence that would gradually encompass the entire block. The arrogance of the signboard's sleek architectural rendering of the residence hall earmarked for Maxwell and Halsted was not lost on me. I tried and failed to picture my father's romantic immigrant world that once occupied this corner. Thanks to Granddad's stories, I saw just a pathetic fish peddler who had tried to challenge Great-Granddad's authority only to watch the cops toss the poor man's kippered herring, halibut steaks, and A1 haddock to the "huddled masses" eager to receive this manna, apparently from heaven.

Across the street, a university chancellor was being framed for murdering a man whose body was dumped practically at his office doorstep. The evidence was circumstantial yet compelling—and completely illogical.

"What's all the noise?" Audrey said when I phoned her.

"I'm on South Halsted. Lots of construction."

"What are you doing there?"

"I need to talk to you about the case."

"So talk."

"In person. When are you done tonight?"

No response. I repeated the question. "After seven," she said and hung up.

I walked north on Halsted and stopped in front of a man about my age holding a large sign that read, "Extinguished Flame, Campus of Shame." He handed me a flyer outlining the so-called premeditated process by which the neighborhood was "stolen."

"Why are you doing this?" I asked.

"To fight back," the man said.

I looked at the paper and read of an alleged scheme developed decades earlier and implemented gradually. First there was the piecemeal purchase of land followed by buildings demolished or mysteriously burned. Then the phony rumors of the city's plan to impose eminent domain on property owners who refused to sell. Bit by bit, a struggling neighborhood capitulated. Those who had defiantly remained moved out and took with them any hope of new investment reinvigorating a once-thriving marketplace for the poor.

"It's an old story," I said. "Nothing changes, nobody cares."

"I care," the man said and then politely told me to fuck off.

I deserved that, I supposed, and continued walking. At Roosevelt Road, I turned east a few blocks and then back north on Desplaines Street, in search of the new Maxwell Street Market. But instead of a neighborhood block party atmosphere, I saw throngs of people milling about a concrete expanse bordered by the expressway on one side and anonymous warehouses on the other. Tables and booths selling everything from tacos to ceramic statues of the Virgin Mary lined the margins, while the blues and jazz performers who would have been scattered throughout the old market were now exiled to a designated area. Sequestered from the privilege of intramural university ball fields and stylish condos, the Maxwell Street Market was now a flavorless bone thrown to the poor.

As I headed back to campus, I thought of Tate's comment about having access to the trustees. Typically, trustees were prominent members from the business, legal, and financial communities mixed with a smattering of career educators and a few students. In Illinois, trustees had the final decision regarding the university's use of funds appropriated by the state's general assembly.

112

Historically, political corruption and cronyism had cracked this ivory tower—despite its ostensibly honorable façade—early and often.

I stopped at a cybercafé, bought thirty minutes of Internet time, and downloaded the trustees' website. Twelve photographs appeared in four rows of three. Under each picture was a hyperlinked name caption. I scanned the photos, unsure what I was looking for but curious about those people known by the term "trustee." It was a cryptic title, under the radar of the general public except when one was caught paying for call girls with the taxpayer's dime.

Had there been several women trustees instead of only one, my brain might not have registered the familiarity of her face, and I might not have noticed among the staid portraits of corporate manhood the glowing, confident smile of Susan Conway. I clicked on her link and examined her resume, which boasted titles of "Principal and CEO" and several corporate chairmanships—and then I checked her voting record.

27

Through the opaque glass of her office door, I saw the fuzzy outline of Susan Conway sitting behind her desk holding a phone to her ear. I heard the excited inflection of her muffled words while she offered encouraging advice to a prospective client. When the conversation ended, I tried the doorknob and was surprised it wasn't locked.

She looked up and said, "You should've called first."

"Your line was busy." I walked in and closed the door.

Conway's chair screeched backward. "You're very unprofessional, Mr. Landau. And I really don't have time—"

"Why didn't you tell me you were a trustee?"

Conway stared at me. "Why would I? What does that have to do with Snooky?"

I walked to one of the leather chairs in front of her desk and sat. "That depends on what else you might not be telling me."

"Out of respect for your friendship with Snooky, I've been trying really hard to like you. But your cheeky arrogance is making it difficult. And right now I can tell you, sir, that I don't like you and I want you to leave my office."

"By the way, I took your advice and checked the bylaws."

"What are you talking about?"

"The rules that govern faculty members conducting private business from their offices—and then there's that evangelizing thing."

"I've done nothing illegal!"

"I don't know. With the language they use, it's a really gray area. Ultimately the ethics committee should decide."

Conway closed her eyes and sighed through her nose. "What do you want?"

"For five years you were on the record for voting against the redevelopment of Maxwell Street. Then in January, you voted for it. What changed your mind?"

"The buildings were in disrepair. There was no evidence of the cultural continuity that once defined the neighborhood."

"And you just realized this in January?"

"I hadn't been paying attention. I'd been relying on my memories as a child and the stories my grandfather told me. Then it was pointed out to me how much things had changed."

"Perhaps it was Chancellor Tate who pointed out to you how much things had changed?"

Conway stared at her desktop. Then she said, "Several people discussed this with me. Dr. Tate may have been one of them."

"Did you know Snooky was laundering kickback money from Baron Construction to Tate and Representative Mildish?"

"It was none of my business what Snooky did with his clients' money."

"Why are you protecting them?"

"I don't know what you're talking about."

"I'm talking about a half-billion-dollar construction contract, and I'm talking about murder."

Susan Conway stood then walked to the door. "Get out!"

I placed one of my cards on her desk. Before leaving, I promised to call next time.

28

Back home, I put the glass elephant on the windowsill and collapsed on the couch. As my brain waves gradually slowed, I thought of checking the university's bylaws to see what they actually said, then wondered if a junkie took Snooky's elephant. And what was Voss's memory theme about? His tone had a childish "I know something you don't know" quality. I hated goddamn games.

Two hours later, I awoke to Punim mewing loudly while holding a small plastic fish in her mouth. I put a variety of hearts, livers, and kidneys in her bowl and fixed myself a sandwich of avocados, sprouts, tomatoes, and cucumbers. Then I cracked open a cold diet ginger ale and turned on the Cubs game, where they were about to throw out the first pitch. By the third inning, it was time to head over to Taudrey Tats. When I walked out of my apartment, I couldn't recall if there had been any scoring or who they were playing.

Audrey sat in the hydraulic chair with her face buried in a fat paperback. Her index finger moved quickly down one side and then the facing side. By the time I had walked to the edge of The Kitschen, she had twice turned over new pages.

I said, "You're kidding, right?"

"What do you mean?" The book was Atlas Shrugged.

"You read that fast?"

She gave me a blank look. "I lose myself. It's like there's me looking at the words, and then another part of me interpreting. It's the same for my art. Part of me draws, part of me interprets. When they both agree, then I feel free."

I took that for a yes, although I had no idea what she was talking about. "Someone called the police from your phone the Monday morning after they found Snooky."

Audrey blinked a few times. "L.A. made the call."

It was my turn to give Audrey a blank look, and then I remembered her dark-haired friend visiting from California. "Why did she call?"

"To tell them we knew the deceased."

"So when I walked in here the next day, you already knew Snooky was dead?"

"Part of me did," she said sounding a touch impatient. "But I was denying that part until you walked in and told me he was murdered. Then it hit me that Snooky was gone forever and I fell apart. I'm hungry."

Audrey was hungry. "What did L.A. say about her conversation with the police? I assume they sent someone over."

"Nobody came over. She said they didn't seem that interested. Can we go eat somewhere?"

We walked to Broadway and then headed north until we stopped at a Chinese restaurant. On the way Audrey started talking about a potential client who wanted his entire back covered in a mural. "It's going to tell the story of wolves devouring humans until the humans become endangered and have to be put in protected sanctuaries . . ." She was still talking when we sat down. "Am I boring you, Jules?"

"Did your dad know your meth-head client Jason?"

"You're joking."

"How do you suppose Jason got your dad's home telephone number and why would he call him?"

"You said he had his business card."

"The card had only his office number."

"Then he must've copied it from my address book."

"You have your dad's address?"

"Of course. I told you I know where he lives."

She had a good memory. "Why would Jason call your dad?"

"Maybe he was looking for me."

"He knew where to find you."

Audrey did her best to look offended. "You think I'm up to no good, Jules?"

"It's your dad I'm trying to figure out."

"You get to be friends with repeat customers. I knew Jason was a drug addict, but I treated him with respect. If he was going to kill himself with drugs, there was nothing I could do about it. That's just his story. And he always paid me in cash. It was just business."

"You let anyone look in your address book?"

"It sits on the counter. What do I care who looks at it?"

"What could've been so important that Jason could not have waited until he saw you at the shop?"

"The guy was out of his mind. Maybe he was going to ask me for money again."

"You gave him money?"

"Once. He paid me back many times with tattoo business."

"The calls were only ten or fifteen seconds long. Would your dad have told you Jason called?"

"He would've left a message on my cell. During the day it would have been Anna, his personal assistant, answering the phone. She's there every weekday to feed the cats, tidy up, run errands, and leave something in the fridge for dinner. Anna has my cell number, and she would've called me if I had a message."

"Why would anyone call you at your dad's house?"

"Because the landline I have is just a courtesy phone for customers to make local calls. When my cell rings, I always know it's going to be a business related call."

"You're friends with this personal assistant?"

"Sort of. I feel sorry for her. She seems kind of desperate. I pay her on the side to let me know what's going on. Dad needed someone to take care of him. I met her first and described what she was getting into. I told her he's just a big baby with a bad temper. She drew the line at changing his diapers."

Our food arrived, and while we ate I feigned interest in the wolf mural she was planning for someone's back and listened as she spoke excitedly of what such a project could mean for her reputation. As her words washed over me, I studied her lovely face and thought how the promise of sex gave women an extraordinary power over men. She spoke with a bubbling, self-absorbed, childlike joy, as if she were the creator of worlds and her client's back existed solely for a chapter of her story. The wolves would be beautiful yet bloodthirsty;

compassionate yet ruthless. And they would feast on entrails ripped from human torsos.

After dinner, we strolled down Broadway. Audrey continued talking about what she could do with the bloody realism of the mural while I enabled her discourse with innocent questions about the world of body art.

She stopped abruptly. "I'm really sorry about the other night," she said and laughed. "I had too much wine. And I really need to get home."

"Where is home, anyway?"

"It's probably better you don't know." Audrey gave me a quick hug and walked away.

29

At eight o'clock the next morning, I drove back into the park across from Tate's house while eating one of Santiago's burritos. I had hoped the personal assistant would get an early jump on things but had to wait until ten-thirty before a beat-up blue Subaru wagon with Pennsylvania plates stopped in front of his house. A nice-looking woman of above-average height with a lean build and light brown hair stepped out. She wore a sleeveless shirt. Her arm muscles were well-defined, as if she had known a life of heavy lifting. I guessed mid-forties.

I called in her license plate to Johnny Bonds, who called me back with the name Anna Piantowski. Her car was still registered in Pennsylvania. A short time later, Anna Piantowski emerged from the house holding a piece of white paper. I leaned against an enormous oak tree directly across the street from her car. When she crossed the sidewalk, I walked quickly to block the driver's side door.

"Hi, Ms. Piantowski. I'm a friend of Audrey's."

She seemed unimpressed with this fact. "She's probably at work."

"I'm also a private investigator." I showed her my license. She took it from my hand, studied it, handed it back. I noticed the cell phone on her belt. "I'm investigating the murder of Charles Snook. He did some work for Dr. Tate. Audrey said you take phone messages during the day. Do you remember a man named Jason calling in the last two weeks?"

"I don't remember, and I've got a lot of errands to run." She held up the piece of paper and then stuffed it into her pocket. On her forearm I noticed a tattooed outline of a heart enclosing the letters "SC."

"Each call lasted less than fifteen seconds. The time it takes to ask if someone was home and then leave a message. Maybe he asked for Dr. Tate."

Anna Piantowski's jaw muscles momentarily popped up. "I don't keep a message log. If someone called for Dr. Tate, then ask Dr. Tate if he got the message. Now do you mind getting out of the way?"

"I don't mind, but first let me tell you some facts: Three calls were made in the afternoon hours to this house; three calls were answered. The drug addict who made the calls has since had his brains blown out the back of his head. And here's a possible fact: If the drug addict wasn't calling for Audrey or Tate, then maybe he was calling for you."

Anna Piantowski was now a wolf about to tear out my throat. "Someone called and hung up," she said. "I said, 'Hello, hello?' and they hung up. It happened a few times."

"And you were not going to tell me this because . . . ?"

"Because I'm in a hurry and didn't think about it."

"Why do I get the feeling you're not surprised to see me?"

Anna Piantowski pursed her lips, and I noticed her hands had become fists that accentuated her forearm muscles. "Look, mister, I have work to do. I'm going to ask you one more time to get out of the way."

I did as asked. As she drove away, I saw her left arm bring the cell phone to her ear.

* * *

I walked back to the picnic table and called Kalijero. "I'm across from Tate's house," I said. "I just had a not-so-friendly chat with his personal assistant, who's in his house five days a week. She just called someone from her cell."

"You want to know who she's been calling?"

"I want to know who she's calling right now."

"I need proper legal authority to track someone."

"She lied to me when I asked if a recently murdered drug addict had called the house."

I heard a grunt, then, "I guess that's justifiable. Give me a couple hours."

The phone rang as I walked back to my car. "Do me a favor," Dad said. "Meet me at Halsted and Maxwell." He sounded troubled. I asked if the end of a barrel was pushed against his head. "Just shut up and meet me there," he said and hung up.

Forty minutes later, I once again stood at the appointed corner amidst the anarchy of a construction zone. The chain-link fence had advanced another fifty yards or so. For several minutes, I watched the backhoes dig up enormous buckets of dirt before I noticed an apparition of a man in an argyle sweater standing on the opposite corner leaning heavily on a cane. I crossed the street and Dad surprised me by hooking his left arm around my neck and pulling me into an embrace. I carefully hugged him, fearful I would crush the bones of his back.

"I didn't mean to sound sore on the phone," he said. I suggested we sit in the shade. Dad gestured for me to lead the way, and he followed me to the front stoop of an abandoned three-flat—soon to be demolished. I helped him lower himself to the third step.

"Why here?" I said.

"First, tell me what's going on."

I told him about meeting Tate at the barely-legal-teen bar, the dead junkie, my -encounter with Voss at the lakefront, the conversation at Area B headquarters, my get-together with Susan Conway, and that morning's conversation with Tate's housekeeper.

"You didn't say how the junkie got dead," he said.

"Old age."

"Funny. And what about that young broad?"

"What about her?"

"Don't let your prick think for you."

"Snooky adored her."

"Those nicknames in Snooky's book, the names I didn't know. Figure them out yet?"

"All but one. Butch is still a mystery. I don't think Butch was part of the Maxwell Street scam."

Dad let out a heavy sigh. "You once referred to our family as a bunch of petty criminals."

"Sorry. Maybe petty was the wrong word. How about small-time?"

Dad surprised me with a laugh. "In 1887 a Clark Street saloon keeper knew someone in the recorder's office who owed him a favor, and my grandfather got his first job making phony real estate sales in return for kickbacks. When he was city collector, bribes from property owners magically transformed unpaid taxes into paid taxes. As city sealer of weights and measures, he saw that cash gifts resulted in accurate scales. As ward committeeman, he had poll watchers kidnapped to make sure the elections were fair. By this time he was making good money. Enough to get his son elected to the superior court at age thirty. Enough to get his chauffeur off a homicide charge after he ran over a woman from Highland Park."

Dad took out a handkerchief and wiped his forehead. Then a broad grin spread across his face and, as if under a spell, he continued. "But the Maxwell Street Market," he said and laughed again. "That's where Granddad was king! He had his own handpicked policemen. The peddlers feared him and paid him regularly or they were out! He created permanent market stalls and sold and resold them for hundreds of dollars. At the height of his power, he threw himself a fiftieth birthday banquet and was presented with a diamond star purchased by the grateful merchants of the Maxwell Street Market!"

Dad turned to me and said, "To this day, you can find books about Capone or Hymie Weiss, and somewhere you'll find your great-grandfather's name. He's even mentioned in Bellow's Humboldt's Gift—I got the book if you don't believe me."

My father looked pissed off. His voice had acquired enough edge to instantly explain how this skinny apparel salesman could also collude with people who never mourned the loss of an associate's finger because of a delinquent payment. He had that certain chromosome required of men who had no impulse to rationalize how they acquired wealth or dwell on who got hurt in the process. It was the American way to make money; the fact he had hoodlum blood in his veins was a badge of historical honor and fuck you if you had a problem with it. I supposed I had a segment of that same chromosome but only enough so that I could go through life emotionally neutral about having a felon for a father and, perhaps, being a tad proud of it.

"These people he sucked dry," I said, "these were his people."

"He was a man of his times. Some he helped and others he didn't. But he always took care of family. You don't think Capone shafted other Italians?"

"Capone was a killer."

Dad eyed me suspiciously. "Your great-grandfather was a highly respected man. You should command such respect one day."

Dad looked away. I wanted to remind him of the difference between respect and fear, but his last comment provoked an unexpected insight. His 1923 birth situated his consciousness astride two spheres: the poor immigrant world that equated money with reverence and the newer, enlightened world that valued integrity over wealth. It seemed Dad would go to his grave with the former world still holding sway in his deep brain regions.

I said, "Why are we here talking about this?"

"Your investigation, Julie. There's nothing new here. They're all involved. Politicians, contractors, accountants, trustees, chancellors. The junkie sticking needles in his arms, the broad scratching out tattoos, they're all involved. It's the same old story being told over and over for a hundred years."

"You think it's a waste of time? You hired me, remember?"

Dad shrugged. "Find out what happened to Snooky and make them pay. If you do that, nothing's wasted. But don't think you'll change anything. One corrupt official goes down, another takes his place. That will never change."

Dad stared straight ahead with both hands resting on top of his cane. I studied his profile trying to find a hint of myself in his face but saw only those sunken cheeks and hollowed-out eyes.

"What's the deal with Voss?" I said. "He's talking in riddles. Is there some bad blood I should know about?"

Dad looked as if he was considering my statement. "I don't know of bad blood with Voss. And if there was, I think I would know about it. Either way I don't give a shit what that prick thinks. He can't touch me. Fuck him."

"I was more worried about him touching me."

Another dismissive wave. "He's got nothing on you. That's the key. Just don't give him anything to use against you. I think you know what I mean. Cross the t's and dot the i's."

"You need a ride home or what?"

"I have a ride," Dad said and pointed at the limo parked down the street. Then he took a folded manila envelope from his sweater pocket and handed it to me. "Here's another installment. This time in hundred-dollar-bills. Thirty of them."

Dad made a comical effort to raise himself. I lifted him up from behind with my hands under his arms. He had the weight of an aluminum lawn chair.

I said, "Are you sure this prostate thing isn't more urgent?"

"This isn't about my goddamn prostate! I'm just old, that's all. But I'm not going anywhere. Not yet." Dad waved at the limo. "We'll talk soon."

The limo stopped in front of us. The driver helped Dad into the car. They pulled away a few feet then stopped. Dad's window lowered. "And don't worry about Voss, I mean it. Just don't give him anything."

I watched the limo disappear into traffic and wondered how long an old guy in Dad's physical shape could live. My cell phone rang.

"You're in luck," Kalijero said. "Piantowski's phone had GPS technology. Her call to someone named Susan Conway connected before she left Tate's street."

30

According to cell phone records, the majority of Anna Piantowski's calls originated from a location on Pulaski Avenue in the Polish Village neighborhood. Driving down the street, you were challenged to find a sign that didn't include "Polski," "Waclawowo," or "Jackowo." Piantowski lived above the Zapraszamy Bakery. I hadn't eaten since breakfast.

Behind the counter, a girl about sixteen wore a bright red dress under an embroidered white vest covered in sequins and pearls. Partially covering her golden blond hair was a matching headscarf. She smiled sweetly, and I smiled back. I was thinking she might not speak English when she said, "We got free samples."

She offered me a large platter of bite-sized pastries full of fruit. I asked if they sold anything similar to a burrito. She thought for a moment, then pointed to a list of ingredients on a chalkboard and said, "We can make a giant pierogi and put anything you want in it."

"Perfect," I said having no idea what a pierogi was but from the list picked potatoes, onions, and cabbage. She disappeared into the back and then returned to take care of someone else. When the customer left, I asked her if she knew the lady who lived upstairs.

"Nope. I don't know nobody up there."

"Who owns this place?"

"I dunno." She smiled again.

A few minutes later, a man emerged from the back holding a large fan-shaped dumpling and handed it to the girl. I paid for my pierogi and walked around to the alley where the stairway to Piantowski's apartment was located. I loitered in the area while eating and keeping an eye out for a blue Subaru. It was about two o'clock when I finished the potato pie. By two-fifteen, my eyelids weighed ten pounds each. I found a small park in an adjacent neighborhood of brick two-flats and spent a drowsy hour waiting for my blood sugar to stabilize before walking back to the bakery and climbing the steps to Piantowski's apartment. There was no answer to my repeated knocking, so I sat on the landing and waited. One hour later she appeared in the alley holding a bag of groceries. Apparently preoccupied, she kept her gaze downward as she climbed the steps and practically stepped on me.

"What the hell are you doing here?"

"I'd like to ask you a few more questions."

"Really?" She stepped over me to open the door. "You try to come in and I'll knock your skinny ass down the stairs."

I needed a different approach. "Look, I'm sorry for being abrupt. I just want to talk a little more. I'll give you twenty bucks, and I'll stay right here and talk through the door." I took out a twenty from my pocket and held it up.

Anna Piantowski looked at the money. "Wait here." She returned empty-handed, grabbed the twenty from my hand, and jammed it in her pocket. Then she took out a cigarette and leaned against the door. "Okay, what do you want?"

She was about to flick her lighter, when I said, "You called Susan Conway after driving off this morning."

Her arms dropped. "You're a cop! You're supposed to tell me that!"

"I'm working with a cop trying to find out who killed Charles Snook, a man who knew Susan Conway and Jerry Tate. Along the way I've come across drugs, money laundering, and dead people. That combination gives cops lots of snooping power."

Anna Piantowski lit her cigarette then took a deep drag. "You said the druggie that called the house is dead. Finding his killer will help you?"

"I know who killed the junkie. Why was Tate's home phone number on his cell phone?"

"No idea. Tate's not into drugs, if that's what you're thinking."

"How do you know Susan Conway?"

"She's a client."

"Why did you call her as soon as you drove off this morning?"

"I had a question."

"About one of Tate's errands?"

"I said she's also a client. I shop for both at the same time. I'd forgotten if she liked onions in her chili."

"You forgot if she liked onions. It's so simple and logical. But I just can't shake the feeling you and Conway aren't telling me everything. Conway told you I might be stopping by, didn't she?"

"So what if she did and who cares anyway? I don't know anything. I run errands for rich people. That's it."

"What's Tate blackmailing her with?"

Piantowski took another long drag, exhaled, and flicked the butt. I watched it sail over the railing and land in the alley. "You're crazy," she said.

"C'mon, Anna, I gave you twenty bucks, give me something. These people don't give a damn about you, and all I care about is finding Snook's killer."

"How the hell would you know who cares about me? You don't know anything about these people. They happen to be my friends, and you're asking me to talk behind their backs."

"Maybe you can tell your friends that as long as they're hiding information, people like me are going to keep asking questions."

Anna Piantowski giggled and shook her head. She saw me as a ten-year-old playing Dick Tracy. Without another word, she opened the door to her apartment and closed it behind her.

* * *

I got lucky and found a parking place in front of my apartment. Good thing, too, because I was dead tired. So tired I didn't think much of hearing the ballgame on my television from halfway up the stairs. When I opened the door, I saw Kalijero sitting on the recliner with his feet on the coffee table. On his lap sat a bowl of tortilla chip crumbs. "What the fuck, Jimmy, you got a warrant?" I asked.

"You know how friggin' easy it was to break in? At least put on a dead bolt."

"What're you doing here?"

"I did a little more snooping into Piantowski's and Conway's phone records." Kalijero pointed to a printout on the coffee table. "Look closely and you'll see a definite pattern with the same four phone numbers going back many months. Three of the numbers we know about. The other I'll let you figure out. I just got a double homicide dumped on my desk."

I picked up the papers. "This almost seems too easy."

Kalijero shrugged. "It's the times. Technology makes snooping damn simple. Especially when you got a drug dealer in the mix. Tate's number on that meth-head's phone is like a golden ticket to legal spying. Hell, you could buy the info online if you wanted."

With technology, the government could find out anything they wanted about anyone they wanted. I'd never felt so safe.

31

Wednesday, August 1, the ninth morning of my investigation. Sunlight hitting the glass elephant on

132

the window glared brightly, momentarily blinding me. There was no spectrum reflecting off the wall. Maybe that was a good sign. Although some cultures saw rainbows as symbols of hope and prosperity, other cultures saw them as harbingers of death and destruction.

Three people clearly benefited from Snooky's murder: Tate and Mildish, whose kickbacks would go undetected, and Baron Construction, whose multimillion-dollar contract would go unquestioned. But were they killers? Could one or all of them kill another human being, someone they knew, liked, and respected, and then live with it forever? There was also Susan Conway. Her opposition to the redevelopment of Maxwell Street threatened to derail the Tate-Mildish plan—until someone changed her mind.

I studied Piantowski's phone records while eating my morning oatmeal. The pattern of phone numbers Kalijero mentioned began last November, continued through December and into January, right up to the university's final vote. Piantowski's first conversation with Caller X lasted seventy-six seconds. She then called Conway, who, four minutes and twenty-two seconds later, called Tate. She probably left a message, since that call lasted only twelve seconds. Then she called Piantowski back and the two spoke for twenty-eight minutes. This flurry of exchanges took place at least once a week, then ceased in mid-January. Caller X was never heard from again. I dialed Caller X's number. A female voice announced the name of a law firm. I hung up.

Flesch, Bozik, and Wigdor, LLC, was the top criminal defense firm in the city. Sixty-two-year-old Alan Flesch never turned down a client who could afford his one-grand-per-hour rate. And when he received his quarter-million-dollar retainer, he was yours, as if he were the one in danger of being sentenced as Bubba's shower mate. It was said the worst you could do with Alan Flesch was a few years in Club Fed. His most recent high-profile case involved a dying infant brought to the emergency room with twenty-eight broken bones and a fractured skull. Despite the testimony of numerous bone specialists affirming that the trauma was not accidental, Flesch produced his own experts claiming the presence of a rare bone disease. His closing statement evoked images of grieving parents already given a life sentence in the guilt-ridden flames of hell for not recognizing their son's illness. What could be a worse punishment? The parents were found guilty of neglect and given three years in a minimum-security prison.

Carrying a nearly empty briefcase and wearing my only suit—a brilliant Gucci knockoff, charcoal gray with silver pinstripes purchased from the basement of an old friend of Frownie's—I entered the Monadnock Building and took the elevator to the tenth floor. I loved the Monadnock Building for its blend of historical beauty and modern technology. Flesch's office was full of natural light coming through the original huge windows of pre-air-conditioned Chicago.

Since nobody sat in the reception area I walked toward a woman seated at a desk outside a corner office. "Are you Mr. Flesch's secretary?" The woman was sixtyish with kind eyes. "Chancellor Tate gave me Mr. Flesch's name. I just wanted to drop off a card." From the briefcase I produced one of my business cards and handed it to her.

"Private investigator?"

"I'm just starting out. If I could get a shot with Flesch, it would really help my career. I wouldn't even take a fee unless I actually got results." There was an advantage to having a baby face.

Betty put the card down. "We use the Altshaw agency but I'm sure Dr. Tate wouldn't mind if you used his name over there. Ask Mr. Altshaw for an informational interview. These guys love talking about themselves."

"That's a great idea," I said and thanked her for her kindness.

32

"Eddie Altshaw's scum of the lowest kind," Frownie said over the phone. "Flesch and him go way back. What makes you think he's gonna give you anything?"

"Cash."

"You think you got enough cash for that bastard?"

"Why not? I just want to know what Tate used to blackmail Conway. For me it's a game-breaker, and it's no skin off Altshaw's nose."

"You're not seeing the big picture, Julie. Tate's Flesch's client. Flesch is Altshaw's client. If Tate gets in trouble, the money stops flowing."

135

"Let's just say he goes for it. How many thousands will it cost?"

"I've been away too long. More than one, less than a hundred."

I was out of my league, but I thought it was worth a try. Thanks to my father's last donation, I had five thousand to play with. It was painful to think of parting with it so soon, but this piece of the puzzle was too big to ignore.

The ease in which I was allowed to see private investigator Eddie Altshaw surprised me. When I arrived at his office, it was as if he expected me. And if he was scum, he was the best-dressed scum I had seen in this business, although the long unlit cigar bouncing up and down between thin, sharp-edged lips on an egg-shaped head was distracting. Think Humpty Dumpty in an Italian suit.

"What do you want?" Altshaw said.

"Susan Conway."

Altshaw looked around the room and threw up his arms. "I give. Who the fuck is Susan Conway?"

"A job for Flesch's law firm late last year."

Altshaw's face glazed over and froze in my direction. Then his lips started manipulating the cigar again, and he grinned broadly. "Why do you care?"

"I want to know what you got on her."

"Why do you care?"

"It may be relevant to a murder case I'm working on."

"Why do you care?"

I pulled a pile of cash from my briefcase and put it on his desk. "That's three grand."

Altshaw started laughing. "Keeping the family business alive. I bet I don't have to count it, either!" Still laughing, he shouted for someone named Irv, and a short, clean-cut guy appeared. Altshaw scribbled something on a Post-it note and handed it to him. "You ever think about changing your name, Landau? Or maybe move to a different city where your name doesn't give you away?"

"Why should I? I'm not the only Landau in the phone book."

"No? Well, I'll bet you're the only one in this business. Irv, take this gutsy little prick to the vault and give him a peek at what's in that box number."

Irv smiled and motioned for me to follow. Before I left the room, Altshaw said, "You know, kid, I would've taken half that amount." He started laughing again, and I felt compelled to join in. "Go ahead, laugh all you want now. But if anyone finds out what you're about to get from me, you're done in this town."

I followed Irv down a stairway into a garden-level storage room with bars on the windows. In the corner of the room next to an outside door was a walk-in vault. Irv dialed the combination, opened the door, switched on a light, and gestured for me to enter. I obeyed his command and saw floor-to-ceiling walls of safe deposit boxes. Irv pointed to a box and told me to try to open it. I reached up and pulled a few times on the latch when a sharp pain pierced my side and dropped me to my knees only to be met with another blow to the face. My last memory was the sensation of being dragged around like a sack of concrete.

I woke in the alley, slumped up against a brick wall outside the door through which Irv had deposited me. Despite feeling as if a day had passed, I was able to replay the events that had actually occurred within the last half hour. I touched my left cheekbone and was grateful Irv's fist had not revisited the right side of my face, which was still healing. As I stood, pain radiated through my left side and stabbed me with each step. I found my car, drove home, then limped up the stairway to the couch where once again I lay with an ice pack on my face.

Staring at the cracked paint on the ceiling, I wondered if I had reached a crossroads. That is, I had to decide how this incident would affect not only the investigation but the definition of myself. The world was full of sociopaths, some of whom had no qualms about associating with killers and others who didn't mind knowing a person targeted for death. And then there were those who slept soundly after pulling a trigger at close range. Murder helped the flow of money seek its own level. How low did money have to dribble before it led to Snooky's killer?

33

Pinkish urine brought to mind the emergency room until I remembered my ten-thousand-dollar deductible. Having already parted with three grand, I thought I'd give it a day or two.

"Altshaw saw you coming a mile away," Frownie said. "Flesch warned him."

"I never saw Flesch, only his secretary." I was sitting upright on the couch balancing the ice pack on my face.

"He's got his whole office bugged. He hears everything. Maybe one day you'll realize the kind of people you're dealing with."

"I gotta get whatever Altshaw has on Conway."

"Forget about it."

"I can't forget about it. If I can prove Tate's blackmailing Conway, it'll break the case wide open."

"Then try some other channel. Don't confront Altshaw directly; he might kill you next time. What about the tattoo broad?"

"She thinks her dad's a killer, but there's this sick love-hate-father-daughter thing going on. It's potentially volatile. I can't take her seriously."

I hung up with Frownie, knowing I needed an insider, someone connected enough to have a foot on both sides of the line. Frownie was out of the question and Kalijero had too much at stake. The only other option was Satan himself. But what would I have to give up in exchange?

* * *

Back on the stone amphitheater seats near Diversey Harbor, Voss said, "Holy shit, Landau, not again!" He referred to my plum-colored cheekbone. "Who'd you piss off this time? Sniffin' around some other man's cooch?"

"Tate's lawyer is Alan Flesch. Flesch hired Eddie Altshaw to dig up dirt on a woman named

Susan Conway. I need to know what he's got on her."

"And you thought you could just stroll into his office and ask him? Just knock him down like you was driving a limo?" Voss laughed hard enough to create a tsunami across his stomach. "If it makes you feel any better, you got thumped by a former Golden Gloves lightweight champ."

"What will it cost to get Altshaw's info?"

"You know what I want."

"C'mon, Voss. Everything I got on Kalijero is hearsay. There's nothing written, no ledgers, no diaries, nothing. Whatever Snooky had he took with him."

"Let's pretend I believe you. Tell me what Kalijero was involved in. Better yet, wear a wire, and I promise to personally deliver whatever it is Altshaw has on Conway." His words inflamed my battered body. I saw a red stream filling the toilet bowl. How much blood was Snooky worth?

"You want to tell me about some bad plasma between us I should know about?"

Voss's face clouded over. "I got nothing against you except your name."

"What did my name ever do to you?"

"Let's just say your name doesn't smell like a rose. Any other questions, Landau?"

"Back to Altshaw. What if I gave you ten grand?"

"What if you gave me a hundred grand?"

He might as well have said a million. I walked away from Voss thinking there had to be another way without whoring myself out. Wearing a wire for the likes of Voss might get me Snooky's killer, but my name would be poison in this town, and if I didn't have my name, I didn't have anything. I went over my conversation with Tate three days earlier. He had referred to himself as the novice, the outsider who was approached for his access to the trustees. At the time I had trouble believing his innocence, as if he were helpless to resist the forces of greed. But if Tate really was just the victim of his own weak character, then the new channel Frownie suggested I find would have to run through the Honorable Jacob Mildish.

34

After consuming sixteen ounces of a cranberry, dandelion root, and juniper berry concoction, I stood in the bathroom waiting to see the result of the remedy. Still a touch pink but no worse. I relaxed in the recliner, feeling confident my kidney was on the mend but exhausted and aching. I needed to stay focused on a strategy for interviewing Mildish. As I drifted off, I imagined my father standing before a judge who read through his rap sheet while weighing the pros and cons of his life. Dad listened patiently while staring at the floor. When he looked up at me, the phone rang.

"Hi, Julie!" Audrey said. "I haven't heard from you in two days."

"Don't call me Julie. I've been busy."

"You sound ticked off."

"Sorry. Had a tough day."

"All that construction down on Maxwell Street where Snooky was found. Does that have something to do with your case?"

"Maybe. Why?"

"Well, I just remembered something. My dad served on a committee that had to do with all that. It was called Citizens for the Preservation of Maxwell Street Market."

"Interesting. He was against the redevelopment and then became an active supporter. Ask him what changed his mind."

"I don't want to talk to him."

"You spoke to his housekeeper to make sure she knew what she was getting into, but you won't ask him a simple question?"

Deep sigh. "Obviously, someone offered him money to change his mind. It happens all the time."

"Doesn't say much for your father."

"He's a shit. All he cares about is money. He would kill for it."

I told Audrey I needed to sleep and she signed off, telling me not to be a stranger. I drifted off still unsure if Audrey really thought her dad was a killer or if she was just telling one of her damn stories.

35

I spent the night in the recliner. Wedged between my legs, Punim stared at me. She darted to her food bowl. My side and cheekbone ached but not as bad as the night before. After a week of plum-colored blotches on my face, I didn't care how I looked. Punim feasted while I showered.

The Illinois General Assembly wouldn't be back in session until November, which meant that Mildish would be out giving speeches and kissing the asses of constituents or vice versa. On this day he was scheduled to discuss the ongoing state budget issues at the public library. The talk was to begin at eleven at the Eller Auditorium on the lower level of the colossal building. I arrived an hour early to get a feel for the place and stake out a location to ambush His Honor as he departed. I walked to the back row of the four-hundred-seat room and stared at the enormous mahogany stage that typically accommodated dance or music programs. Had I not known what was going on, I would've assumed a foreign dignitary or a rock star was making an appearance. Spaced uniformly throughout the room, beefy bodyguards in ill-fitting suits aired electronic ringtones through two-way radios. I took an aisle seat and watched them nervously gad about their assigned areas. I wondered how a state representative justified such security. But this was Chicago, after all. You didn't have to be politically astute to know "state representative" was comically euphemistic for a guy like Mildish, whose connections and money put him in a power class that would've made Great-Granddad proud.

One of the bodyguards approached me. "There's almost an hour before Representative Mildish arrives." When I realized he had nothing more to say, I thanked him for the information. The secret agent stepped away, alerted a comrade through his radio, and spoke quietly. Moments later, I had an agent on both sides of me and one behind.

"What is your business here, sir?"

"I'm waiting for the show to start."

"Mr. Mildish won't be here for an hour or so. How about waiting in the lobby until we're ready to seat people?"

"You think you could do me a favor and give him this?" I handed Boss Agent my card. He ignored it.

"I'm going to ask you one more time to step into the lobby."

I found his behavior in a public library shocking, and the smart-ass part of me wanted to pursue a scene of outrage. Luckily, my submissive side knew I had nothing to gain. I retreated to the lobby, where tourists milled about the marble floor and looked at paintings and photographs of local philanthropists. Businessmen and women clutching briefcases and folders trickled in. They looked nervous, as if scheduled to perform in a talent show. A few ventured into the auditorium, which inspired the rest of the herd to file into the auditorium. I entered last, reclaiming the aisle seat in the back from which I had been ejected. Several dozen empty rows remained between me and the hundred or so people who sat up front. When Mildish finally waddled onto the stage draped in his black pinstripes, I thought stockholders' meeting or crime syndicate conference—take your pick. This man clearly had no interest in avoiding stereotypes and seemed even to encourage such comparisons with the silk cravat and the bejeweled rings jammed on to his fat fingers.

Reading from a prepared speech, Mildish reported on community development projects, citing issues dealing with senior housing, abandoned property, landmark designations, and zoning ordinances. The kindliness of his voice defied his mobster appearance; it was as if he were reading a bedtime story. Fifteen minutes later, the speech ended and Mildish exited stage right. As if on cue, his front-row constituents stood and calmly stepped down into the orchestra pit and through a side door. In a short time, a line backed up through the pit and stretched down the aisle, almost reaching the lobby. Apparently His Honor had an office behind the stage where he held private meetings. A real phantom of the opera.

I approached one of the secret agents. "What's the password to get to meet with Mildish?"

"You have to make those arrangements beforehand."

I took out a business card and a hundred-dollar bill. "I'll pay extra for return service."

He glanced at the bill then carefully took it from my palm with thumb and forefinger before stepping away to speak quietly into his radio. Agent Two appeared, took the card from Agent One and left. A few minutes passed before Agent Two returned and handed the card back to Agent One, who stepped closer to me. I handed him another c-note and he gave me my card. On the back was written, "Guild Books, 2 p.m."

* * *

A North Side hangout for aspiring artists—I was surprised Mildish knew such a place existed. I arrived at the appointed time to see His Honor seated comfortably in Guild's coffee bar, reading a one-act play. A leather folder lay on the table.

"This place always brings me fond memories," Mildish said as I approached the table and sat. He put the play, A Marriage Proposal, down. "As a drama student, I was obsessed with Chekhov. Oh, my, now the other eye?"

I didn't take the small talk bait. "Everything's starting to come together," I said.

"With your investigation of Mr. Snook's murder?"

"There are only a few people who would have benefited from Snooky's death. These people were involved in illegal activities involving millions of dollars. Snooky knew about all of it."

"As I said at our meeting last week, Mr. Landau, I don't know anything about Snooky's murder. If you have some evidence suggesting that's not true, why don't we look at it together? We can do it at police headquarters if you like."

"Last week I cared only about my friend's death. But I was naïve to think I could just step over anything lying on the path leading to a murderer. You must have realized this. Whether you're involved in a killing or not, you're a big player in a big picture, and if I have to use this information to find out who killed my friend, I will."

"Coming from a family well versed in the machinations of Chicago politics, I'm surprised it took you this long to see this big picture. And by implicating me in some transgression, you hope to accomplish what? I didn't make the rules, Mr. Landau. I'm guilty only of playing the game as it has been played in this town for well over a hundred years. If I were truly a killer, if I were truly worried that you could destroy my life, do you think you'd be alive right now? And do you think you'd make a difference in the big picture?"

"Well, do you think I could at least get an A for effort?"

"You have quite the cavalier attitude. Some might say reckless. But humor me if you don't mind. Let's use Maxwell Street as an example. If you had been paying attention, you'd know the state's historic preservation department employed the spouse of a university trustee and two spouses of Baron Construction principals. It was all over the news but what happened? Maxwell Street was sacrificed with little outrage."

For the first time, his casual, cold-blooded manner gave me the creeps. "How many people are you willing to kill to have your precious ass covered?" I asked.

Mildish stared at the table as if he had not heard me. Then he said, "I guess you'll always view me as a killer. And I'll just have to accept this disturbing fact."

"What did Tate use to blackmail Susan Conway?"

Mildish held my gaze before closing his eyes and sighing. Then he started nodding his head. I got the feeling he had been anticipating this question. "Why is that important?"

"Depends on who killed my friend."

Mildish loosened his tie then dragged a handkerchief across his forehead. "Miss Conway is a favorite of wealthy religious conservatives. They trust her with their money because they think she's one of them. They send her clients. She gets to invest their future earnings, and in return she helps them find the sharpest students—potential converts—who have demonstrated business intelligence and possess the kind of ambition much sought after by these types. It's a lucrative situation for her. Unfortunately for Miss Conway, Dr. Tate was shown photographs of Miss Conway engaged in activities her clients would not look upon approvingly."

"Details, please."

Mildish squirmed in his seat and for the first time looked uncomfortable in his pinstripes. "Miss Conway prefers the company of women over men. The Bible-thumpers frown upon that."

I took a few seconds to process his words and the images conjured up in my brain. "It's hard for me to believe someone as professional as Susan Conway would be so careless with her personal life—knowing how much was at stake."

Mildish's face went through several contortions before he opened the leather folder and handed me several eight by ten photographs of two naked women intertwined on a bed. I immediately recognized Anna Piantowski and remembered her tattoo of the letters "SC" inside a heart.

"You were told these sex photos were going to be used for blackmail?"

"I had nothing whatever to do with it."

"But you knew it was going to happen so you pulled a few strings to get copies for personal use."

Mildish ignored my comment. I supposed I should've been thankful nude adult women were his fantasy. "There are many aspects to getting a job done," Mildish said. "Business, Mr. Landau, is a competition like any other race or sporting event. Just as athletes try to find an advantage, so do businessmen."

"I see, you work for the same company, just not in the blackmail department. I'm sure Baron didn't know anything about it, either—although he probably has his own copies."

"Men are free to pursue their own self-interests. I won't take responsibility for the actions of others."

"Of course you won't. Why run the risk of being guilty of something?"

I stood to leave. Mildish said, "I'm sure you're a good, decent man, Mr. Landau. And I'm confident that you will do everything in your power to find your friend's killer without hurting innocent people in the process."

"As long as the innocent people don't interfere with the pursuit of my self-interests, they have nothing to worry about." I turned to leave then stopped and said, "Do you often take those photos out in public or just in the men's room with your pinstripes bunched up around your ankles?"

Mildish had no comment other than the hollow, vacant stare of his black eyes.

Susan Conway's door was open. From the hallway, I watched her work on her laptop, analyzing complicated spreadsheets, I imagined, creating profitable investment strategies that would help her clients feel God's love.

Without looking up she said, "You might as well come in."

I did as told. "You knew it was me?"

She wore a floral print blazer over a white blouse with a ruffled collar. She looked up from her computer. "You're the only person who ever lingers outside my office like a criminal. Fall down Rollerblading again? I see you landed on the other eye this time." She leaned back in her chair with a blank expression.

I sat down. "I'm in the mood for chili. You ever been to Chili Mac's? I'll buy."

Conway maintained the same vacant look, although her eyes narrowed. "What the hell do you want, Mr. Landau?"

"It's a peace offering. I'd like to buy you a lunch of terrific chili."

"I detest chili."

I guess she didn't get Anna Piantowski's memo informing her she liked chili either with or without onions. I stood and said, "Maybe I should close the door," and did so without comment from Conway. I retook my seat. "I know why you changed your vote."

Conway shrugged. She seemed resigned, defeated. "And what are you going to do with this new information?"

"You've lost your spirit, Ms. Conway. I hope it's not as bad as you think."

"And what do you care about what I've lost or what I think?"

"I have no ill will toward you. I'm just trying to find out who killed my friend."

"And I bet you'll stop at nothing to get what you want."

It hurt to be viewed as so insensitive. "I'm not here to intimidate you. Can you implicate Tate in Snooky's murder?"

"Information on my personal life would not have shut me up about murder. Snooky was my friend, too."

"You don't think Tate was involved?"

"I don't know anything about the murder. And I had no impression Tate knew anything, either."

"He was threatening to ruin you!"

"He was just the messenger! The others are using him as a shield. He's in too deep to refuse." That explained why Anna Piantowski would continue working for Tate while her lover was being blackmailed.

"The others being Mildish and Baron?"

"I told you Snooky never used names. Tate approached me about the photos and begged me to change my vote. For my own good, he wouldn't tell me who was behind it all. He had real fear in his eyes."

"Did Snooky know about this?"

"I never said a word to him. I realize now he may have been killed because of our friendship. They couldn't risk retribution if he found out I was being blackmailed. He knew everything, after all. He kept the books." Conway pushed a tear off her cheek.

Had Snooky been a hack bookkeeper, I might've believed he was killed to cover tracks. But he had spent over twenty ears gaining the trust of bookies, loan sharks, gamblers, and a generic assortment of other lowlife hoods who lived on the fringes. These were his people. He knew the game and the consequences of breaking the rules— Snooky didn't have a death wish.

I told Susan Conway I was convinced her friendship with Snooky had nothing to do with his murder, and she seemed to appreciate my words, although I doubted we would have lunch together anytime soon.

37

The phone rang at three a.m. "Your dad asked me if Voss was holdin' somethin' over your head," Frownie said.

"You couldn't have held on to this breaking news until seven or eight?"

"Voss can't wait. I gotta know. Does that cocksucker got somethin' on you?"

"What the hell could he have? And don't you think I would've told you about it?"

"I don't know what to think. Your first murder case and I'm thinkin' you see it all as a game. Well, let me tell you, it ain't no game."

"Frownie, you're overreacting."

"Yeah, sure. You know everything, Julie. But actually, you don't know shit." He hung up. Thanks, Frownie.

I couldn't get back to sleep. I sat in the living room and studied the streetlamp through the warped window pane and tried to imagine what Frownie felt. His consciousness straddled Prohibition, the Great Depression, Capone's rise and fall, and the crime bosses that followed. Great-Granddad's influence peaked during the tenure of Mayor "Big Bill" Thompson only to crumble with the rising Sicilian population of his Twentieth Ward domain. He was eventually kicked out of politics with—as the Tribune reported—"Scarface Al applying the boot." Somewhere along the line, Frownie got to know Granddad, then my father, and finally me. How or why the relationship endured had never been revealed. But I knew some people made money while some went to prison. I also knew Frownie was right: I didn't know shit.

About four a.m., I took a walk down Halsted. The late July air was damp but pleasant. Produce trucks raced up and down the street, servicing the numerous bodegas and breakfast nooks preparing to open. The smattering of drunks, dope addicts, and whores gadding about were just part of the scenery. When I returned to my apartment, the sky was beginning to lighten.

My legs felt heavy on the stairway. I tilted the recliner back to its farthest position. I had foolishly thought uncovering the blackmailing of Susan Conway would break open the case. Instead I learned that greed and corruption were alive and

153

well in Chicago city politics. Who knew being a lesbian was even frowned upon by anyone anymore? I drifted off thinking I'd wake up to discover the last ten days had all been a dream and Snooky was home dusting his collection of rain-forest bird statues hand-carved from tagua nuts. Once again, the phone woke me two hours later.

"I'm taking the morning off," Audrey said. "Come with me to a gallery."

"I'm trying to focus on the case."

"Perfect! Come with me to take your mind off things awhile and that might help you see more clearly."

I supposed she had a point.

* * *

Next door to Audrey's shop, a thirty-something woman wearing a sequined lavender head scarf was on her knees in the display window of Vagabond Boutique, dressing a mannequin in a 1950s housedress. Beside her lay a large orange tabby cat. Our eyes met long enough to surpass my comfort level. I blinked. Her gaze followed me into Taudrey Tats, where Audrey waited to wrap her skinny arms around my torso. She squeezed tight with the side of her head plastered against my chest just under my chin. I squeezed back, and it felt good, though it seemed pretentious on her part.

I let up a bit, but she squeezed harder. Audrey manipulating her sexuality, leading me around by a ring through my nose. Pathetic.

"All right already," I said and freed myself. "I'm a big boy."

She studied me. "You got punched in the other eye?"

"Maybe."

She shook her head. "Well, then, let's go."

I volunteered to drive, but she flagged down a cab. "It feels more urban-appropriate," she said. I didn't bother asking what that meant. She gave the driver an address on the northwest side.

"Where are you taking me?" I said.

"A gallery I stumbled on last year. I go every few months when there's a new exhibit." She described the artwork at The Eclectic Narcoleptic as typical of "extreme development fused with intellectual neo-expressionism."

Audrey hummed an unidentifiable tune. I tried to relax, but my thoughts stuck to the case. In particular, Voss's mysterious grudge. Did the Landaus piss off the Germans somehow? Or maybe it was the Greeks he hated, particularly Kalijero. Did he blame me for his inability to settle an old score with Kalijero? Why wouldn't Kalijero tell me about this conflict? Maybe he didn't know.

The taxi let us off in front of a converted firehouse in another brick-bungalow neighborhood. "The artist is H. R. Musick," Audrey said as we walked into the sparsely populated engine bay. "His disparate pop-art characters interacting on photographed backgrounds create vignettes of absurd theater. It's a brilliant demonstration of the subtext of real life."

We looked at a picture of a child dressed in an old-fashioned sailor's outfit sitting cross-legged on the back of a giant black swan as it floated across a pond. The child's toy schooner floated next to them.

I felt compelled to ask, "That's the real life you live in?"

Audrey responded with something about each picture having a million worlds and each world having a million stories and that truth was everything and nothing—or something equally bizarre. Then she recognized a woman across the room and ran over to her. I continued the tour seeing only the events of the previous ten days. Fear of not finding Snooky's killer creeped in. Angles, I thought. There had to be another angle. Snooky was family, but he wasn't blood. If someone wanted Landau blood, why didn't they kill me?

Audrey's voice startled me. "What stories do you see?"

The painting in front of me depicted young girls, bunnies, a World War II fighter plane diving with guns spitting out orange flames, and a black bear. "I see Snooky lying on a pile of construction trash with two bullets in his head." Audrey had no reaction. She started telling her own story about the picture's characters. Tate killed Snooky, I thought, because he was perversely jealous of Snooky's relationship with Audrey. Or maybe Tate killed Snooky because he knew too much about Tate's financial dealings. Both scenarios seemed improbable and had nothing to do with bad blood.

"Tell me what you're thinking?"

I looked at Audrey. "I need a story of irrefutable evidence."

We walked to the firehouse's tower, a sixty-foot-tall structure used for drying hoses. At the top of the structure was the original 1912 bronze bell. "I'll start spending more time with him," Audrey said. "Maybe we can figure out who actually pulled the trigger."

"Your life isn't complicated enough? I mean, you've got real issues to deal with regarding your dad."

"If Dad is a murderer, things become much less complicated."

As soon as I attributed her unapologetic indifference to the world as part of a shallow, immature personality, she blindsided me with a simple observation that demonstrated intellectual depth and sensitivity. Add a generous sprinkling of sex appeal and you had a woman difficult to resist.

We shared a cab back to Taudrey Tats, where Audrey had planned to spend the afternoon preparing sketches for her wolf-mural client. Next door, the Boutique Lady remained in the display window, meticulously pinning all kinds of trinkets to a dress. From her knees, she looked up and stared at us while we said our goodbyes.

"Your gaudy neighbor likes to stare."

Audrey turned and waved to Miss Boutique, who smiled and resumed decorating. "She thinks you're in love with me."

Audrey's sudden relapse annoyed me. "The shock value of your blunt honesty is zero. In fact, it's a real turnoff."

Audrey stepped back and searched my face. "Okay," she said and walked into her shop.

38

The Friday lunchtime crowd kept me circling the neighborhood longer than usual, and with each pass I noticed the black Cadillac limousine parked in the loading zone across from my apartment. No doubt it idled with the air-conditioning on. Eventually I found a space two blocks away and started walking. About half a block from my building, the limo bullied across both lanes of traffic and stopped in front of me on the wrong side of the street. The passenger rear window lowered to reveal Mildish's cherubic face. Undisturbed by the blaring horns and obscenities directed at his driver, Mildish said, "Could you give me a few minutes, Mr. Landau?"

Mildish pushed open the door. A frigid gust swept over me. My Honda could drive ten miles burning the gas used to create that arctic blast. Once inside, Mildish tapped on the glass partition. The tires squealed, throwing me against the door as the car swung around and merged back into traffic. "Sorry about that," Mildish said. "I guess none of us is immune to the temptation of power."

"Especially four hundred horsepower," I said.

Mildish chuckled. "It's time I tell you that Dr. Tate murdered Mr. Snook."

When he didn't elaborate, I said, "That settles it. I'll call Area B headquarters and have a warrant issued for his arrest."

I waited until Mildish said, "I made an executive decision—"

"You can't prove it, but you're going to throw Tate under the bus. Why?"

Mildish rubbed his chin and then his eyes and forehead. "To end this once and for all." His voice had that unemotional edge of a professional assassin.

"You mean to end my investigation once and for all."

"It looks bad, I know. It was our fault. Tate was new to this, and we didn't keep an eye on him. We should have anticipated his panic and stepped in. Surely you must know he acted on his own, and we had nothing whatever to do with your friend's murder."

"You want me to accept your executive decision as truth and leave it at that?"

"It's just business."

"And you think your business decision will exonerate you? If you don't like being a suspect, then give me proof of your innocence or someone else's guilt."

I didn't think it possible to sweat inside a refrigerator, but Mildish took out a handkerchief and started mopping his forehead as if sitting in the left field bleachers at Wrigley. "I will testify under oath—" Mildish started to breathe rapidly and rub his hands together. Then he frantically searched his jacket pockets and found a pill to place under his tongue. "Give me a few moments, please," he said. I waited as His Honor's head fell back and his fists pushed into the leather seats, apparently bracing himself against some unimaginable horror. A couple of minutes later, he sighed deeply and relaxed.

"I've never actually seen a panic attack, but that sure looked like one," I said.

"We all have inner demons to battle," Mildish said and leaned toward me just a bit. "It would be a mistake to interpret mine as a sign of weakness."

I should've been scared or at least intimidated. Instead, I leaned toward His Honor and said, "Tell me again how you had nothing to do with those photos Tate used to blackmail Susan Conway."

Mildish straightened himself. "Good god almighty—that was business! His efforts at persuasion were failing. He was showing signs of weakness, so we made a decision. In retrospect, we never should have brought Tate in. We could have used some other channels to get to the trustees. If we were going to kill someone, it would have made more sense to kill Tate than Mr. Snook. We trusted Mr. Snook. Tate was an amateur."

"You tracked me down just to tell me of your executive decision?"

"I have been made aware that Dr. Tate's past includes some shocking behavior. The kind of behavior that should ruin a man's life."

"Killing someone isn't shocking enough?"

"This involves the abuse of a child."

"What does this have to do with Snooky's murder?"

"Dr. Tate murdered Charles Snook. Trust me on this decision."

I struggled to quash my laughter. "I should trust you?"

"Tate will be told that he can either tell the truth about it or be exposed as a degenerate. In effect, this will end your investigation."

I took a moment to digest his words. "You're going to tell a man to confess to murder or be labeled a child molester? You are indeed the all-powerful Oz! What the hell kind of choice is that? Either way, he's finished."

"There's nothing to be gained by putting off the inevitable. If a guilty man can't be brought to justice, then bring the justice to him."

"Your executive decision seems a bit irrational and desperate."

Mildish groaned. "I had nothing to do with Mr. Snook's murder. We hope you'll be satisfied with our decision and let things return to normal. Of course, you'll be well compensated for dropping the investigation." Mildish tapped on the glass partition and the driver slowed at the next intersection before pulling a sharp U-turn.

I stared out the window watching the city blocks pass as we moved closer to my apartment. "So who's going to inform Tate of your executive decision?"

"Do not trouble yourself with such details."

"And what does the Windy City Wizard have in store for me should I not be satisfied that Tate acted alone or acted at all?"

"This is the last time I will tell you that I don't kill people. But if you want to work anymore in this town, you should know that destroying someone's reputation is not beyond my reach."

The limo pulled over in front of my building. I left without saying goodbye.

39

Frownie wore a black silk bathrobe with matching slippers. He placed a small, ornate glass on the end table next to me and then sunk into a huge leather lounger and put his feet up. "These are specially made for single malt," he said. "See the outturned lip? That's supposed to channel the whiskey to the tip of your tongue so the smoky taste is emphasized." I sipped and nodded and sipped again. When I didn't say anything else, Frownie said, "You don't give a shit. So what's up?"

"Mildish is giving Tate the choice of confessing to Snooky's murder or being exposed as a child molester. And he said he'd pay me off to drop the whole thing."

Frownie sipped and held the whiskey in his mouth. When he finally swallowed, he said, "How much he gonna pay you?"

His response annoyed me. "Is that really the point?"

Frownie sipped again and repeated the routine. "Sometimes you gotta step back and reassess things, Julie. Not all crimes are solved. You did your best for now. Maybe somethin' else will come up later. But in the meantime if you can get paid, that's not such a bad thing."

"So Mildish wins and the truth never comes out?"

"What did he win? You got him shittin' his pants so he's gonna pay you. With guys like him, you don't wanna go too far if you can help it. He's a coward and cowards take the easy way out. Destroyin' someone's life is easy for a guy like Mildish. If you had rock-solid proof of who killed Snooky, then maybe you stick to your guns. But if you got nothin', then you gotta ask yourself if it's worth riskin' your life anymore."

"What about Tate? If he's the killer, no way he acted alone."

"What about the molestin' thing?"

"I don't know. It's possible, I guess. Audrey suggested he was a pervert."

"So he cut deals with crooks and he's possibly a child molester. He made his bed, Jules—and you can't protect people from themselves. Remember, Snooky also chose to do business with criminals."

The day had begun with Frownie's three a.m. freak-out about Voss. Twelve hours later, Frownie casually sipped whiskey and told me to take the money and run. Play the game was what he was really saying—and be thankful you got a few bucks for your trouble. The disappointment stung, but I stayed in Frownie's company and listened to him mellow with each sip, gradually sliding into the ocean of memories that shaped so many lives of his generation. Having lived through an economic calamity and a world war, it was not difficult to understand how the promise of easy money influenced Frownie's world. A quick payday was a no-brainer when images of hard-working Americans waiting in line at soup kitchens were as real as the late twentieth century crack whore. Prohibition gangsters and crooked politicians lived in my consciousness only as romantic images of Hollywood history. The bad guys I had recently dealt with were hardly larger than life. Despite having killed a hopeless junkie, I had seen too little of what it really meant to live and die in America. Frownie had seen too much.

* * *

I left Frownie's place troubled by the idea of taking Mildish's money. Lack of sleep caught up to me. At home I lay on the couch where Punim joined me, nestling between the crook of my arm and my rib cage. I fell into a deep, black sleep from which I awoke three hours later with no memory of dreaming but with the idea that I should inform Audrey that her father's life had just become more complicated.

"You sound sad," Audrey said

"Yes, I'm a sad guy. But I need to talk to you about some new developments."

"Good, I can show you some of my wolf drawings! Come by any time before ten."

I splashed cold water on my face. Refreshed from the nap, I was struck by the strangeness of Audrey's response. Considering our sober discussion a few hours earlier, I didn't expect wolf sketches to outweigh new developments in a murder case. But she was an artist after all.

I arrived at Taudrey Tats around eight. Audrey had set up a display rack of pencil drawings. The first sketch showed a furry, angelic face worthy of a Hallmark greeting card. As much Siberian husky as wolf. With each subsequent sketch, the face changed until it gradually morphed into a vicious, bloodthirsty hellhound.

"It's the potential in all of us," Audrey said. "Hungry sexual violence just beneath the surface."

I didn't want to consider the possible scenarios that may have influenced this interpretation. "Let's get some tea or coffee," I said, and Audrey suggested a place down the street called Blind Roasted.

"The owner really is blind," she said as we walked. "He buys coffee and tea by sense of smell."

The shop was softly lit by small spotlights illuminating landscape paintings of various Asian and South American countries whose seeds and leaves we drank. Audrey ordered a cup of Peruvian dark whole bean, and I got a cup of lemon lavender mint. We sat at a table under a watercolor of Brazilian fruits and vegetables.

"Your father will be given the choice of confessing to Snooky's murder or being exposed as a child molester."

Audrey raised her eyebrows and stared at me as if waiting for the punch line. "Who told you this?"

"The people I'm in touch with are deadly serious about protecting their asses. They're tired of having this murder hanging over their heads, so they're outing Tate as the guilty party."

"He's not going to admit to anything."

"I said they're deadly serious."

Audrey turned pale. She looked confused and then incredulous. "They're going to kill him if he doesn't cooperate?"

Her sudden awakening to the gravity of the situation appeared genuine. I wanted to believe that from this realization the real Audrey would emerge, an Audrey who didn't speak ambiguously or forget crucial details, an Audrey who stayed focused on the tragedy at hand and didn't digress to frivolous thoughts. I wanted to like Audrey. I wanted to trust her.

"At the very least they'd ruin him, that's for sure. And they threatened to ruin me, too."

She slumped in her chair. "I hate him," she said. "Ruin him but don't kill him."

"He's got money. Do you think he'd run?"

Audrey stared at me. "What's worse, death or life in prison?"

"Depends who you ask. I can't picture your dad in prison. If he did run, he'd probably be okay if he stayed away from Chicago."

"You sound as if you want him to run."

"I'm putting myself in his place. Choices are easier when you have money."

"What if he went to the police?"

"He'd run the risk of incriminating himself. The others involved would pull every string they had. But if he's truly innocent, maybe he'd do it."

"But who exactly is going to give my father this ultimatum?"

"I don't know, but guys like Mildish have connections for everything. They probably know someone who specializes in giving people lose-lose propositions. Maybe you should consider telling him what's going to happen."

Now she looked past me. I was about to repeat myself when her head began nodding slowly, and she said, "I should go." After unhooking the enormous bag from the back of her chair, she hoisted it over her shoulder and walked out.

40

It was dark when I got home. I left the lights off, fired up the laptop, then grabbed a diet ginger ale and a bag of black market tortilla chips. For some reason, I also grabbed the glass elephant from the windowsill and put it on the coffee table. An elephant's emotional attachment to other elephants was said to equal that of a human's. Elephants dwell upon and grieve over loved ones. Their grief was said to last many years.

I came across a website quoting a British World War II commander who credited elephants with helping defeat the Japanese in Burma. I flashed to orange flames of the diving fighter plane's guns depicted in the artwork at the firehouse. Next, I found the fighter pilot exhibit at O'Hare International Airport, an airport formerly called Orchard Field but renamed in 1943 after the death of World War II hero Edward "Butch" O'Hare. Then I thought of the strip joint, O'Hare's Tailspin. Snooky's alias for Kalijero had just been revealed: Butch.

The next thirty minutes were spent staring at the shadows on the wall, listening to my thunderous crunching, trying to decide if I should tell Kalijero anything about Butch. When the bag was empty, I gulped the last of the ginger ale and dialed his number.

"Yeah, well, that kind of crap is standard operating procedure," Kalijero said, referring to Tate's predicament.

"What do you mean?"

"I mean when pros like Mildish bring in fledglings like Tate for dirty business, they think of ways to get rid of them if they can't be trusted."

"I don't believe Mildish really thinks Tate killed Snooky."

"Doesn't matter what you believe. If Mildish decides Tate did it, then he did it. But I gotta be honest, Jules. We're focusing on larger fish."

"A university chancellor being framed for murder by a state rep? Too small? Just toss it back."

"Don't be an ass," Kalijero said. "Look at the overall view. The police brass know what a crook Mildish is. If Mildish doesn't already know about their secret strip-club-whorehouse, then he could easily find out if he needed some dirt. Voss knows I facilitated the whole thing, and I just found out that Voss has been greasing palms on the Liquor Control Commission, and on and on it goes. Everybody in this town has something on everybody else. It's a balancing act. When something upsets the balance, you get shifting loyalties, and then bodies start showing up in construction sites. This is how the city that works works."

"And an antisocial lunatic named Voss is in charge. Business as usual."

"Don't give me the babe-in-the-woods routine, Landau."

"You're right, Jimmy. Why should I be surprised to hear nothing has changed in a hundred years?"

"Why should it change? Are people any different? Is greed losing its popularity? Look, if I hear something new, I'll let you know."

"Oh, by the way," I said. "I figured out who Butch is, the alias in Snooky's book."

The ensuing silence told me Kalijero understood what I wasn't saying. "Okay," he finally said then hung up.

I resumed staring at the shadows and thought that my friend's murder had become an afterthought sinking into a swamp of big-city political corruption. I needed to find a way to keep the investigation moving forward. I thought I would have to be more aggressive and stop relying on the obvious. A good accountant was an asset to a petty mobster until the accountant made a mistake. What was Snooky's mistake?

* * *

A plan of action eluded me, as did sleep. From the beginning of my investigation, I had always had a plan for the following day. At one a.m. I tried to surrender to an unnamed force I always imagined ran my life. This was my way of dealing with the fear and doubt pounding on the door. The next four hours were spent thinking I would never sleep again. At five a.m. I sat up in bed and vaguely recalled traveling the convoluted paths that had brought me to this station in life. Dreams disguised as sleep.

I dressed and stepped outside into a warm breeze of early August that felt almost tropical. It was quiet enough to hear the rustling of the ash trees that lined the sidewalk, and for a few moments I understood how people fell in love with cities. I headed south, not feeling at all special or cool despite legally carrying a handgun. By the time I reached the Armitage neighborhood, the sun was above the horizon and I was hungry. I walked into a diner known for its herbivorous fare. Not coincidentally, it was across the street from Taudrey Tats. The restaurant was already half-filled with young, sleepy-faced white kids mellowing out with a good breakfast after a hard night of partying. I sat in a row of two-tops along the front window and watched the neighborhood slowly transform into Saturday morning. My waitress was young and cute and absurdly cheerful for such an early hour. I ordered vegan buttermilk pancakes with fruit sauce.

I wondered if Tate had learned of the judgment recently passed on his life. A man of wealth and privilege suddenly in a world crumbling into shame. The waitress brought my breakfast. The primeval joy of ravenous hunger meeting hot food temporarily eclipsed my worries. When I looked up from my plate, a woman I recognized as the gaudy Boutique Lady stood on the sidewalk watching me. She wore the same sequined lavender head scarf. She smiled and waved as if we were old friends. I acknowledged her with a nod, and she hurried to the entrance. Moments later, she stood in front of me.

"Can I help you with something?"

"You really don't eat meat?"

I stared a moment. "Have we been introduced? I mean, who are you?"

She took a seat. "We looked at each other through the window the other day, and we have Audrey in common. And now here you are sitting by yourself eating breakfast." She reached across the table and offered me her hand. "I'm Susie. I don't eat meat, either."

I shook her hand. "You want to talk to me about something?"

Susie gave me a blank look. "I know it's none of my business but I'm really curious about all the screaming and yelling."

"What screaming and yelling?"

"I just assumed Audrey discussed it with you. A few weeks before the murder. Every time he came over, they ended up shouting. I could hear them through the walls."

"Who was shouting?"

"Audrey and that man who was killed."

Suddenly, I noticed Susie's pretty blue eyes and chestnut hair flowing from under her scarf. How did I not notice this before? "That man was called Snooky. What exactly did you hear?"

"I can't say for sure. Just a lot of: 'Why?—Because I can't!—But why?' Back and forth they would go until the man would storm out."

"Did you ever ask Audrey what was up?"

"She would just laugh and tell me how her father was trying to run her life, and that he couldn't accept she was grown up and on her own."

"Hang on. She told you that man was her father?"

171

"At first she spoke as if he was. But then when I saw how they acted around each other, it couldn't be her father. I mean, it was too weird. And then she told me he was her accountant sent by her father, who I assumed was the other older man who began hanging around during the same time."

"What did the other man look like?"

Susie described Voss, from his comb-over to the gold tassels on his loafers. "Let me make sure I'm getting this. Before Snooky's murder, fat-comb-over-man was visiting Audrey?"

"Oh, yeah, quite often. Was that her father?"

"Are you and Audrey friends?"

Susie hesitated. "I've had this shop for ten years. So when this kid moved in next door, I offered her any advice she might need, and we became fast friends. I thought she was interesting. But over time, I became less comfortable with her clientele."

"Do you remember a bald guy with a lightning bolt tattooed across his head?"

"Of course! I don't know how she could associate with those creeps. Even if it was just business. You know, I kind of assumed you would have stopped by already to question me. I mean, don't you guys question neighbors of people who knew crime victims?"

I almost said "not necessarily" or "it depends" but recognized the lame excuse. Instead I said, "Did you tell Audrey I was in love with her?"

Susie looked horrified. "I said you seemed interested in her. And I said that only as a courtesy because Audrey wanted me to agree with her. She said you were in love with her."

I thought Susie might be my age or a little younger, but definitely not older and definitely well educated. I said, "Audrey is a strange one. And we both know she likes to tell stories."

"You seem sympathetic to her weirdness."

"Well, I know some things about her past. I guess that makes me more tolerant."

"Why would you believe anything she told you?"

Good question. "I don't know. Maybe I shouldn't."

I offered to buy Susie a vegan blueberry hand pie, but she politely declined saying she had come in early to finish several alterations promised at Vagabond Boutique's nine a.m. opening. She invited me to stop by anytime.

41

"So what do you got?" Voss said, once again at Diversey Harbor on the amphitheater steps.

"I want to test this elephant memory of yours. When did you first meet Audrey?"

This time, Voss's entire head turned red. "What the hell is that? You drag me down here to talk about Kalijero and then you start questioning me? Listen, you little bastard, I ask the questions around here, and I'm sick of your goddamn games. You know, I could have your whole face turned into one big purple welt!"

"Whaddya gettin' all defensive for? It's a harmless question."

173

"I told you I traced the phone call to her building after the murder! Now tell me what you got!"

"You sure about that? You sure you never saw her before the murder? Never been to her tattoo shop?"

Voss stood up. "Bullshit!"

"Because I got sources who swear you were hanging around there weeks before Snooky died."

"Bullshit! Why would I hang around a goddamn tattoo joint?"

"I don't know. But I sure as hell don't need to be an elephant to remember a face as ugly as yours."

Voss made a move toward me and stopped. He looked ready to erupt. "You don't know what you're doing, do you? This all could've been real easy, and you could've made a few bucks. But because your name is Landau you think you can just run people over. Just run 'em down, leave 'em lying on the street for someone else to drag away, and with no consequences!"

"Why don't you stop talking in your damn riddles? I don't know what the hell you're talking about."

"Now you want to be Sherlock-Fucking-Holmes. And all because of that little scumbag bean counter." Voss chuckled. "I heard Snook begged for his life like a little bitch—"

I grabbed his silk collar with both hands and pushed him hard against the stone step, bouncing his head off the concrete. He shrieked, "You're dead!" and although he outweighed me by at least one hundred and fifty pounds, I sat on his chest thinking how much I wanted to crush his skull like an egg.

I settled for one more bounce, and he screamed something unintelligible and then I put my mouth next to his ear and said, "I may be dead, but you're forgetting about my family curse, the one that lives in my brain and tells me that dying is no big deal and that neither is killing. So if you're really going to kill me, you better make sure you do it the first time because I will find you and laugh my ass off as I crack your head wide open."

Voss had no response. I slowly shifted my weight off but still maintained pressure on his collar to keep him down. Then I let go and stood over him to see what he would do. He wasn't wearing a shoulder holster and I didn't see a gun on his belt, but I had to assume he had a weapon somewhere, maybe on his ankle. If he went for it, I would kick him in the face and be long gone before he could right himself and put me in his sights. But all he did was lie there panting, covered in sweat, eyes bulging. I cautiously walked backward up the steps to where they met the grass. Then I took one last look at Voss and walked into the park crowded with people enjoying an August afternoon.

* * *

Over the phone, I updated Kalijero on the morning's events. He responded with, "Meet me at Area B," and hung up. An hour later, I was again sitting on the backless wooden bench outside the detectives' room waiting to be summoned. I read the new postings on the bulletin board, which included an announcement from the Chicago Police Pipes and Drums Club, an order for all tactical gang and area enforcement teams to return to civilian dress, and an official recognition of the Chicago Police Marine Corps League birthday.

Kalijero opened the door and waved me in. I saw Deputy Chief Hauser, exactly as I remembered him six days earlier, behind a metal desk leaning back in a steno chair, arms folded against his chest—although it looked as if his crew cut and matching mustache had been tidied up. I sat on one of the wooden folding chairs and waited. Hauser said nothing and stared into space while Kalijero sat leaning forward staring at the floor. Finally, Hauser said, "Voss threatened to kill you?"

"He said, 'You're dead.'"

"Why did he say that?"

"I had just banged his head against a concrete step."

"No, asshole, I mean what does he want from you?"

I glanced at Kalijero and said, "I don't know."

Kalijero chimed in, "Go ahead."

"He thinks I have information that will put Kalijero behind bars. But it's become obvious to me he knows who killed Charles Snook—"

"It has?" Hauser said. "Do you also got info to put Jimmy in the can?" His stare bored into my skull. I felt a headache coming on.

"I don't know anything except my friend is dead, and nobody gives a shit. And I'm pretty damn sure Voss knows—"

"Landau, do you have any idea what you're into?"

"I'm investigating the murder of my friend Charles Snook. That's all I know."

"That's all you know? Well, you're gonna need to know more than that if you want to live long enough to find your friend's killer."

I looked at Kalijero and he said, "We're watching Voss. But it's like what I was telling you. It's all a balancing act. And Voss complicates things. He moves around like he's invisible. He's so connected he's taken for granted. He's a cold-blooded son-of-a-bitch who plays all sides all the time. He's got so many alliances, fallback options, doomsday triggers, that everyone is afraid of him. So they just let him be. They just write him off as the cost of doing business. You get what I'm saying?"

"I should write off Snooky?" I asked, just to clarify.

"Just back off for now," Kalijero said.

"There's a line that has to be crossed," Hauser said.

I took turns giving both of them a hard stare. "Okay, so you're waiting for this line to be crossed. Because when it's crossed, Voss has gone too far. You take him down and at long last, the curse has been lifted." Neither commented. "And when you got Voss dead-to-rights, does he tell us who killed Snooky and why?"

Hauser sighed loudly then started massaging his forehead. Kalijero stared at the floor shaking his

177

head. I said, "Oh, I forgot. Snooky's not a big enough fish—"

"You can fight the system all you want," Kalijero shouted. "But that won't change the fact that you'll still end up dead! And for what? Is knowing who killed Snooky more important than staying alive? Can't you just accept that Snooky made poor choices and they finally caught up with him?"

I stood up. "My god! How did I miss it? Snooky killed himself! He forgot to look both ways when crossing Maxwell Street."

I walked out of Hauser's office with no expectation of shouts beckoning my return. They had done their job. They had warned me I was a discarded cigarette smoldering on the sidewalk of life waiting for an oxford wingtip to grind me into the cement. But Hauser and Kalijero couldn't comprehend a life driven by the alignment of the reckless gene of my forefathers with the corrupt powerbrokers of the day. Just as Snooky's life had no significance, so I knew my life meant nothing to those who pulled the strings. I also knew I had nothing to lose.

42

"What did I ask of you?" Frownie said over the phone. I was relaxing on the recliner, trying to keep my eyes open. "Let me die first. That's all I asked. But I guess that's asking too much."

"Don't you think this is overblown?" I said. "Like maybe Hauser and Kalijero are trying to scare me so I don't risk messing up their big score?"

Frownie called me a son of a bitch under his breath. "It's no different than when I was your age. Neighborhood tough guys, mobster families, government bureaucrats. All one big crime company. Maybe they're bluffin', but I don't want no more of it. And I don't want to hear from you again until you're done with it. If I'm not around when it's over, then at least I'll be in the grave before you."

Frownie hung up before I could protest. The finality in his voice shook me and left me with a vague feeling of loneliness. The police cared only about Voss, Voss cared only about Kalijero. My investigation had defaulted to Audrey and Tate with Audrey no longer just a sexy, free-spirited artist taking a personal interest in the investigation. I drifted off with the realization that Audrey could not be trusted. I had no idea who she was.

I awoke feeling something had changed. While chopping vegetables for an early dinner, I searched for arguments why the path to Snooky's murder should run through Taudrey Tats. Voss wanted Snooky's book, so he forged some sort of relationship with Audrey? Would Voss resort to murder just to acquire a ledger? Maybe they cut a deal. But for what? What would Audrey require to be a party to murder? And then there was the arguing. What the hell did Audrey and Snooky argue about?

While I ate my vegetables, Punim devoured a pile of livers and kidneys. When she was done, she jumped onto the other wooden chair at the kitchen table and started grooming herself. I worried about

179

who would take care of her if something happened. Could she survive on crappy commercial cat food? The possibility that someone wanted to kill me produced such thoughts. I was about eighty percent sure it was a bluff, but you never knew. It seemed absurd that my time could be even close to expiring, although I couldn't deny the feeling that I had drifted into unexplored-life-experience territory. I had dipped my toe into the cold waters of organized crime—twice beaten into unconsciousness, no less—and it really wasn't that bad. A twenty percent chance of dying? I could live with that.

The door knocker slammed hard against the strike plate. A smiling dark-haired girl stood in the doorway wearing a denim skirt and a white T-shirt with a picture of Bambi. I knew who she was but her name evaded me long enough for her to exclaim, "L.A.!"

"Of course," I said. "How are you?" Her hair was draped over one shoulder.

"Audrey's having a little party tonight at the studio, and we want you to come."

I hesitated. "Really? What time?"

"After eight."

"When did you get back into town?"

"Gotta go. I'll see you later." As she turned to leave, I saw a tattoo depiction of lunar phases running across her neck.

43

At nine o'clock Taudrey Tats was crowded with twenty-somethings and younger, most of whom were dressed in black or darker shades of purple and red, and most of whom smoked something. An electric guitar instrumental played just above the din. Outside a light drizzle cooled the air, providing a stark contrast to the hot smoky studio. I stood inside the door and surveyed the crowd. I spotted Audrey and L.A. in the back talking with two skinny guys wearing black jeans that looked way too tight.

I made my way along the perimeter of the room toward a cooler loaded with ice, then squeezed past a woman wearing a yellow zebra print miniskirt and talking to a guy in a nineteenth-century gray military frock coat. It reminded me of a straitjacket with silver buttons. Zebra glanced at me. I smiled. She quickly scanned my linen sport jacket before turning back to the guy and dragging deeply on her cigarette. Most of the people in the room had similar haircuts, as if they all had encountered the same three-year-old playing with scissors.

Hard lemonade and wine coolers filled an ice chest. On a small table sat gallon bottles of bourbon, gin, and vodka. I took the tallest glass, filled it with ice, and continued my journey. I caught L.A.'s eye. She waved enthusiastically and pointed me out to Audrey, who also started waving.

"I told you he'd come," L.A. said. The two guys eyed me suspiciously and turned away; each held a cigarette and a drink in one hand.

"You're supposed to pour something over the ice," Audrey said.

"You couldn't have put a few cans of soda in that cooler?" The two guys looked back at me. Both were attempting to grow facial hair. "Did you say anything to your dad?" I asked Audrey.

"About what?"

"What do you think? What we talked about yesterday."

Audrey appeared confused, then irritated. "Yeah," she said.

"You going to tell me how he reacted or what?"

Audrey looked around the room and then back to me and said, "Why should I tell you anything? What difference does it make?" Her pupils floated in a red spider web. Then she said, "What're you going to do about it?" She turned around and disappeared into the crowd. L.A. grabbed my wrist, stifling my impulse to grab Audrey by the back of the neck.

"If you're gonna be here, then be here," L.A. said and let go. The two guys stared at me as if Uncle Jules had crashed their party.

I thought of leaving but instead fetched a raspberry wine cooler. Drinking bad Kool-Aid was easy. Ten minutes later, I was on my second bottle, my brain now thoroughly awash in sugar and cheap booze. I leaned against the wall and scanned the room of mostly black, jagged haircuts. Two shaved heads caught my eye. They seemed out of place, but when I moved closer, I saw they both had a number of small tattoos scattered over their skulls. Their faces were pale and scabby. Audrey's bread and butter.

"You seem more relaxed." L.A. looked up at me with that same smile.

"Where's your drink?" I said.

"I don't drink."

"How did you and Audrey become friends?"

L.A. stared at me thoughtfully. "We watch out for each other. That's why I'm here. To keep an eye on her."

I looked back at the druggies and saw that Audrey was now talking to them. "You didn't answer my question. And if you really care about her, why don't you get her away from those meth-heads?"

"Why would I?"

"Because they're sick and dangerous! They're the walking dead. And why isn't she more picky about her clients? They're gonna rob her of everything. She got a death wish or something?"

L.A. laughed. "You're drunk on two wine coolers!"

"I'm a little buzzed, big deal. You've been watching me?"

"I'm looking out for you just as I'm looking out for Audrey."

One of the druggies had left Audrey's side. I searched the room but couldn't locate him. I looked back at L.A. and said, "What the hell are you talking about? Why am I here?"

L.A. just stared at me with that stupid grin and said, "Tell me about all the famous people your family knew."

"What do you mean?"

"You know, in the old days. When you couldn't buy alcohol. The Roaring Twenties."

"What did Audrey tell you?"

"I don't know. Stuff like your family knowing gangsters and being really powerful, making lots of money."

"And how did Audrey find out this information?"

L.A. shrugged.

"Did she tell you what she was arguing about with Snooky during the weeks before his murder?"

L.A.'s smile disappeared. "I never saw them argue—not when I was here."

"I thought you tell each other everything?" L.A. stared at me either deep in thought or just speechless. I said, "I'm done with this bullshit game. The two of you dance around like innocent little girls playing dress up. Oh, aren't they cute! And sexy! And yes, we're old enough. Do you see life like Audrey does, just one big story to make up as you go along? Can't deal with reality so you make shit up and hide behind it?"

Audrey emerged from behind me and stood next to L.A. "Is he having fun yet?" Her bald friend joined her.

"He's a crabby drunk," L.A. said. "And he worries too much."

Druggie was smoking a cigarette. I looked at him just as he took a long drag. He blew a cloud of smoke in my face and said, "What're you doing here?"

Audrey shook Druggie's arm and told him to chill out.

"What the fuck do you care?" I said. I was a tough guy now.

"You're that investigator dude. You're trying to find out who snuffed out Audrey's bookkeeping bitch." Druggie then bounced his lit cigarette off my chest.

I jammed the heels of both hands hard into his bony chest, knocking him into another couple who fell over like bowling pins. I took another step toward my target but was stopped by several hands grabbing my arms and jacket collar. Then I heard a comforting voice.

"C'mon, Jules," Susie from Vagabond Boutique said. "Let's go home." She took my hand and led me through the commotion. I heard Audrey's voice following us all the way outside to Susie's car, but I was paying more attention to a sudden wave of nausea than anything I heard. I sat in the passenger seat and closed my eyes while Susie stood on the sidewalk arguing with Audrey. When I opened them again, Susie was in the driver's seat looking at me.

"Where do you live?"

I gave her my address and leaned my head back. She said she had locked the shop and was observing the party from just inside the door. The way kids interacted these days fascinated her. Then she saw me standing with Audrey and the druggie and got the sense that something bad was about to happen.

"My head's throbbing."

"How much did you drink?"

"Two wine coolers."

She laughed loudly. "Don't drink much, eh?"

"Don't rub it in."

"What in the world were you doing there?"

"I was invited," I said, trying to sound ironic. "Audrey knows more about the murder than she's telling me. I thought maybe I could catch a slipup if she was stoned."

"Any success?"

"Some. Everything is a game to her. I'm starting to think her little dark-haired friend might know something, too."

"Audrey didn't want you to leave. That's for sure."

"What do you mean?"

"I mean, all the way to the car she kept saying, 'Don't let him leave yet!' But I've been around long enough to know you didn't belong in that crowd. I mean, they're mostly skinny punks, but there was a lot of them and only one of you."

She stopped in front of my building. I leaned a bit closer, thanked her, then said, "You have beautiful eyes." She smiled. "I'm sorry—"

"For what? You're a sweet man."

I closed my eyes, shook my head a few times. "Nobody has ever called me a sweet man. If you knew me better, I doubt you would, either."

"Well, why don't you get some sleep and then think about whether you want me to know you better." She was sharp, all right.

I took the stairs slowly, one at a time, planting both feet then waiting for the nausea to subside before continuing. I was not exactly born to party. Halfway up the flight, I heard the sound of creaking floorboards. Punim only weighed eight pounds. A few more steps and I saw under the crack of my

186

door. A shadow of something moved across the floor. I un-holstered the .40-caliber. Whoever it was showed no fear of being caught. It occurred to me the nausea may have saved my life. The next step released a loud groan that silenced the world except for the murmur of a television from the second floor. The prudent action would be to walk away, call in a burglary-in-progress, and wait outside. The intruder would most likely escape out the kitchen door, or jump out the window into the space between the buildings, or run out the front. But by waiting, I had only a one-in-three chance of an encounter. I didn't like the odds.

The jamb had been torn away from the casing. The door opened with a slight nudge from my foot. I shouted that my gun was drawn and suggested the intruder reveal himself to live another day. I pushed the door as far back as I could until it bounced off the hinge pin. I stepped inside, turned on a lamp, then surveyed the living room down the barrel of my Glock, before turning down the hall that led to the kitchen in the back of the apartment. As I stepped past the shadow behind the opened door, a foul but recognizable odor once again assaulted my senses. I swung around just in time for something hard to smash against my wrist and send the gun skidding across the floor. A bolt of pain rocketed through my left side, buckling my knees before a thud on my back sent me all the way down. Conscious enough to realize one more hit to the head might finish me, I managed to wrap my arms around a pair of bony legs and jerk the guy to the floor. I attempted to climb on top of him, but a blow to the left cheekbone knocked me back. I scrambled to the front window where I grabbed the ledge and pulled myself back up. The intruder stood inside the open door with a crazed look in his eyes. I recognized his tattooed skull as one of the scumbags from the party. His right hand was wrapped in some kind of white material.

"Where's the money, fucker?"

"I got eighty bucks in my wallet. You can have it." I took all the bills out of my wallet and held them out. "Take it and go!"

"You've got a grand somewhere! We all know it."

Where do they get this from? "You're crazy! I don't keep that kind of money lying around. Just take this cash and get out. Go!"

He said nothing, just stared wild-eyed and panting. I tried to locate my gun and thought it might be underneath the recliner. I moved toward the chair, but Druggie stepped closer and raised his white fist. I said, "I'm giving you a chance to get out," but it was useless. There weren't enough brain cells between his ears to understand running away was better than beating me to death. I stepped back to put more space between us, and he charged me with his hand held high like a lancer coming in to finish me off. But Druggie failed to consider how the distance between us changed the equation. I waited until he committed himself to the kill and stepped aside to let him put a dent in the drywall. When he turned to me again, I kicked him as hard as I could in the stomach and watched him collapse to the floor.

I pushed the recliner until I could see the Glock, then called the cops. My left side ached. Druggie lay in the fetal position, moaning. I looked closer at his hand and guessed he had created a plaster-of-Paris fist, something boxers did to cheat. When I heard the police open the downstairs door, I dropped to my knees, slid the gun about five feet away, and raised my hands above my head. Two uniforms entered with their pistols drawn. "I live here," I said. "I made the call." One officer knelt beside Druggie and radioed for medical. The other kept his gun out and told me to stand. As I struggled through the pain, Kalijero walked in and ordered the uniform to holster his weapon. Then he helped me to the couch.

"You've taken more beatings in two weeks than guys with thirty years in this business," Kalijero said. "What happened this time?"

I told him about the party and surprising the intruder. "He wouldn't leave," I said. "I gave him a clear path out of here, and he came at me like a psycho."

"How did he know where you lived?"

"I don't know. But someone is telling meth-heads I have a lot of cash."

Kalijero leaned back and started rubbing his forehead. "Somewhere that broad's got a role in all this."

The paramedics arrived. "Voss," I said. "Voss visited Audrey before Snooky died. I think maybe Voss thought he could get the goods on you easier if Snooky was dead."

The cops stood in front of Druggie watching the paramedics work on him. I struggled to my feet through the pain of cracked ribs. One of the paramedics walked over to Kalijero and said, "DOA."

"What?" I said. "Who's dead?"

"The body on the floor is deceased, sir," the paramedic said and walked out.

"Just take it easy, Jules," Kalijero said.

"I've killed two people in two weeks."

"He was already dead! Look at him. He was skin and bones, for chrissake. You did him a favor."

"A dead man in my apartment. There'll be an investigation."

Kalijero shrugged. "Routine. Some paperwork. Relax."

The paramedic returned with a black body bag. I watched them maneuver the corpse inside and zip it up. "I kicked him in the stomach," I said to the paramedic.

"Probably an internal rupture. Bled out. That usually does it."

I wrapped an ice pack around my side with an Ace bandage, held another against my face, and sat at the kitchen table while one of the uniforms asked me questions. Kalijero listened but said nothing.

When the other cops left, Kalijero asked me what I was going to do now. He had that don't you think it's time to give up look. "I'm going to ice my body, try to sleep, and continue my investigation."

"Maybe you should go to the hospital."

"Not with a ten-grand deductible. I'm gonna lie down, and after that, I don't know what."

Kalijero stared at me. "There's a lot going on, and I'm not going to pretend I know everything. But it's all dangerous for you. Fear makes powerful people do crazy things. Lay low and let things play out. You can start over again."

I didn't respond but sat with my eyes closed, content to let Kalijero do whatever he wanted. When I heard the front door close, I put down the ice pack and eased myself up. Another wave of dizzying nausea took over, and I barely made it to the toilet before an acrid flow spilled out of me. I sat on the bathroom floor and thought about Kalijero's words. I was a dead man if I didn't forget about finding Snooky's killer. They would kill me purely for my association with Snooky. Blaming a genetic abnormality for my lack of fear sounded callow. Maybe I was just stupid. For whatever reason, I wasn't buying what Kalijero was selling. And sitting there on the bathroom floor, having just been the catalyst for another man's premature death, I had never felt more alive.

44

Cracked ribs healed on their own terms. I reminded myself of this as I lay in bed trying to get comfortable. Several weeks of shallow, interrupted sleep awaited me. At seven a.m. the phone rang.

"I had a hunch people didn't sleep too late after killing someone."

I didn't recognize the voice. It sounded young. "Who is this?"

"I mean no harm, sir. My name is Ellis Knight. I'm writing a story for The Partisan about the

191

growing meth problem, and I thought maybe you'd like to share your thoughts."

"How did you get my number?"

"You're part of the public record, sir. Meet me at Mocha Mouse, ten o'clock. How about it?"

"How about you go fuck yourself?" I hung up.

I prepared more ice packs, fed Punim, and lowered myself onto the recliner. It was Sunday, and my left cheekbone was once again a throbbing plum. I needed to get the door fixed. Punim leaped onto my lap. The pain caused me to jump, which sent her dashing down the hall and probably onto the porch landing, where she often slept during the cooler hours of a summer morning.

I thought about Tate. He should have aged thirty years by now. His frame of mind would tell me if he was the novice in over his head or playing some other kind of game. My apartment's door knocker bounced. I shouted, "What!?" An assassin would not have bothered knocking. Audrey walked in, her face red and tear-streaked.

"I'm sorry," she said. "This wasn't supposed to happen. You weren't supposed to get hurt, I swear. Nobody was supposed to get hurt."

"You knew about all this?"

"They had it all planned out. I heard about it yesterday morning, and I couldn't get them to change their minds. They would've hurt you, so I wanted to get you out of the way. They were supposed to just take a few things and go, but you left the party early."

"You sick bitch. You couldn't have warned me? Don't you think I could have stopped them?"

"If they thought you would be here, they would've ganged up on you! They could've killed you! They saw you at the party, so just one went. I couldn't stop it from happening, I swear."

I waited for the sobbing to subside and said, "He thought I had five grand stashed away. Where did he get that idea?"

Audrey wiped her eyes and then gave me a confused look. "I don't know."

She may have been telling the truth for a change. Voss most likely told the meth-heads I carried around a lot of cash. "I guess I should thank you. I could've been beaten up by two meth-heads instead of one."

"Let me pay for the door."

I leaned my head back and closed my eyes. "Very thoughtful. You may leave now." I had no interest in parting smiles or thoughtful stares or any other ambiguous gesture. She was good, all right, so good that her motives were buried deep within the bowels of a story that had yet to be told. Had my character's chapter ended as a lifeless bloody pulp—then so it was written. But what part of her story would reveal why she colluded with Voss?

* * *

Leave me the fuck alone was my only thought when the phone rang again a couple of hours later.

"Christ almighty, you didn't take the money from Mildish?" Dad said. "And I gotta hear this crap from someone else?"

"I'm not walking away. Fuck the money."

"You think Snooky wouldn't want you to take the money?"

"Dad, you hired me. Remember?"

"Don't use that against me! If I had known how complicated it all was, I would've let it go."

"And when I didn't hear from Snooky and found out he was dead? I would've gone after his killer. Money or no money."

"And now you're a marked man. Too stupid to see how many people would profit from you being dead."

"But not Voss, the most important of them all. He wants something from me. If I'm dead, he doesn't get what he wants."

Dad said nothing, only breathed roughly through his old man lungs. I hated when he thought so loudly. I imagined him holding the phone with one hand while massaging his forehead with the other. "Dad, c'mon. What did you think a murder investigation would be like?"

"I don't know. Not so complicated."

"A couple of days ago you told me nothing has changed, that it was the same old story."

"It's true."

"Then why are you surprised? You know all the stories from the old days. You read the same articles I did. The Tribune called Great-Granddad a terrorist eighty years before it became a household word. Kidnapping poll watchers, threatening jurors, extorting money from peddlers, his chauffeur killing a pedestrian, and the guy that was gunned down in the primary—"

"He was innocent! It was a frame-up, even the papers said it was Capone's gang who shot that guy."

"That's not the point. Was the boss of the 'Bloody Twentieth Ward' all those years ago really any different than today's Voss of Internal Affairs?"

This time only a short silence. "Maybe not. But for god's sake, don't be reckless. Don't go getting killed over this. Think about what that would do to me and Frownie—"

Dad's voice broke off. I had never heard or seen him cry. God forbid a Landau should show such weakness.

45

You were never sure who knew what in this business. That's what Frownie always said. For that reason, I decided to follow up with the phone call invitation to Mocha Mouse, arriving at a quarter to ten. Kind of Blue played over the sound system of the Jazz-themed coffee shop. At the corner table farthest from the door sat a kid with black horn-rimmed glasses and a mop of dark wiry hair piled high. He was staring into his laptop. His powder-blue dress shirt and stupid smirk gave him a nerdy, smart-ass appearance that fit perfectly with the voice on the phone. I walked toward him, and as if he had planned the whole scene, he looked up and smiled just as I approached the table. Knight introduced himself. "You look like a walking car wreck." Affecting a Bogart accent, he then said, "Of all the coffee shops in all the towns in all the world, he limps into mine."

"Ever had cracked ribs?" I said.

"Is that a question or a threat?"

"I'm not sure." I sat down.

"Dude! How does it feel to be a tragic hero after killing two meth-heads in two weeks? You think you can kill 'em all, Detective?"

I studied his idiotic grin for a moment and said, "Why do you say two meth-heads?"

"I read the police blotters and I thought I'd take a chance. Am I wrong?"

"A deranged addict pushed a gun into my back and another one wanted to bash my brains out. But Ellis Knight would have talked them down, right? Maybe get them some therapy?"

"Whoa, I'm not blaming you, dude. I'm just asking. Should they all be killed?"

"I'm here, Knight. What do you want?"

"I want to know if you think meth addicts should be killed. It's not an unpopular stance these days."

"Thou shall not kill."

"Thou shalt not murder."

"I killed in self-defense. That's the only reason to kill."

Knight lowered his head and started typing on his laptop. When he was still typing a minute later, I said, "What're you writing?"

"Sometimes ideas pop into my head, and I have to get them down. What you just said, 'the only reason to kill,' conjured up a lot of ideas."

"How about you get to the point of why you think I have anything to add to your article."

Knight leaned back and folded his arms. "There's a lot of money to be made in meth. And there's a lot of possible angles to consider. You think Charles Snook got clipped because he was gonna expose a high-ranking university employee as a meth dealer?"

"Who put that crap in your head?"

"Or how about some payback involved with your family? Snook was like family, right?"

"You're just making this shit up."

"You know I can't reveal my sources, Detective."

"There's no story here."

"Then why was Snook killed?"

"I don't know yet. And what does his murder have to do with anything?"

"I've been given ten thousand words to describe the big meth world out there. That's a lot of room to stretch out and see all the different microcultures affected by it. You got the scumbags with hot plates cookin' themselves to death. You got suburban assholes looking for kicks, and now I think you got mobbed-up operations eating their own to protect profits. And with all those wheels spinning, a couple of meth-heads get spit out toward Detective Landau, and Detective Landau wastes them."

Had I entered the Twilight Zone? "I get it. You're developing a plot for a book."

Knight laughed. "It's human interest, dude. Los Angeles. Ever been? You should go, dude."

"It's not human interest, it's bullshit. And what's Los Angeles got to do with anything?"

"I gotta feeling you can find some truth if you look hard enough over there. I mean it's Los Angeles, dude. Film noir, right? Unsolved murders like that black-dolly thing. That was a real black-haired chick who got hacked up. Never solved."

"Black Dahlia, you idiot. Is there a Los Angeles connection to all this you're not telling me about?"

"I'm just sayin'—"

"Audrey's friend lives in Los Angeles. She's even called L.A. Long black hair. Red eyebrows. You know her?"

Knight ignored my question but couldn't hide his unease. "I mean, like, it's possible Mr. Snook's death is related to meth. It's possible you subconsciously want to kill these druggies—hell, I'd like to kill them. Or maybe there's an old score being settled, something to do with the Landau heritage. And it's an opportunity for you, too! The article will give you some street cred. You'll get a name as something more than a son of the Chicago Landaus, more clients. Dude, I'm gonna make you famous!"

"Okay, Knight. I like to kill scumbags. And that includes lying tabloid journalists. If you print any bullshit about me or Snooky, you're a dead man." Cursing through the pain, I pushed myself up and walked away knowing Knight still wore that same smirk on his face.

* * *

I opened the outside door to my building and saw a man on his knees in front of my apartment.

198

He hummed loudly while chipping away at what remained of my door jamb. He didn't notice me until I had almost reached the landing. "Audrey sent me," he said and stared at my purple eye. "The guy upstairs let me in. You're pretty trusting to leave your place wide open like this."

"I got nothing of value, except my cat, and she wouldn't go quietly."

He didn't hear a word. "I just gotta clean up the rest of the broken wood, cut a new piece, measure everything up, reattach the hardware, and I'm done."

"Great," I said and spent the next two hours listening to the alternating sounds of carpentry and the whistling of unidentifiable tunes. I popped a couple of Tylenol and tried reading the Sunday Trib, but my mind was under siege from physical pain and a growing anxiety over the sluggishness of my investigation. Frownie had warned me that when such feelings arose it was important to revisit a main character to see if anything about their story had changed. A lot had happened since I last spoke with Tate. It was time to renew our acquaintance.

46

Low-hanging clouds had turned Lake Michigan slate gray. Driving to Evanston, the heavy sky reminded me of November, when temperatures dropped into the forties and the humidity remained at seventy-five percent to make you as uncomfortable as possible. Add a little wind to the mix and you wondered why du Sable, the "Father of

Chicago," didn't hightail it back to Haiti during his first November.

As expected, the park across from Tate's house teemed with people picnicking, throwing a ball around, or just looking out over the lake. I thought my chances were pretty good of catching him at home on a Sunday, although there was no sign of life in or around the house. I rang the doorbell. Tate answered in his robe and slippers.

"I see by the lovely colors on your face you're making friends again," Tate said. "Bluish purple suits you."

"I was in the neighborhood."

"I doubt it." Even in a robe he looked dapper, as if he belonged in silk.

"We haven't spoken in a while," I said. "What do you say?"

Tate stepped aside, and I followed him into the living room. I sat on an elegant wood-trimmed love seat in front of the huge picture window that looked across the street to the park. Tate sat opposite me in a matching chair. "How's the investigation going?" There was no hint of sarcasm in his voice, and his body language appeared genuinely calm.

I said, "You had any interesting offers lately?"

"Offers for what?"

"I'll phrase it differently. How about choices? Have you been given any choices lately?"

"What the hell are you talking about?"

"You haven't spoken to Mildish or Baron recently?"

"They can both go to hell."

"How about Audrey?"

Tate's face darkened. "I told you to leave her out of this. She knows nothing about my personal dealings. She has nothing to do with anything!" Tate stood and walked to the other end of the room. He stared out the window that looked into the backyard. After several minutes he returned to his chair and said, "You have something to tell me?"

Suddenly, I wondered if I was set up to tell Tate of the ruinous choice he would face. Mildish assumed I'd run to Tate with the bad news, and Tate would run away and disappear on his own. Instead, I ran to Audrey, thinking she would break the news to him. Another mistaken assumption. Audrey preferred her old dad got the news directly from Mildish operatives.

I noticed his leather and satin slippers matched his pajamas. "Actually, I hoped you had something you wanted to share with me—just in case you had planned on going somewhere. Something about Snooky's murder, perhaps, like how your phone number got on a dead meth-head's cell phone?"

"What are you talking about?"

"A junkie attacked me. Your business card was found in his pocket."

Tate laughed. "You really think I associate with dope addicts?"

"No. But Audrey does."

Tate laughed again. "Audrey? You're suggesting Audrey had something to do with Snook's murder? What was her motive?"

"I know she's the drug fiends' tattoo artist of choice. I know a meth-head dialed your personal phone number. Do you think he wanted to discuss graduate programs?"

"What? My business card and a phone call?" Tate stared into the floor. "I love that girl," he finally said. "And she knows I love her. What in god's name would motivate her to have a man killed and then frame me for murder and drug dealing? I just can't believe it."

"Snooky was in love with her. Do you agree?"

Still looking at the floor Tate said, "Of course he was. All men our age fall in love with young women like Audrey—and I'm no different."

I waited, unsure of what I had heard. "That comment suggests something extremely disturbing. Care to rephrase?"

Tate lifted his head. "Men desiring younger women is completely natural. As long as it's consensual and she's of legal age, what does it matter?"

Up to this point, I had felt a degree of compassion for Tate. Now he encompassed every loathsome and sickening image my brain could offer. "But we're talking about your daughter—you sick bastard!"

The red shot up from his neck to his white hairline like one of those cartoon thermometers that ends up spurting through the top. "You're crazy!" he shouted. "Who told you that?" He stood over me, ready to tear me apart.

"Audrey," I said.

"Audrey told you that," he said quietly and buried his head in his hand. "She wants to ruin me."

"Why does your daughter want to ruin you?"

Tate pulled his hand away. "For God's sake, she's not my daughter!"

"Do you even have children?"

"Yes! I have a daughter. She lives with her mother. At least I think she lives with her mother—in California. Oh for Christ's sake! I don't believe this."

"Then why don't you tell me who Audrey is, and maybe I can figure out why she wants to ruin you."

His head dropped back. He stared at the ceiling awhile and then popped up. "I met her at that club you saw me at. She sat next to me at the bar."

"What did you talk about?"

He seemed not to have heard me. "She bewitched me. It sounds idiotic, but that's how I felt. At sixty-two years old, I was an infatuated teenager. The long dark hair, the big black eyes. And her attitude. Her brazen disinterest in the world. She seemed to know who I was, but how was it possible? I don't remember what we talked about except that she had recently moved here from Los Angeles and wanted to start her own business. She needed to buy equipment. Of course, I helped her."

"Why do you think she picked you?"

"They tell us what we want to hear. I know I'm in good shape for my age. I took care of her. I listened to her stories. I gave her whatever she wanted."

"When did things change?"

"A few months ago, she started coming over less often. She said her business was taking more and more of her time. Snook verified that her shop

203

had increased revenues. He was concerned with the amount of cash she kept on hand. And he was worried about some of her clientele. Naturally I, too, became concerned and asked her to be more discriminating in who she worked with. She accused me of being elitist and from that point on, it was clear that she was done with me, although every now and then she would pop in and act like nothing had changed."

"What if Audrey knew of the dirty dealings around Maxwell Street and was going to expose you and the others? Snooky couldn't allow this, so Audrey lashed out—had him killed. What do you think?"

"But why? I just can't imagine her doing that."

I pondered his question a moment. My last conversation with Knight popped into my head. "Got any enemies in Los Angeles?"

Tate scratched his chin and looked around. Then he startled me with a laugh that was as phony as it was loud. "Well, I have an ex-wife in Los Angeles," he said, as if he were about to tell a joke. "But it's been over ten years, so I think she would've exacted her revenge by now."

"Wanna tell me how to get in touch with her? Or you gonna make me dig it up?"

"I really don't see the relevance—"

"Oh, c'mon, Tate. Just pretend you know I'm on your side."

Tate walked into the kitchen then returned with a piece of paper. "That's her name," he said as he handed it to me. "Jane Prenevost. At least that's her maiden name. She went back to it after the divorce.

I don't have her number—and she could've remarried and taken a different name for all I know."

Los Angeles. My gut told me I had to make the trip, if only to talk with someone who knew Tate in a context removed from Chicago politics, and to see what the girl called L.A. was like two thousand miles away from Audrey. Unexpectedly, I now had a story of my own. Once upon a time there were three women. Two were from Los Angeles, two were tattoo artists, and two had direct connections to Tate. What were the chances that a third connection would give the story the ending it deserved?

47

I still didn't know where Audrey lived, but I had a hunch. "You just figured that out?" Susie said after getting over the shock of my eye. We were splitting a vegan meatball marinara sub at the diner across the street from Taudrey Tats.

"So in the back, there's a full bath?"

"You ever wonder what that cinderblock wall was for? Behind it is a cozy suite the owner of the building put in to cheat on his wife during business hours. Definitely a building code violation."

I asked if she had seen Audrey's friend and described L.A. to her. "She shows up every few weeks," Susie said. "I've never met her."

Susie finished her portion and excused herself to open the boutique. I remained at the table and watched for signs of life at Taudrey Tats. As noon approached, Susie propped open the door to her store, and soon after Audrey turned over the "Open" sign. I paid the bill and crossed the street.

"You grimace with each step," Audrey said as I walked in. She was sitting in The Kitschen chair sipping coffee while paging through a magazine on her lap. She looked somber. Maybe she was human after all.

"Cracked ribs don't heal in four hours," I said and sat on a drafting stool. I looked around. The place was spotless. "Was there a party here last night or was I dreaming?"

"You're angry. I don't blame you."

"Where's L.A.?"

"She takes the cheap overnight flights. We cleaned until her ride picked her up around three."

"Home to Los Angeles?"

Audrey held her gaze on me and nodded. "She's barely legal, Jules. The perfect age for the over-thirty crowd."

"Tell me about Voss."

She hesitated. "Who's that?"

"A few days after the murder, you called me and said a cop stopped by. He wanted to know if I had Snooky's payoff book. I referred to him as Detective Kalijero, and I told you there was no book. The next day you gave me a description of the man. It wasn't Kalijero; it was Voss."

Audrey shrugged. "He was a cop. That's all I know. Since you acted like you were sure you knew who it was, I assumed you knew what you were talking about."

"Did Snooky tell you that Voss wanted information from him to use against another cop named Kalijero?"

"I never heard of Voss before that day he just showed up."

"You'd never seen Voss before that day you called me?"

"I just said that." She had an edge in her voice. Any residual feelings of guilt had disappeared. She returned her attention to the magazine as if I had left the room.

I laughed and said, "Did you ever see Snooky's Steuben Glass animal collection?"

Audrey closed the magazine and walked to the display rack. She stared at the drawings until I saw a smile creep onto her profile, and she said, "He was very proud of it." Just like that, the coquettish little girl returned. "The 'Mouse and Cheese' was my favorite."

"Mine was the 'Contented Cat.'"

"Are you going to keep the collection? I'm sure Snooky would approve."

"The house was ransacked. Everything was smashed to pieces, including the glass animals."

Audrey turned to me with a genuine look of sadness. "I didn't know that. But why? I mean, even if they were looking for something, why destroy those figurines? Obviously nothing could be hidden in them."

"Bad guys like to send messages. Although one of the animals survived—the glass elephant. I took it home."

Audrey thought for a moment and then giggled. "I remember it. It was cute but out of place with the rest."

"Why?"

"It was just a cheap imitation. It wasn't crystal like the others."

"I think you're wrong," I lied. "It refracts beautifully on my wall just like lead crystal."

Audrey rolled her eyes. "So when you're not solving murders, you're an expert in crystal? Trust me, it's a fake."

"Trust me, Audrey. I knew Snooky. He didn't buy imitation anything."

"The elephant was given to him, smarty pants. He didn't buy it."

Audrey had swallowed the bait. Voss would never have spent good money on lead crystal to send as a message. She knew it was fake because she knew Voss sent it to Snooky. Audrey took one of the drawings off the rack, laid it on the light box, and started to draw. I walked over to her and watched as she worked on the texture of saliva drops falling from a wolf's fangs.

"Audrey, who gave Snooky the elephant?" I said, knowing the answer but giving her some more rope.

"One of those police detectives."

"Who?"

Audrey turned to me. "Voss. Or maybe the other one you mentioned—" She caught herself and returned to the drawing.

"You don't know Voss, but you chatted long enough to know he gave Snooky a glass elephant. Did you make a deal with Satan, Audrey?"

"What are you talking about?"

"Why would you want to help Voss get information on Kalijero? What did you get in return? Was it worth Snooky's life?"

Audrey dropped her pencil and turned to me. Her eyes had become narrow black slits. "You're making up crazy stories because you don't know how to figure it all out. You're at a dead end. Well, that's not my fault. Stick with the facts!"

"How about this fact: Voss told me he gave Snooky that elephant. If you knew it was a gift, then you must've known this fact before Snooky was dead. Since you said you had never heard of Voss until after the murder, it's a fact you're a liar."

Audrey shook her head wildly. "You've got me all confused. I don't know who gave the elephant to Snooky. Why don't you just get out of here!"

"Another thing. Tate told me you're not his daughter. He said you picked him up at that sugar-daddy bar."

"He's a liar!" she said and shoved me in the chest. I stumbled in agony toward the door, cursing loudly, employing every vile word I had ever learned regarding females. Before leaving, I glanced back and saw Audrey sitting in the tattoo chair crying into her hands. I didn't pretend to know why.

Bent over on the sidewalk, I breathed through the pain. At some point, I was aware of a hand resting lightly on my back. I looked up and saw Susie's face.

"I heard the shouting, and here you are," she said. "What can I do? Do I need to take you to the hospital?"

"There's nothing to do. I just have to avoid getting shoved around."

"You want to come in and sit awhile?"

"No," I said but didn't like the sound of my voice. I took her hand. "I mean, I would, but I better get home and lie down." I told her I would be going out of town and asked if she would take care of Punim. She agreed and we made plans for her to come over that evening for a meet and greet.

"What's in Los Angeles?" she said.

"It seems to be a common denominator for some characters in my investigation, including an ex-wife, Audrey's red-eyebrow friend, and a Partisan writer who knows more than he's telling me."

48

Parked in front of my apartment building was Frownie's beloved 1935 Lincoln Model K Roadster convertible. He sat behind the wheel, reading a newspaper.

I rapped my knuckles against the rumble seat before coming up to my mentor on the driver's side. "Are you lost, mister?" I said.

Frownie turned his head and looked in horror. "My god. Your face is all fucked up again?"

"It's not as bad as it looks. What brings you here?"

"Why you holdin' your side like that? Someone hit you in the ribs, too?" Frownie shook his head.

"I'm here to take back what I said about not wanting to hear from you again."

"I didn't take you seriously," I said, which wasn't completely true.

"You see, when you get old like me, you sometimes decide you don't want to deal no more with your friends and such gettin' hurt." He stopped and then said, "I got guilt, too. I knew your old man didn't want you doin' this kind of work. But I liked that you wanted it and were so enthusiastic and all. And I thought, it's your life, why the hell not learn the gumshoe business?" Frownie reached out and grabbed my arm. "Anyway, I'm here for you, kid. While I'm still aboveground, I'm always here."

I took Frownie's hand in both of mine. "I've got to go to Los Angeles for a couple of days. For the case."

Frownie nodded. "Got enough money?"

"I'm fine."

Frownie took his hand back and stared through the windshield. I could tell he was recalling some friends or associates from long ago. "I used to know a lot of people in L.A.," he said. "I wish I could make a few calls for you, but they're all dead." Frownie laughed. "I've outlived my usefulness."

"Bullshit," I said. "I've got a lot more use for you if you'll just stop worrying."

Frownie looked at me and smiled. "Okay," he said. "I'm glad I saw you." Then he started up the roadster and drove off.

* * *

211

Susie came over at five-thirty with two orders of vegetable chow mein. Punim displayed a passing interest in our guest then disappeared.

"Maybe she'd like to meet a lovable orange tabby guy," Susie said.

I discouraged the idea, explaining that Punim had reached the point where personal space was her highest priority and that one male in her life was enough. I showed her the container of organ meat. Susie pretended not to be revolted.

We sat on the couch eating out of containers, making small talk, Susie purposely avoiding any discussion about my trip to L.A., which I appreciated. I asked about her life and she described a New England prep school education topped off with four years at Bryn Mawr. "I lived a WASP stereotype," she said, "then I moved here and opened a business."

"Your parents must've been proud."

Susie almost spit out her food. "Oh my god, no," she said. "Opening a second-hand clothing shop in my family ranked just above running off with the circus." That one sentence told me a lot about her life. I anticipated she would then ask for my story, instead she looked at her watch and said, "I gotta get back to the shop."

We stood in the doorway anticipating each other's body language. I wasn't sure who made the first move, but my hands found their way to her waist and we kissed. "Call me when you get back," she said and I watched her walk down the stairs.

* * *

I could see the setting sun as we landed. Through the smog it looked like a giant egg yolk. I had never been to Los Angeles, but I was used to navigating freeways, and I remembered L.A. had once mentioned her sea turtle tattoo would be the "envy of Echo Park." The neighborhood was easy to find, as was a cheap motel on Sunset Boulevard called The Jenny, where I guessed, among other things, rooms could be rented by the hour. With a creepy yellow neon sign and purple stucco walls, how could I resist? Forty bucks a night sealed the deal. I slid three days' worth of cash under the thick plastic window to an old man who said nothing as he pushed back a key.

Apart from some chipped paint and the graffiti on the small dresser, the room wasn't that bad. A few blocks down the street, I found a vegan Thai restaurant and had a "tentil loaf" for dinner—the best tentil loaf I've ever had. A mix of white hipsters, Latinos, and Asians filled the sidewalks and neighboring streets, which bustled with bars, nightclubs, and music venues of every kind. A funky hip-hop-soul sound caught my ear. I followed the music across the street to a small club where a band from Seattle called Theoretics wowed the crowd. I leaned against the bar and ordered a Guinness on tap. I could nurse a Guinness for an hour and look like I belonged there.

A few minutes passed before I thought how absurd it seemed to have the feeling of being watched. Everyone watched everyone in a crowded nightclub. From the periphery, I thought I glimpsed a face and turned my head to see no one in particular. I moved to the other end of the bar, but the distraction continued. A pint of Guinness later, I was buzzed enough not to care about any trickery being played, imaginary or otherwise, and for a couple of hours enjoyed the idea of being a private investigator visiting Los Angeles.

The next morning I noticed my eye was turning greenish yellow. I had a late breakfast at the same Thai restaurant. From there I walked around the neighborhood looking for tattoo shops or perhaps a friendly tattooed person. The Los Angeles sunshine revealed the drastic contrasts of the area. Clapboard houses shared streets with craftsman bungalows and modernist lofts. Tacos and burritos lived alongside Maine lobsters and wasabi-marinated yellowfin tuna.

Finding a tattoo studio on Sunset Boulevard didn't take long. A small business between Manny's Laundromat and a newspaper/smoke shop was my first stop. From the sidewalk, I observed a Latino boy organizing ink cups and needles and putting tubes in a metal device I assumed was for sterilization. Two Latino men in white tank tops were examining drawings on a display rack. Both were covered in tattoos from the elbows to the wrists. I walked in and waited at the glass counter. Neither man seemed to notice me until the boy walked over to them and whispered. They glanced my way and continued talking. A couple of minutes later one of them approached me.

"How can I help you?" he said.

I asked him if he knew a tattoo artist called L.A. and he said he didn't. Then I described her as short with long black hair, and he laughed since I had just described his sister and all his friends' sisters. "How about with red eyebrows?" I said.

The man thought for a moment and then yelled something in Spanish to the other man who shook his head. "Sorry, man. Can't help. You a cop or something?"

I faked a laugh and said, "I'm just trying to find someone." Then I handed him a card. "If you get any info or see this girl, there's a hundred-dollar bill in it for you." The man seemed unimpressed but took my card anyway. I thought two hours of pay was generous, but what did I know?

I stepped outside and, like the previous evening, a figure caught my attention from the corner of my eye. I turned my head to an empty sidewalk and just when I thought I might have developed some type of optical affliction, I noticed an old red sedan with tinted windows parked at the end of the street in the direction I had been drawn. I started a fast walk toward the car only to see the tires disappear in a cloud of dust before squealing onto Sunset Boulevard. Not yet twenty-four hours in Los Angeles and things had already gotten complicated.

Who knew I was in Los Angeles? Frownie, Susie, perhaps Tate. I continued walking. Four blocks farther I found another tattoo studio, Indra's Tats, between a dental clinic and an unnamed restaurant with the words "Giant Tasty Burgers" on a banner hanging from the gutter. The façade of the clinic was decorated with a mural of smiling Anglo and Latino teens holding up the earth. The studio

215

was modern and enormous with a dozen or so artists, each with their own work space enclosed in movable glass and aluminum walls. In addition to artwork, huge trophies lined shelves and countertops.

I was greeted by a pleasant young woman behind the glass counter who said an artist would be with me shortly and invited me to relax on one of the leather couches that surrounded a large glass table covered with copies of Illustration Magazine and a hardbound volume of The Tattoo Encyclopedia. After I sat, she offered a variety of coffee drinks. I declined and quickly explained the reason I was there. She smiled, nodded, and told me she was sure an artist would help me in just a few minutes. The staff was a United Nations of white, Asian, and Latino artists, all neatly groomed and dressed in sport shirts and khakis. Surprisingly, none had exposed tattoos. I began paging through the encyclopedia, stopping at the section dedicated to symbolism. In particular, the ancient Greek utilization of moon phases interested me.

Nick, a husky Polynesian-looking guy, appeared. He shook my hand and sat on the couch across from me. "I'm sorry for bothering you," I said. "I'm not interested in a tattoo. I'm just looking for a woman tattoo artist called L.A."

Nick told me I had no reason to apologize. "People come in here all the time to chat, use the bathroom, ask directions. We're not just artists; we're part of the community. All are welcome anytime. As for this woman you're looking for, I don't know her. But it's possible one of the other artists might. Why don't you come back later when I have had time to ask around?"

I thanked Nick, and he walked me to the door as if I had been an honored guest in his house. If he had been any friendlier, I might have gotten a tattoo out of guilt. In the next two hours, I found four more studios. No one had heard of anyone named L.A. At each location I spotted the red sedan somewhere in the vicinity, either parked or passing by. Whoever was driving wanted me to know they were hanging around.

At the intersection of Sunset and a narrow, tree-lined side street, I was lured away from my present task with the promise of scenery that didn't include murals of Jesus holding sparkling balls of light. The street bordered the top of a steep grade and was lined with garages underneath homes that must have commanded a fabulous view of what I thought was the park in Echo Park. I followed the street until the slope was shallow enough to easily traverse into an area of mature deciduous trees. From the shade, I looked over an empty parched landscape of brown grass that extended to the freeway at one end and a baseball stadium at the other.

Although I didn't see any signs of life in the park, I felt uncomfortable, as if I had walked into a crowded room full of strangers. Back on Sunset Boulevard, I stopped at a lemonade cart. Both arms of the Latino man behind the cart were covered in tattoos. Within the collage, I could make out a skeleton wearing a sombrero, a bandito-like character riding a motorcycle, and the Virgin Mary. I pointed to the largest sized cup, and the man smiled and nodded. I watched him cut a bunch of lemons in half and squeeze them into the juicer. Then he dumped in a sugary concoction, cold water, a scoop of ice, and turned on the blender. I said, Muchos gracias. He smiled and nodded. I turned to walk away and stopped.

"Where did you get your tattoos done?" I said. Again, he smiled and nodded and I said, Donde? and pointed to his arms. His face lit up, and he spoke rapidly in Spanish while pointing in the direction I was headed. I smiled and nodded.

It took almost an hour before I found the next studio. The building was tall and skinny and looked like a converted three-flat. It stood alone between a used-car joint and the parking lot of an abandoned warehouse. I thought of fire-bombed cities where a lone chimney was all that remained. My lemonade and ice long gone, I urgently needed a bathroom. I stood outside the glass door and saw four white guys barely in their twenties. One was in the back working on the lower spine of a young woman. The other three were hanging around up front, leaning on the glass countertop. Their haircuts were either high-and-tight or crew cut. Each wore a light blue oxford cloth shirt and jeans. When I walked in, they straightened up in unison and looked at me as if I had caught them watching porn.

"Hi, guys," I said.

"Can we help you?" one of them said.

"You'd help me big-time if you let me use your bathroom."

Three smiles and three arms with pointed fingers directed me to the back. When I returned, I

218

thanked them and asked if they knew an artist called L.A. They looked at each other and shook their collective heads. "She's short with long black hair? Blue eyes?"

One of them coughed and then said, "Who did she apprentice with?"

His question surprised me. "You guys go through an apprenticeship first?"

They all kind of chuckled, as if they had a moron in their midst. Then one of them said, "Yeah, unless you're just a scratcher." They all laughed for real.

"And you guys don't want to be a bunch of scratchers," I said.

"Dude, our ink guns cost six hundred dollars apiece. That sterilizer? Five grand. The apprenticeship, ten grand—"

"Whoa. You paid someone to apprentice you?"

"Hell, yes. You're paying to learn from a master who has the knowledge to pass on. It's sacred shit. Have you ever heard of Hiroshima?"

"The city that got nuked?"

Loud laughter. "No, man. Hiroshima is a world famous tattoo artist in Japan. That's who we apprenticed with. He gave us the knowledge to open up our own place."

"You got cash, you get some knowledge, you got a career," I said.

"Their parents are investors," the girl shouted from the tattoo table and giggled.

There was an uncomfortable pause, and then I said, "You guys gonna do piercings, too?"

More loud laughter. "We are tattoo artists," they said. "No blow-job studs or eyebrow rings."

"That reminds me," I said. "This L.A. woman. I forgot to say she has red eyebrows. Long black hair, blue eyes, and red eyebrows."

The three guys still came up blank, but the guy in the back yelled, "I think I know her. She hangs out at that Adinkra Arts place."

I walked to the back. He was coloring a winged heart just above the girl's ass-crack. "How well do you know her?" I said.

"I don't know her. I've just seen her around. Those red eyebrows are a trip. She hip-hops at this club we go to. She hangs with black guys. The guy she dances with is an artist at Adinkra Arts."

"Is it far from here?"

He pulled a tissue from a plastic box of sterilized wipes and aggressively cleaned the excess blood off the winged heart. "It's just down the street. Maybe half a mile. But the neighborhood changes. Not necessarily dangerous as long as you don't act like a tough white guy." The girl got up off the table, and they walked to a full-length mirror. She stood in front of it while the guy held up a small mirror behind her. She smiled and then threw her arms around him.

"What do you think of my tramp-stamp?" she said to me and then revealed her backside.

"Lovely," I said.

"You got a ride waiting for you?" The guy pointed to the front where the red sedan was parked.

I could just make out a silhouette behind the wheel. "I'm not sure," I said and wished the guys luck. I ran out the door straight into a hailstorm of dust and debris as the car peeled out down the street. Part of me welcomed the chicken-shit game being played. It gave me an excuse to lose my temper and act tough.

As I continued down the street, the red sedan appeared again, blazed past me, and turned sharply onto the next side street only to re-emerge minutes later to perform the same maneuver. Block after block the car taunted me, and with each pass the routine became more juvenile than sinister—which pissed me off even more.

A hundred yards ahead I saw a large wooden circle above a storefront covered in strange black and white symbols. As I neared the façade of the building, I recognized the silhouette of the African Continent. This time the red sedan sped by and turned onto the street that bordered the far side of Adinkra Arts. It was time to act out. I ran to the opposite side of the building, picked up a chunk of broken concrete, and waited behind a half-dead sumac tree. When the car turned the corner and raced to the stop sign at Sunset, I ran to the rear window and threw the concrete as hard as my aching ribs would allow. The pain was torturous, but the satisfaction of seeing the rear window explode into shattered glass eased my suffering.

Out jumped the driver, a skinny white boy with black rimmed glasses and a pile of dark hair. "Are you fucking kidding me?" he shouted, and in that instant I recognized Ellis Knight, the reporter from The Partisan.

"Knight? What the hell are you doing?"

Knight locked his hands together behind his head and looked back and forth from me to the smashed window. He had an expression of wide-eyed panic. Then he let his hands drop and said, "You're a terrible detective. I followed you all the way from Chicago, and you didn't even notice!" He started giggling, and it occurred to me he might be nuts.

"You're following me?"

"For the story! Don't you get it? I got ten thousand words, dude. We've got meth, murder, incest, dark-tattoo-world shit, twisted-daddy-complex sex. And then there's you, the detective from a family of crooks going back to the bad old days. The possibilities, dude. They're endless."

For a moment I felt vulnerable, as if the success of my investigation was at the mercy of this little prick's recklessness. "Who've you been talking to?"

"Sources."

"Did your sources tell you to drive like a goddamn maniac?"

"I thought I'd sprinkle a little drama into the mix." Knight looked at the destroyed window as if for the first time. "C'mon, man, why did you do that?"

"Some lunatic in a big red car follows me around driving like a psycho, and I need a reason to smash his window? You're lucky I didn't smash your face. You think you can act like an asshole and not suffer the consequences?"

Knight looked puzzled. "You're not getting it, are you? You're not seeing the opportunity here. Dude, this is your chance to really make a name for yourself. You'll be the guy who busts it wide open, and I'll be there to get it all down—as it happens!"

"You're a joke, Knight. Stay away from me."

I walked toward Adinkra Arts expecting him to follow, but he stayed put. Once inside, I saw several African-American men of varying ages in cargo pants and T-shirts. Two of them were working on clients while the others were either drawing or performing mundane cleaning tasks. The space was long and narrow with recently constructed drywall in the back, creating an area hidden from view. A teenager behind the counter paged through a magazine. "Hello, sir," he said, drawing the attention of three others, one of whom was built like an offensive lineman and would be their spokesman. "How can we help you today?" the big man said in a gentle voice that defied his appearance.

"Hi, guys, I'm looking for a girl named L.A. I was told she works here."

They all looked as if they misunderstood. The big man said, "L.A. like Los Angeles? I never heard of no chick named L.A."

"Yep. Long black hair, blue eyes, red eyebrows."

A few quick, sideward glances from the others and then he said, "We never heard of anyone named L.A."

"I just want to talk to her. She knows me from Chicago." I handed a card to the big guy.
Movement in the back distracted me, and I caught a glimpse of what I thought was a short black-haired woman disappearing around the corner.

He looked at the card, mumbled "Private investigator," and then with one hand started dragging the edge of the card along the tips of the other hand's fingers. "What brings you to L.A., private investigator?"

"Murder."

They all laughed. "You think this L.A. chick killed someone?"

"You mean the chick you never heard of? She didn't kill anyone. But this chick you never heard of has a friend who might know something about killing." I took out a hundred-dollar bill. "The dead man was a close friend."

The big guy looked at the money and then back to me. "Put the cash away, bro. We know someone with those red eyebrows. But her name ain't L.A." Still strumming his fingertips, he walked to the back and disappeared behind the wall. The kid behind the counter returned to his magazine, and the other two drifted around in the immediate area talking quietly to each other. After ten minutes the big guy reemerged from the back. He handed the card to me and said, "She never heard of you."

"What do you mean she never heard of me? I just spoke with her a couple of days ago. Let me just see her—"

"Sir, she said she never heard of you." My ribs ached just looking at the big man's glare.

"It took the two of you ten minutes to decide she never heard of me?"

"Sir, Audrey said she never heard of you. That's really all we got, so unless you'd like a tattoo—"

224

"Audrey never heard of me?"

"Goodbye, sir."

I stood on the sidewalk outside the door. Then I walked onto the asphalt parking lot and looked around. There was no sign of Knight or the red car.

49

The next morning I lay in bed staring at the popcorn ceiling, wondering why I had chosen this path in life. Scumbags, morons, and dopers messing with your head, laughing their asses off while you run around like a crazed hamster searching for crumbs. That giggling schmuck Ellis Knight, using me to achieve some tabloid-journalism fame fantasy. Two little girls pretending to be grown-ups, telling stories while my friend's body lies on a pile of debris. And then the professionals—politicians, lawyers, hoods—smacking you around like the neighborhood idiot. He's not a cop, after all, who cares?

I called Kalijero. "You got any connections at The Partisan?" I asked.

"Landau? Where the hell are you?"

"Los Angeles. You know anyone at The Partisan?"

"That alternative rag? What the hell are you doing in L.A.?"

"There's a punk named Ellis Knight who's trying to write a story on Snooky's murder. He'll include all possible angles while enthusiastically blurring truth and fiction. He's hinted at knowing everything we've talked about. And I mean everything—get it?"

In the ensuing silence, I imagined Kalijero swallowing a few times then taking a deep breath. "Yeah. What do you want?"

"Anything. We've got to figure out who or what his connection is to all of this."

Kalijero agreed in that grudging way of someone who knows they have no choice.

* * *

I dialed Tate's number. "Where does your ex-wife work?"

"Why? What did you find out?"

"Nothing. But there're a couple of dozen Prenevosts in the phone book."

"It's a closed chapter. I don't see how opening—"

"Who's opening anything? Maybe someone has been in touch with her. I swear, Tate, for a man who knows he's being framed for murder and drug dealing, you always seem to be holding back, like there's something you're not telling me. Does she have something on you, Tate? And by the way, how did you know she lived in L.A?"

"We still have a few friends in common."

"Chancellor, tell me where she works, if only as a nice gesture—just in case you need a character witness down the road."

"She's a public defender," he said then hung up.

I called the main number for the Los Angeles public defender, asked for Jane Prenevost, and was connected to the Compton branch where the receptionist asked, "And what is this regarding?" I gave Tate's name. "If Mr. Tate needs representation, he must first complete a financial statement to verify he cannot afford a private attorney."

"Jane is expecting Mr. Tate's call—just ask her!"

"Hold, please."

"What do you want, Jerry?"

"Do you know Chancellor Tate is being investigated for murder, extortion, bribery, and conspiracy?"

"Who is this?"

"I'm a private investigator from Chicago. I'd like to ask you some questions."

"We've been divorced ten years. I don't know what he's into, and I don't care. There's nothing I can help you with."

"Your ex-husband's being framed for murder." I waited for my words to sink in and said, "I'm sure you work with investigators, Ms. Prenevost. You never know what kind of information could help solve a case."

I could hear her breathing and tapping something on the desk. "Someplace public. Bring ID. I've never known a private eye who wasn't a jerk. And don't tell me to call Jerry to verify anything. That's not going to happen. And don't give me a lot of details. I don't want to know anything. Whatever he did or didn't do is his problem."

An hour later, I sat waiting in the Thai restaurant near my motel with a pot of tea and a couple of egg rolls. It was the post-lunch period when the remaining guests sat around talking, and the waiters didn't give a damn. But even if it had been high noon on Michigan Avenue, I would've immediately recognized the woman who walked in holding a briefcase as Jane Prenevost. Tall with brown hair braided to the middle of her back and younger than I expected, she would've been perfect for television's next beautiful district attorney avenging the unfortunate victim of sociopathic behavior, or the law school professor dedicated to proving the innocence of a death row inmate. She walked directly to my table and, without saying a word, sat then opened her briefcase.

"Can I help you?" I said.

"Cut the crap. You're the only one sitting alone and the only man under fifty." I nodded and waited for her to finish whatever she was doing and close her briefcase.

"Okay," she said. "Prove to me who you are." I handed over my driver's license, my FCC card, and my PI card. One at a time she examined them with a penlight. "Where's your FOID?" she said.

"I didn't bring my gun."

"Really? I thought you guys all liked carrying your guns around."

"It gets complicated bringing a handgun into California. You must've been very young when you met Tate." I poured her a cup of tea.

"I was twenty; he was forty. That shouldn't be a surprise. Are you new at this? You're pretty young. I'm from Chicago, and I recognize that affluent North Side accent. Why would an educated person choose to be a private investigator?"

"You're an educated woman, Jane, you went to law school. Why would you choose to defend killers, rapists, and child molesters?"

We locked eyeballs a few seconds, and then she looked away before sipping her tea. "I assume Jerry hired you?"

"No. The man your ex is accused of killing was a good friend." I explained my relationship to Snooky and where I was in my investigation. "I'm working purely on assumptions right now. I don't think Tate's a killer. But there seems to be a conspiracy against him by individuals who have no logical connection to each other."

"What exactly do you want from me?"

"Just give me a character reference with a little context." I thought of Audrey. "Tell me a story, like how you met, et cetera."

Jane picked up a fork, cut off a chunk of egg roll, and chewed while staring at a tall glass of water. "I met him at a park in Chicago with my two-year-old daughter, Lisa. I had gotten pregnant my senior year of high school. My boyfriend decided he wanted to live in California and open a bicycle shop. So he moved out here while Lisa and I stayed with my mother and waited for him to get settled. You can probably guess the rest. Then one day I was pushing Lisa on the swing when a handsome older man approached us and started talking."

"A prince to the rescue."

Jane smiled faintly. "Even though he was wearing a nice suit, he got down on his knees and let Lisa pull his hair in all directions. She laughed and laughed, and then we were all laughing."

"I can guess the rest."

"Okay, here's some character context. I was surprised he wanted a child with me. Lisa was about five when her sister was born. She had a hard time adjusting to not being the only kid and started acting out. First she would just say mean things, like she hated us and hated her sister. Then she became destructive, broke lamps, vases, glasses. We ended up shipping Lisa off to live with her biological father."

Jane's expression defined the word "guilt." "Do you blame Tate for that?"

"Yeah. But I blame myself, too. Jerry's a sick guy, but he's not a killer."

"Elaborate on the sick part."

"He already had a lifetime of younger women under his belt by the time I came along. At age forty, he tried to change. I was his experiment. I give him credit for lasting twelve years with a woman who had the audacity to continue getting older."

I said, "Let me guess. He started using his money and good looks to go after the late-teens-early-twenties demographic. So you moved your family from Chicago to Los Angeles and Tate didn't give a damn."

"I got Lisa back and he got his freedom—although he'll always be a prisoner."

"What kind of a relationship does Tate have with his daughter?"

"No relationship. Not even his name. She's Audrey Prenevost.

"And what's Audrey Prenevost doing now?"

Jane repositioned herself in her chair. The question made her uncomfortable. "She's here in L.A., working as a tattoo artist."

While the tattoo-themed coincidence sparked my imagination, Jane waited for the negative reaction she plainly anticipated. "A talented tattoo artist can make great money," I said. "How did she get interested in body ink?"

Jane shifted in her seat again. Now she looked downright ashamed. "Apparently it runs in the family. Lisa is a tattoo artist in Chicago."

The front door to Taudrey Tats flashed through my brain. I tamed my smile, fearing the satisfaction of being on the verge of solving a puzzle would be misinterpreted. "Just curious," I said. "Did Lisa take your last name or her step-father's last name?"

"Neither," Jane said. "She uses her biological father's name, Moreau."

"That's an interesting name," I said, still thinking about the front door, how it introduced, "The Sole Proprietor and Mistress of Poor Taste, L. Audrey Moreau."

* * *

Now that I wanted to find the little bastard Knight, I didn't know where to start. I walked around the neighborhood advertising my presence but failed to attract a red sedan with a smashed rear window. I decided to drive my rental back to Adinkra Arts and park on the side street where shattered window glass still covered the ground. Across the street, I saw a bench set back from the sidewalk in the shade of a locust tree. From there I watched a slow but steady stream of people enter the shop for varying lengths of time. The clientele reflected the neighborhood both racially and economically. A yellow cab pulled into the parking lot and honked twice. The neighborhood didn't strike me as the type where people took cabs, but what did I know?

An elderly woman joined me at the other end of the bench, and then a handful of kids showed up. A few minutes later, I was surrounded by a small crowd. When the bus approached, the crack detective realized where he was sitting. When the bus pulled away, the crack detective felt two enormous hands gently pressing on his shoulders. I turned my head and caught a glimpse of brown fingers before a sudden increase in pressure inspired images of snapping chicken bones. Then two men with handkerchiefs covering all but their eyes sat on either side of me.

"That was my car you smashed up," the voice from behind me said.

"Knight was trying to run me—"

His fingers dug into the space above my collarbone, shrinking me down in pain. "Careful," said the guy on my right. "The dude was walking around like he got tender ribs. Does that hurt?" He jammed his fingertips into my right rib cage. Disappointed by my non-reaction, the other one did the same into my sore ribs on the left side. I howled; they laughed.

"I want four hundred for the window," the voice said.

The guy on my right took the wallet from my back pocket and counted out the money. "Check it out," he said. "He's actually got the cash. You just saved yourself a lot of pain."

The hands on my shoulders loosened their grip. I stood and looked at the three masked men. I was pretty sure the one who had been behind me was the offensive lineman from Adinkra Arts. Their eyes betrayed the squint of gaping smiles. "Just what the hell is Ellis Knight to you?"

"He ain't nothing," the big guy said. "He just gave you up to save his own ass. You showed up at the right place at the right time. He owes you one." More laughter.

"Where is he?"

"In a cab on his way to the airport."

"Give me a break and leave some of the cash."

The big guy looked hurt. "We're just taking what you owe us," he said. His partner handed me the wallet, four hundred lighter. "You're smart to carry a lot of cash when you're snooping around a neighborhood like this. It gives you better odds of surviving a robbery."

* * *

It was dark when I walked into my apartment. Punim lay on the recliner thrashing her tail as if waiting for an explanation of my whereabouts. "It was just a couple of days," I said and called Susie to tell her I had returned.

"Did you find what you were looking for?"

"I think I got the big picture," I said and promised to talk again soon.

I called Kalijero next. "I'm back," I said. "What do you got on Knight?"

"Knight's a local punk from a wealthy family. Northwestern grad. Wants to be a true-crime writer. He's gonna expose that corrupt underbelly."

"What else?"

"Tomorrow The Partisan is running a short piece on meth-heads popping up dead. They want to know why the police don't care. Why they're not pursuing leads. Your two stiffs will be examples. No names mentioned yet."

The resignation in Jimmy's voice troubled me. I had never really bought his fatalistic façade. The idea of his long and distinguished career at the mercy of Ellis Knight and the two Audreys was probably more than he could bear.

50

At nine o'clock the next morning, I drove to The Partisan office, located in a ten-story building of red granite, with huge windows and two stone columns framing the main entrance. One of the country's oldest skyscrapers, it was the type of building that conjured romantic visions of Great-Granddad's late-nineteenth-century Chicago— although the black fire escapes traversing the outside walls evoked feelings of desperation and doom.

The Partisan occupied the fifth floor, where a plaque said carriages were once manufactured by the Studebaker brothers of South Bend, Indiana. I asked the receptionist if Ellis Knight was available. She dialed an extension, waited, and then pushed a button and announced over the intercom that Mr. Knight should come to the reception desk. Someone yelled, "He's not here," and she asked if I wanted to leave a message.

I walked back down the five flights, sat on a marble bench, and watched people breeze through the bronze and mosaic lobby. The thought of sitting there all day hoping a goofy kid made an appearance seemed ridiculous, especially since a journalist could work virtually anywhere he wanted. Then it occurred to me that writers often have a favorite hangout. We had first met at Mocha Mouse. It was worth a shot.

Driving through bail bonds row, I noticed a sign boasting, "Access to All Public Records—All the Time!" I remembered Knight's first phone call, when he informed me I was now "part of the public record." I pulled over and checked the list of recent phone calls on my cell phone. I called the first number I didn't recognize. Knight picked up on the second ring. "I want to make a deal," I said.

Knight hesitated. "Dude, I had no choice. It wasn't my car. And then you showed up." He sounded nervous.

"C'mon, Ellis, getting knocked around is no big deal."

Knight chuckled. "Yeah, I guess I didn't see it that way. But I swear if you hadn't showed up like you did, they would've bashed my head in. I mean, they're good guys as long as you don't cross them. And I didn't think he'd mind if I borrowed his car."

"Where are you? Let's talk."

"Just don't kill me. I'm at the Mouse."

Twenty minutes later, I walked into Mocha Mouse and again saw Knight sitting at the corner table farthest from the door. My first thought was how much I still wanted to wipe that cocky grin off his face.

"You still got that agonized look when you walk," Knight said. "How can the bad guys take you seriously when you're so pathetic?"

I eased myself into the chair across from him. Once settled, I grabbed the collar of his polo shirt and yanked him toward me. Then I forced the side of his face against the table and lay on top of him. The move sent spasms of pain through my side, but it was worth it to see his glasses go flying and a couple of buttons pop off his shirt.

"Let me explain something, Knight. I am going to find out who killed Charles Snook. I'm still wondering if you have information that could help me find the killer. I'm willing to make a deal, one that would be mutually beneficial. Or I could make sure you are arrested as an accessory after the fact for having knowledge that a crime was committed. The choice is yours."

I pushed myself off the table and watched the pitiful, red-faced Knight grope for his glasses. His shirt hung open from the collar to mid-chest, revealing a stained undershirt. As soon as he had composed himself and retaken his chair, I started feeling sorry for him. Then he said, "For me to be an accessory, you'd have to prove that I received, relieved, comforted, or assisted the killer in order to hinder or prevent the killer's apprehension, trial, or punishment." My pity vanished; his grin returned. "But tell me about your deal."

"You tell me what you know, answer my questions, and I'll make sure you get the inside word on what's happening to all the various parties related to my investigation."

"Ha! You think I need your help to get this story? You're funny. Go ahead, ask a question."

Suddenly, I was playing his game. "How well do you know the girl with the red eyebrows who works at Adinkra Arts?"

"Remember when I asked you if you'd ever been to Los Angeles? That's where I lived until high school when we moved here."

He waited for my response, wild and grinning. I said, "You knew L.A. when you lived in Los Angeles."

"Bingo! But I didn't get to know her personally until she started coming here to visit. I would see her around, but didn't realize who she was because she looked different. But she recognized me and we hit it off!"

"Her name is Audrey, isn't it?"

Knight leaned over the table and said, "You're on the right track, my friend!" He fell back into his chair. "You've lit the fuse. Now follow it."

"The Audrey that lives here. Her real name is Lisa—"

"No shit? How did you find out?"

"I'm not gonna tell you just yet. Any idea how Lisa and Audrey know each other?"

"Nope. She wouldn't tell me.

237

"I'm supposed to believe you don't know anything about Lisa?"

"It's the truth! I don't know how they know each other. Those chicks live for their weird world of secrets."

"You giving me all the facts, Knight?"

"Facts are just by-products of the process. Give me process, Detective Landau! Sniff it down and dig it up, dude! That's where the story is!" Knight opened his laptop and began typing. His grin was eclipsed by a severely furrowed brow under which this strange kid's eyes fixated on a hidden world of process. I resigned myself to participating in his game and hoped if I gave him enough process, he'd give me enough facts. I got up and walked away from the table fairly certain that my absence was unnoticed. That week's issue of The Partisan was stacked on the floor next to the door.

Sitting in my car, I looked through the stories of neighborhood activism and political misdeeds next to reviews of local hipster bands and art exhibits. On page twelve, my eye caught a sidebar adjacent to an article debating the effectiveness of methadone. The headline read, "The Only Good Meth-Head Is a Dead Meth-Head." The article described "power-junkies injecting meth into the veins of society, pushing in dreamland and drawing out bloodstained cash from an addicted underclass supplying a steady stream of money to all those attached to the political tit. The infected milk nourishes city hall, police, big business, and then down the line . . ." There was no byline, but Knight's voice was unmistakable.

51

The significance of my Los Angeles trip to premeditated murder remained in the periphery, although I felt confident that the partial decoding of the two Audreys would somehow help bring my investigation to a conclusion. Despite the abundance of motivation to go around, evil was still the missing ingredient. But I knew evil when I saw it.

I called Kalijero. "Voss is the engine behind this train wreck, right?"

Deep sigh. "So what? What're you going to do about it?"

"I'm gonna take him down."

Kalijero laughed. "Really? You going to arrest him?"

"That balancing act you were talking about. Imagine the leverage you would have if you could prove Voss played an active role in murder. It's the ultimate trump card for you and your pals. What's pimping and money laundering compared to murder?"

"When the corpse is a meth-head—"

"I'm talking about Snooky! Voss used Lisa—"

"Who the hell is Lisa?"

"The tattoo girl. Her real name is Lisa Audrey Moreau. Voss used Lisa to try to get information on you. Snooky wouldn't rat you out, but Snooky and Lisa used to laugh about the code names he made up for his clients. She must've told Voss about the names which helped him figure out the connection to Mildish, Baron, and Tate."

"So why kill Snooky?"

"After Snooky and Lisa had a falling out, Voss gave up on her. Voss assumed Snooky kept records of everything, and that his murder would be written off as just another mob flunky getting clipped. Voss and his cronies ransack his house for evidence against you. Plus he can lean on Mildish and get a cut of the Maxwell Street action."

"So the tattoo broad—Lisa—unknowingly participated in murder because Snooky wouldn't go along with her plan to ruin Tate's reputation?"

"There's more to it; I just haven't figured it out yet. Maybe something to do with meth. By the way, why does Voss have such a hard-on for you?"

"I was once married, you know. Voss's sister. Let's just say we weren't a good match and leave it at that."

"Enough said. I think there's a real chance Lisa's life could be in danger. If I give you solid evidence something's going down, will you act?"

Kalijero cleared his throat. "She's a potential innocent victim, a potential character witness, and a potential suspect. Assuming you convince me, I'll act."

52

From my vantage point at the diner, I could make out Lisa bent over a drawing table. She seemed frozen except when she stopped to erase something and wipe the page clean. A middle-aged man with a gray ponytail entered the shop. Lisa stopped what she was doing and greeted him. Then she walked to a filing cabinet and took out what I assumed was a drawing he had requested. He studied it for a few seconds before sitting down in the barber's chair.

I called Susie. "I'm across the street at the diner. Can you get away for a few minutes?"

"How important is this? I've got a few browsers and my assistant is new."

"I would be extremely grateful."

She hurried across the street. I waved through the window and moments later she joined me. I said, "I found out in Los Angeles that Audrey's real name is Lisa and I'm convinced the short, fat, comb-over guy you saw in Lisa's shop played a role in Snooky's murder. His name is Voss. Lisa appears to have been involved, although probably not intentionally. Things are coming to a head, and it would be a big help if you could keep an eye on Taudrey Tats. Tell me if something seems strange."

Susie stared at me wide-eyed. "Everything you just said seems strange. Lisa? I won't ask. But, like—what is it I'm looking for and how should I look for it?" She seemed equally baffled and annoyed.

"It's all about keeping Lisa safe from comb-over man. Ideally, engage her in conversation. Does she seem preoccupied, like someone who feels threatened, or is she the same Lisa? Maybe she'll confide in you. If you hear any yelling, try to remember what it's about. Call me if you see her little dark-haired friend with the red eyebrows or anyone else who's hanging around that's not a tattoo customer. I know I'm being vague about what I want, but just trust your instincts."

"And what exactly am I getting into?"

"I just need another pair of eyes and ears. Although, conceivably, there could be a potential for danger."

"You want to be more specific?"

"Voss is a cold-blooded bastard. Others have called him a psychopath or a sociopath. One of the two. Lisa—I don't know what she is. She may be guilty of something, but I think she's also a victim—somehow. Either way, I'm going to get the truth and, in the process, if Voss decides Lisa is a liability, her safety might be at risk."

Susie drummed her fingers on the table and glanced back at her shop. "I'd best be off," she said.

* * *

I had been going non-stop since nine a.m. and needed some downtime to rest my aching ribs and try to assimilate all the components of my investigation. Once I was on the recliner, Punim wedged herself between my thighs. Her front paws disappeared beneath the white fur on her chest. She stared at me in that neglected-cat way, sending a barrage of guilt darts into my torso. It was just the two of us after all.

My fear for Lisa's safety was genuine, second only to my fear of her dubious mental state, which could jeopardize my plan and possibly put her in more danger. If Voss was truly running the show, I had every reason to believe he was aware of my last visit to Taudrey Tats, when I accused her of making a deal with Satan. Lisa didn't know enough to recognize the sharks swimming around her. But if

242

approaching her was too hazardous, what was my next step?

I called Knight. "I've got some process for you. Are you still at Mocha Mouse?"

He didn't try to hide his delight. "All right, my man! You diggin' in? Gettin' deep? I knew you'd come through. Get thee to the Mouse!"

For the second time in five hours, I walked through a coffee shop named for a saxophone-playing rodent and approached the far corner table where Ellis Knight happily waited with his open laptop. "I brought some process with me," I said and held up a manila folder before sitting down. "Here are some of the details involved in the process, courtesy of a police photographer." From the folder, I took two pictures of a man face down on a pile of construction debris. One of the pictures was taken from only a few feet away. Two close head wounds were clearly visible. "Meet my friend Snooky."

Knight stared at the pictures. "Why is he wearing a suit?"

"That's what CPAs usually wear when they're working. But here's a more casual picture." I showed him the druggie I had fought in my apartment. He was on his back, eyes open. A stream of blood spilled out of his mouth and flowed down his cheek, gathering in a puddle by his ear.

Knight recoiled, then recovered. "Whoa. What is this?"

"I just got one more," I said and showed him the police photo of the druggie who had held me at gunpoint in the alley, lying on his back, eyes open, legs folded queerly to the side. Around his head was a halo of blood, brain, and skull. Knight retreated again but this time didn't bounce back.

"Dude, what's your point? I mean, okay, I'm grossed out, you win."

"It's just part of the process, Ellis. It's a brutal process, you know? And I'm really scared that Lisa could end up in one of these pictures."

Knight frowned. "You're trying to freak me out. Just because she knew the dead guy means she's gonna end up dead, too?"

I thought I was penetrating his juvenile façade, dude! "Why don't we cut the bullshit and you just tell me what you know."

Knight looked agitated. "I know that guy got bumped off, and he worked for Lisa. And I know how much she hated that chancellor dude even though she was banging him."

"Tell me why she hated him."

"She wouldn't tell me."

"Who wouldn't tell you?"

"L.A.-Audrey. Get it? She started calling herself Los Angeles Audrey and then just L.A.. These two chicks have some really weird connection she won't tell me about. It's through L.A. that I know stuff."

"L.A's real name is Audrey Prenevost."

"Yeah, that sounds right."

"You asked if Snooky was murdered because he was going to expose Chancellor Tate as a meth dealer. That came from Audrey Prenevost?"

"She suggested the meth thing a few times, but it wasn't, like, written in stone. I mean, she's kind of playing with my head, too. She throws out ideas to try to get me to be creative."

"Tate has nothing to do with meth. He's being framed. I have a clue as to why Lisa is trying to destroy his life, but there's more going on that I don't know. What do you think she could she have against him?"

"I don't know."

"What about Audrey Prenevost?"

"She'd know more than I would. You haven't explained why Lisa might end up with a bullet in her head."

"Has Audrey Prenevost ever mentioned the name Voss?" Knight shook his head. "I guess you really don't know shit."

Knight typed a bit and then waited for more. "C'mon, Detective, give me something! I won't use his real name or nothing."

"He's the Duke of Darkness."

Knight's face lit up. "Awesome! Is he, like, some psychotic meth king? Tell me more."

My first inclination was to downplay the meth as just a smokescreen to what was really going on. But I stopped myself. "Get Audrey Prenevost to talk to me and I'll think about it."

Knight stared thoughtfully for a moment and then started nodding his head. "I think I can do that."

53

"What if Voss is trafficking meth?" I said to Kalijero.

"Where are you?"

"I'm home. It makes sense—"

"Don't move until I get there." The line went dead.

It was rude to hang up on people and I reminded Kalijero of this fact when he entered my apartment.

"You'll get over it," he said. "Sit down." I did as told. "Remember what I said about moonlighting at that club out by the airport? Big shots getting all the booze and tail for a night? At some point, I was told to start expecting small packages to deliver to the clients' rooms. I wasn't too concerned at first until I found out it was meth. For an extra grand, fat middle-aged men who had forgotten that the thing between their legs had another function besides pissing could screw like porn stars for a night with the girl of their dreams. You can probably guess how popular this extra feature became. My troubles began when I started snooping around, trying to find out where the meth was coming from. I was called into a meeting with some of the heavies at the club. Voss was there. I said we had a good thing going. Why dirty it up with drugs? Voss suggested I could easily be replaced and that my career might suffer a significant setback if I didn't cool it. I told them this meth thing had me worried. Voss assured me his channel into the police had backups all the way to the top. Shortly after this conversation, Snook told me tattoo broad—Lisa—had started asking questions about me. Snook got her to confess that this slimy older man began showing up when she was about to close and that he made her nervous. So I staked out the place and, sure enough, Voss paid a visit to her shortly before closing time."

"Did you tell Snooky about your meth money?"

"I'm thinking Voss had Snook killed. He had the motive. He needed that book to make sure I kept my mouth shut. But we need more than a motive to convict Voss. Lisa knowingly or unknowingly played a role in all this. I think her main motive was fear of Voss, although hurting Tate probably helped."

"Answer my question. Did Snooky know he was laundering your meth money?" Kalijero avoided eye contact. He reminded me of a little boy too ashamed to talk. "You piece of shit! You didn't tell him because you knew Snooky would've dumped you as a client."

"All right! I'm a shit! You don't think I feel bad about all this?"

"What if we get proof? He goes down?"

"If he's trafficking meth, nothing will stop the state from prosecuting. That's the line Hauser was talking about. We're working with the Feds, but they're letting us take the lead. If we don't move in, the Feds will take over, and that'll make us look like idiots."

"If Voss admits killing Snooky, you'd get him for that, too?"

"Yeah, yeah, I'm sure they'd throw that in."

"Don't yeah, yeah me, you shit. Get Hauser's word."

"We'll nail him for murder! I give you my word."

I could've told Kalijero what his word was worth, but I didn't. "What kind of time would Voss be looking at?"

"Five to life, depending on how many grams he was moving and if they get first-degree murder."

"What about Lisa? She had nothing to do with dealing meth."

Kalijero thought for a moment. "Tough to say. They could still nail her for accessory after the fact—depending on the evidence. When this is all over, move on. If everything doesn't work out exactly how you want it, just go back to making an honest living and don't dwell on changing the system or saving the world."

The phony resignation in Kalijero's voice was impossible to resist, and I laughed loudly. I said, "You can't fight city hall, kid. Just accept the facts of life."

"Okay, smart guy, look at your beloved Maxwell Street. All the moral sermonizing about the poor. All the people with their fond memories. All the work put in by historic preservationists begging for landmark status and all. And in the end, Maxwell Street was given all the respect of a ten-dollar whore."

"Well, maybe you've got a point . . ."

Why Kalijero should take a sudden interest in my professional future was a mystery. But the fatherly advice to stay away from a line of work because it stunk or was a lousy way to make a living was nothing new. I did my best to capitulate, to suggest that maybe I agreed with him and that making an honest living did not include tracking down criminals and that the system was hopelessly corrupt and that the seamy side of big-city politics would probably swallow me up and spit me out as nothing less than a criminal myself. By the time he left my apartment, I was fairly certain he thought I was full of crap.

54

The next morning a circular saw tore through my ribs as I pushed myself out of bed. I thought of Kalijero controlling the spinning blade while reminding me that Snooky's murder investigation had given my body the same level of respect Maxwell Street had been given. After feeding Punim, I prepared a couple of ice packs and laid on the couch. I dozed off until the phone rang.

"You weren't joking about Lisa being in danger of getting clipped, were you?" Knight said.

"Those pictures I showed you weren't jokes."

"I called L.A.—I mean Audrey Prenevost—last night and told her what you said. She started acting really weird. She said she was going to call Lisa, but I don't think she will. I've seen her this way before. She freezes up and doesn't do anything, just acts like there's nothing going on. I told her to come into town so we can discuss stuff. You know, dude, she's scared of you. She thinks you're dangerous and angry about what happened at the party with Lisa's emo-druggy-freak friends."

"Audrey Prenevost and Lisa were supposed to be best buds, real soul sisters. Now you're saying she's afraid to call her and tell her that I said her life could be in danger? She must have some dark secrets. Get her ass in town, Knight. Think of the story you could write when we find out."

I envisioned Knight's eyes attaining a faraway look before his cocky smile crept back on his face.

* * *

The outer drive had just transitioned to Sheridan Road when my phone rang. "That dark-haired girl is back," Susie said. "Can't miss the eyebrows, and the giggling is unmistakable. She arrived late last night. I didn't want to wake you up."

I maneuvered the car into a loading zone in front of an apartment building.

"Giggling?" I asked.

"That's how they always act together, like little girls."

I thanked Susie for the information and told her I'd be in touch. A half hour later I walked through Frownie's front door. He put his arm around my shoulders and led me into the living room that looked out over the blue expanse of Lake Michigan. "So how was Los Angeles?"

"It was an interesting trip." I tried to hide the pain as I sank into his couch. Frownie walked to the bar, took a couple of tumblers off the shelf, and filled each about two fingers high with single malt. Then he walked back to me and offered a glass.

I dreaded having to bring up Voss's name again to Frownie, but I was beyond the point in my investigation where I could hold anything back. "I'm going to tell you how I see it," I said. Frownie stood gazing passively out the large window to my right. "Voss is behind Snooky's murder." I paused to let Voss's name penetrate his octogenarian brain, but besides Frownie's leathery arm slowly lifting the tumbler to this mouth, he offered no discernible reaction. When I was fairly certain no valves or arteries had dislodged, I continued.

"Kalijero knew about Voss's drug dealing. Voss needed Snooky's book to make sure Kalijero kept his mouth shut. Eventually, Voss thought that if Snooky disappeared, he could ransack his house and maybe find the book with account numbers, et cetera. And if Voss didn't find what he was looking for, at least Snooky was out of the way."

I waited for Frownie to offer some kind of acknowledgment. Still staring out the window, he smacked his lips, nodded his head ever so slightly. After watching his arm once again toggle between his mouth and his side, I thought of those heat-engine toys that imitate the movement of birds bending over to drink from a glass.

"You think there's anything you overlooked?" This was Frownie's way of saying I missed something.

"Tell me."

"So the answer is, you don't know."

"Holy shit! Fine. I don't know. Now can we just assume I learned something in this investigation and go with it?"

Frownie paced around a bit in his own world. From the other side of the room he said, "You know what you gotta do, don't you?"

"If I can get him on the record taking part in drug dealing and Snooky's murder, all the bullshit loyalties will disappear faster than those junkies he used up."

"So how're you gonna do it?"

"Not sure yet."

Frownie meandered his way back to me. "You ever see a cornered raccoon? Survival is all they're thinking about because as far as they're concerned, you're there to kill them. With those claws they can climb the side of a brick wall and turn your face into a pile of spaghetti. You trap an animal like Voss, that's what you gotta expect."

55

I sat at the kitchen table writing down the details necessary to implement my plan. To nail a man like Voss required impeccable witnesses and recording devices. To a jury, his words must sound explicit, his intentions unambiguous.

The phone rang. "I did it," Knight said. "I told Audrey Prenevost to get the hell back here and she's coming in."

"She got in last night."

"What? How do you know?" Knight sounded hurt.

"I have spies, Ellis. I need you to arrange a meeting for me with her. I don't care where. But do it as soon as possible."

After I assured Knight of his inclusion in the meeting, he hung up. I called Kalijero and told him my idea. "So you give Voss Snook's book and he gives you a bullshit story. What about Butch?" Kalijero asked, using his own code name in Snooky's notebook.

"Relax, Voss won't spot it. I have to show him the book, Jimmy. Voss has to think the book is golden."

"You're just going to give it to him? What if he pulls a gun and walks away?"

"That's why you have to be watching the whole thing. If he draws down, I'll do the same. If he shoots me, you're a witness."

"It must be true what they say about the Landaus. You're all crazy. Get back to me."

* * *

Knight called me a couple of hours later. "She's coming over at five," he said and gave me his address. "Try not to bum her out. I'm hoping for a big night."

Not until I was on my way to Knight's condo did his affluent Near North address dawn on me. Somehow, I didn't see him fitting in with the Magnificent Mile crowd. I parked my Civic in his building's underground garage between a Porsche SUV and a Mercedes SUV. The doorman phoned Mr. Knight, and I was on my way to the fifty-second floor.

Knight opened the door holding a cordless phone to his ear. He waved me in. The living room was large and occupied by a brown leather L-shaped couch with matching love seat, chair, and ottoman. Everything was arranged in a semicircle around an enormous television and glass coffee table that held Knight's laptop. I sank into the couch while my host drifted around the condo in his socks repeating, "Okay, Dad," every ten seconds. Hanging

253

on one of the walls were black-and-white photographs of industrial parks and gutted buildings. Another wall was covered with a variety of antique maps. Just outside the kitchen, the top third of President Nixon's head jutted from the ground in a portrait of his unmistakable hairline.

Knight ended the call in the kitchen and then joined me. "What do you call this kind of photography?" I said and pointed to the photos. He glanced at the wall and shrugged. Then I said, "I like the Nixon head." Knight seemed confused. "That picture!" I pointed to the head. Knight shrugged again. Why did he annoy me so easily?

"That's my dad's stuff—okay, come here." He motioned for me to follow him, and we walked to his bedroom, which was off the hallway about ten feet from the door. "Stay in here until she shows up. I didn't tell her you were coming."

I did as told and sat on the bed. Knight left the bedroom door ajar. My annoyance was unjust since she probably would not have shown up if she knew I was here. Ten minutes later the doorman called, and I heard the cylinder of the dead bolt snap open. Knight fidgeted in the doorway. A minute later he shouted, "Over here, La-La."

Audrey Prenevost shouted back, "Wow, you live here?" When she entered the foyer she said, "Oh my god, look at that sofa!"

From the sound of it she ran into the living room and leaped onto the couch. Then she began talking about the shop in Los Angeles and that in six months her bosses thought she would be tattooing on her own. I peeked around the corner.

254

Audrey Prenevost was lying on her back. I walked out of the bedroom and stopped where the hallway intersected the living room.

"Hi, La-La," I said.

She lifted her head and stared at me. Then she sat upright, "Hey! That's not fair. What are you doing here?"

Not fair? "Don't get all wigged out. I just want to talk."

"He just wants to talk," Knight said. "You don't have to freak."

Audrey Prenevost glanced at Knight and then back to me. In a low voice, she said, "Who's freaking? Jeez, you guys."

"I know Audrey's real name is Lisa. Did Lisa tell you about the last time I visited Taudrey Tats?" I said.

She stared at me. "Why should she?"

"I thought you two shared everything."

She turned back to Knight, who had opened his laptop. "We share what we want to share," she said.

"Did she share why she claimed your father—Chancellor Tate—was her father?"

Knight shouted, "Say what? That chancellor dude is your father?" He had that look of joy one associated with lottery winners. Audrey Prenevost blinked a few times and then pulled her legs up to her chest before burrowing cross-legged into the elbow of the couch. We both stared at her.

"He wasn't a father to me," she said finally. The bitterness in her voice sounded alien, as if someone else had spoken. "I don't even know him."

I said, "But you knew your best friend was your father's girlfriend! You also knew your best friend told me he was her father. Isn't that a little strange?"

Knight typed furiously.

"Just because Lisa's not boring like most people doesn't mean she's strange. You don't even know her."

"I know she was involved in my friend's murder and she's in danger. And here's something else you should know. If you have any knowledge of this murder, you're an accessory. Keep this up and you'll be tattooing with razor blades in prison."

Either Audrey Prenevost's face turned whiter or her eyebrows got redder. She stood up and said, "I'm leaving."

I positioned myself in front of the vestibule that led to the door. "Not until you tell me how Lisa was involved in Snooky's murder." Knight jumped off the couch and joined us.

"Dude, chill out," Knight said to me. "C'mon, La-La, just tell us what you do know." He put his arm around Audrey Prenevost and led her back to her roost in the corner of the couch. Then he jumped back into typing—not missing a beat—as if transcribing a perpetual news crawl in his brain.

I said, "You knew who Snooky was, right?" Audrey Prenevost nodded. "Lisa trusted him, right?" Audrey Prenevost agreed. "Something happened between them. They started arguing. A short time later, Snooky's dead. What were they arguing about?"

I waited. "Lisa wanted names of his clients," Audrey Prenevost said quietly. "And she wanted to know about my father's money. He got paid for something to do with a construction project. Snooky wouldn't give her the information. And there were other names she wanted. But I didn't understand it all." Knight kept typing.

"What was she going to do with the information on your father?"

"I didn't understand all that stuff. I wasn't in that part of the plan. That stuff came later—"

"So there was a plan," I said. "Lisa planned on meeting your father at the bar. She planned on getting into a relationship with him. That part, you knew about?"

"Yes."

From that one small word came a big feeling of vindication. "And then what was she going to do?"

"She wasn't sure. Maybe after a while tell him she was only sixteen to freak him out and maybe threaten to tell the police or something."

"But your father steered Snooky to his girlfriend Lisa because her tattoo business needed a bookkeeper." Audrey Prenevost nodded. "Would I be correct in saying everything that occurred after Snooky started working for Lisa was not part of the original plan?"

Audrey Prenevost thought about it. "I guess so."

"Excellent. So Lisa wanted information on Tate's illegal financial dealings and Snooky refused. Then Snooky gets killed. Okay, Audrey, what was the plan you were a part of?"

"To ruin my father—for those disgusting things he did to me."

I had not anticipated this loathsome suggestion to resurface. "But how did Lisa figure into it? She's old enough to legally date Tate. You could have exposed him on your own."

"Well, we wanted it to look really bad because it was a long time ago, and I'm not really sure what I remember. Lisa helped me put the pieces together. So if he was dating someone as young as Lisa, we thought it would help make him look bad."

Something wasn't adding up. "Does your mother know what happened to you?"

"She's in denial. She says Lisa put false memories in my head."

"There are few accusations more horrible than what Lisa is suggesting. Please, look deep inside. In your heart of hearts, do you really think Tate touched you inappropriately?"

Audrey Prenevost again brought her knees close to her body and hugged them. She stayed that way for a full minute before saying, "No. I don't think anything like that ever happened."

I sat down on the couch close to her. "On Lisa's shoulder is a moon phase sequence. It starts with a new moon black circle and progresses to an almost full moon. You have a tattoo like that, right?"

"I have the same thing on my neck," Audrey Prenevost said. She pulled her hair back to show us.

"Well, not exactly the same. Yours starts with a full moon and progresses to the last stage, just a thin crescent of white before it would become totally black again."

"Yeah, but it's the same idea."

"The other day I was looking at a book of tattoo symbolism. The Greeks saw the moon as a symbol for a sister. The phases of the moon symbolized the evolving relationship. But in your case, the tattoo is more than symbolism, it's blood—or half blood. Lisa is your half-sister, isn't she?"

"Wait a second!" Knight screamed. "Tate is Lisa's stepdad? She was bangin' her own stepfather?"

"Calm down, Ellis. Tate didn't know because Lisa went to live with her biological father when she was a little girl."

"Yeah, but jeez, dude, Lisa knew who he was."

I understood what Knight meant. The concept turned my stomach, too.

"She gave herself the middle name Audrey," Audrey Prenevost said. "After our grandmother."

"On the door to her shop," I said. " 'Sole Proprietor and Mistress of Poor Taste, L. Audrey Moreau.' "

56

"I can't believe it," Knight screamed again. "Tate was banging his own stepdaughter and didn't even know it!"

I said, "Lisa Audrey Moreau hated Tate so much she convinced you that he abused you and then she took him to bed to prove it—sort of."

"He treated Mom like shit."

I took a deep breath. "When Snooky arrived, the plan changed to include Tate's finances. Did she mention the name Voss?"

Audrey Prenevost rested the side of her head on top of her knees. She said quietly, "Lisa said Voss mentioned you."

The power of that small voice uttering "you" rattled my foundation. "Me? What're you talking about? I didn't know Voss."

"We didn't know it was you—until you showed up. After Snooky died."

"Well, what did he say?"

"He said to expect a private investigator."

"Everyone knew Snooky was considered part of my family. Voss's motive was to get info on dirty cops and get a cut of the Maxwell Street redevelopment kickbacks. There's no mystery here. Killing Snooky didn't have anything to do with me."

"Maybe Voss has a deeper grudge you don't know about."

I refused to acknowledge Knight and kept my attention on Audrey Prenevost. "I have one more question. Lisa knew Snooky was dead a few days before I showed up. Yet she fell apart when I told her about the murder."

It seemed Audrey Prenevost had already given this some thought. "She said Snooky created a story full of criminals and that if he had a violent ending, that was how he had written his own story. She didn't know anyone else who knew Snooky besides my father. Voss said to expect you. I guess when you showed up it really hit her. That he was gone."

260

Before I left, I summoned Knight to the door and suggested it would be in everyone's best interest if Audrey Prenevost hung around a few days. Knight's cocky grin reappeared. Then he wiggled his eyebrows a few times—a reference to erotic ambitions, I guessed.

* * *

From my apartment, I phoned Kalijero. "You told me to get back to you, remember?"

"Talk."

"I want to get a message to Voss. I want him to meet me at Maxwell and Halsted. I'll bring the book he wants; he gives me everything on Snooky's murder."

"At Maxwell and Halsted? Oh, let me guess. You want to settle a score at the scene of the crime—like in the movies."

"Let's just say I have a burning desire to meet him there. And why not? Tomorrow evening, after the construction crews leave. There's nothing there except the office buildings a block away. It'll be quiet. Voss can choose the time. So he knows I'm serious, I'll include a grand in cash with the message. I get the cash back when I give him the book."

"You're assuming a hell of a lot, aren't you?"

"C'mon, Jimmy. Tell Hauser I'll be the bait. Wire me up and I'll get Voss to hang himself."

"It's so easy, huh, Landau?"

"I didn't say it was easy, but Voss is an arrogant bastard. He has no fear, he'll shoot off his mouth, I'm sure of it."

Another trademark Kalijero sigh. "I'll run it by Hauser but if he says no, that's it. I don't want to lose my pension this late in the game."

I thought I was hearing things. "Since when do you give a damn about permission from Mommy and Daddy?"

"This is Voss we're talking about! Why don't you just call the son of a bitch yourself?"

"I want him to know the police are involved."

"What about Lisa? You gonna tell her what you're up to?"

"Don't worry about her. You just try to get that permission slip from Daddy and don't worry your pretty little head about it."

I imagined hearing the steam shooting out of Kalijero's nostrils. "I'll give you one hour to meet me in front of Area B with the note and cash. I'll either take it or beat the shit out of you first and then take it."

I spent the next few minutes watching Punim gallop around the apartment, stop momentarily to groom and look around, only to dash off again. I reflected on the limb I had just crawled out on. I called Susie and told her I wanted to stop by within the hour. She didn't object and didn't sound surprised when I didn't tell her why.

I pulled in front of Area B and saw Kalijero on the sidewalk halfway down the block, smoking a cigarette and looking preoccupied. I don't think he even noticed I parked about thirty yards from him. When I slammed the door, he glanced my way, took a deep drag, and flicked the butt into the street. He took his time walking back, avoiding eye contact until he reached me. I said, "How did Hauser react?"

"He said we should've used official informants while we had the chance. I kept reminding him you're a Landau. We finally made a deal."

"So you got the green light?"

"I said we made a deal." Kalijero had such a pained, uncomfortable look, I thought he might cry.

"Just say it already!"

"What is it with you? Maybe if you had a wife and kid you wouldn't be so careless with your life. You got a death wish? Is that it?"

"Hey, Jimmy, you got a family hiding somewhere nobody knows about? Are you going to tell me that you don't get a secret thrill from risking your life sometimes?"

Kalijero frowned. "Fine. Give it to me." I gave Kalijero a sealed envelope filled with ten Ben Franklins and my handwritten note. Kalijero turned around and whistled loudly using his thumb and index finger. I've always wanted to learn how to do that. A black Crown Vic with tinted windows appeared from the end of the block and stopped across the street from us. Kalijero walked to the driver's side, handed the goods through the window, and leaned down to say something to the driver. Then the car sped off and Kalijero walked back to me. "Done," he said.

"What's next?"

Kalijero glanced at the concrete staircase in front of headquarters. "You wait for the phone to ring and a voice tells you the time." Without any more comment, he started climbing the stairs.

He was halfway up when I shouted, "We'll talk later. You can tell me about the deal." He turned and stared at me a few moments before giving me a half-assed salute, the kind of hand gesture one used to acknowledge another person while getting the hell away from them.

57

From the diner, I could see Lisa working on a client. I crossed the street and entered Vagabond Boutique, where Susie stood with a customer in front of a full-length mirror. She was holding a red dress with white flowers to the customer's neck and shoulders. Several other garments were draped over a stuffed wingback chair. I sat on the edge of the display platform and stared out the window between a pearl-snap Western shirt and a pink button-up blouse. When the customer took a few of the dresses into the changing room, Susie walked over to me.

"I don't think those shirts are your style," she said. "I think you'd look better in a black rayon crepe blouse that just came in."

I smiled and got right to the point. "I'm setting up a meeting with the fat comb-over guy."

Susie had no immediate reaction. Then she said, "You're meeting with a psychopath? Where?"

"Where my friend's body was found— Snooky."

"You never told me he was your friend."

"A very good friend. I'm not sure why I didn't mention this before."

Susie took the remaining dresses off the chair and draped them over her arm. "It's just you and this Voss guy, who happens to be capable of anything? And you're telling me this in case you get—something happens?"

"I'll be fine, but if something does happen—"

"I'll take care of Punim. At least tell me the police know what you're up to."

"They know."

She turned to me. "And?"

"It's too complicated to explain right now. Picture a corruption/shit sandwich where police, politicians, and developers are fighting it out to see who takes the biggest bite."

It was an ugly metaphor, but I guess it got through. "Can you at least tell me when the meeting is?"

"Tomorrow night sometime."

I watched her rehang the dresses then walk to the center of the shop where she said something to her assistant. The she turned to me and said, "Well, good luck," before disappearing into the back.

58

An early August evening on North Halsted Street, Chicago. I sat in the overstuffed chair, aware I had nothing to do but wait, but also conscious of having reached a symbolic turning point.

I owed Knight a phone call. I kept it brief. I told him I expected the investigation to end soon. When I refused to reveal details, he responded with howls of protest. I assured him he'd get his story unless I wasn't around to tell it. Then I hung up. He called back seconds later, but I let it go to voice mail.

I should've been tired and hungry, but my adrenaline levels were too high to experience either sensation. I closed my eyes and thought of Voss. How did such a psycho gain such power within legitimate circles of municipal government? I guess it was a stupid question for someone whose great-grandfather shared a headline with Al Capone.

I channel-surfed the rest of the evening. The phone rang around midnight. "Ten p.m. tomorrow," Voss's creepy voice said and hung up. Knowing that a time had been set brought a strange feeling of relief.

* * *

The next morning I phoned Susie and told her about the ten o'clock meeting. "Thanks for letting me know," she said.

"I'm going to stop by the shop and see if Lisa's acting different, like she knows something's up."

"You think she's in on it with the nutcase?"

I paused. "It's possible. I don't know what to think anymore. "

I entered Taudrey Tats just after nine in the morning. There were no customers inside, understandable for that hour, but I was surprised Lisa was nowhere in sight. I shouted her name and waited. From the back, I heard shuffling and the sound of furniture moving. Then Lisa appeared looking as spry and unburdened as the day I met her. "Well, hello," she said. "What brings you to these parts?"

Given her bizarre personality, I should not have been surprised at her reaction. "I wasn't happy how our last meeting ended. And now that my ribs have started to mend, I thought maybe it was time to mend fences."

She giggled while taking drawings off the display rack. "You have such a way with words. I wish I was clever that way. But I have the visual artist's mind."

I decided to test the waters. "Any more folks stop by claiming to be cops?"

She didn't respond but stayed focused on several drawings laid out on a table. Sounding as though it were an afterthought, she said, "By the way, do you still think I'm a murderer?"

"I never said you were a murderer."

She stepped out from behind the table, walked directly up to me, and trained her big black eyes on my smaller, browner ones. "You implied it."

I had forgotten how enticing she was. I felt as if I were the one who had explaining to do. "Your story wasn't adding up, and I called you on it." I stepped backward, toward the front of the shop.

"Well, you stopped by and said hello," she said. "You did your good deed."

My impression was she had no idea of this evening's planned get-together with Voss. I walked toward the front and told her it was nice seeing her. As I reached for the door, she said, "Remember what Snooky told me. 'Every relationship is allowed either one secret or one lie.'"

I recalled her mentioning this alleged statement during our first meeting. "Well," I said as I walked out, "he never said that to me. He always told me the truth."

59

It was interesting how different the world looked about thirteen hours before a moment of truth. Everyone I passed on the street gave off a unique vibe broadcasting something about who they were. A glance, a short stare, or toggling eyeballs paired with a faint smile or pursed lips created an incalculable number of emotional subtleties. Suddenly this world was truly fascinating.

I called Kalijero. "Ten tonight," I said. "At Maxwell and Halsted."

"I'll be over around seven to put on the transmitter, test it out, and go over things."

When Kalijero didn't hang up, I said, "You got something else you want to say? Like everything's going to work out great?"

"Anything can happen. And you have zero experience at this."

"I know what I'm getting into—"

"Hauser sees you as a no-risk freebie. A throwaway. Civilians think they want to play cop and wear a wire. Then the family wants to sue if something bad happens. But if a Landau gets killed, so what? No jury's gonna say a Landau didn't know what he was getting into."

"Jimmy—"

"The only risk is if we screw it up. Then it's my ass."

"What do you mean, your—" Kalijero hung up.

I walked the neighborhood a little longer. I felt tired, like I'd been up all night. It was about ten-thirty when I got back to my recliner. I sat with a notebook and pen, retracing my steps from the morning Dad showed up. I should have been taking daily notes as Frownie had taught me. But viewing the investigation from its endpoint presented a clearer view of the most relevant facts regarding Snooky's murder and Voss's guilt. It would be someone else's job to hack away at all the peripheral rot. My Glock .40 was essential. Being heavily armed with facts was equally vital.

Afternoon melted into evening. A cold front moved through the area, sparking a fast-moving thunderstorm that left behind cooler air and a pleasant easterly breeze off the lake. Kalijero showed up at seven carrying a small cardboard box from which he took a square recording device the size of a Triscuit cracker. He had me take my shirt off, taped the device into the groove of my breastbone, then gave me an earpiece.

"Wait here." Kalijero made a move to leave.

"Where're you going?"

"Where do you think? To my car, so we can test it out."

"You mean there's no one else working with you?"

"Bingo."

Kalijero sat in his car in the loading zone across the street and we practiced using the miracle of digital technology.

"Hey, Jimmy—"

"Don't shout! Just talk normal, like I'm in the room."

"Why does Frownie hate you so much?" Kalijero's mumbling in Greek came through loud and clear. "I'm just curious—"

"Shut up and focus on Voss!"

For the remainder of the test I spoke only when requested. After Kalijero was satisfied, he came back up. "By nine o'clock," Kalijero said taking over my recliner, "I want you in that block strolling around, testing the sound just like we're doing now."

"How much do you need to arrest him?"

Kalijero thought about it longer than I liked. "Confessions with details, showing premeditation, rationalization. You said you can get him talking about how great he is. Prove it."

"When he walks away from me, you nab him."

"No. We can arrest him anytime if we get a recorded confession. But if it gets ugly between you two, I'm coming in. Then you gotta think about getting down, behind some crap. Anything can happen—"

"What do you mean ugly? If he pulls a gun?"

"Remember this morning when I talked about the risk of screwing it up? For example, if I go in before we get the info to bust him, then Voss knows we've been watching him and starts covering his ass. Plus he's got plenty of favors to call in."

"What if I shoot in self-defense?"

"You better make damn sure you can prove it."

Neither of us spoke for a while. Then I said, "I don't want you coming in unless we can put that son of a bitch in prison. I don't care if the microphone blows up. Got it?"

Kalijero got up from the recliner, looked at me, then shook his head in disgust. Before walking to the door he said, "I'm doing this alone because this whole operation is off the record. That's the deal I made with Hauser. If we can't nail Voss with his own words, I'll stay away and just monitor things from afar. But just so you know, if shots are fired, I'm moving in."

* * *

I put on my linen sport jacket, clipped a pen to the breast pocket, and shoved a high-capacity magazine into the Glock. In a side pocket, I put Snooky's notebook. In the other pocket, I dropped a glass vial, a book of matches, and two four-ounce cans of lighter fluid.

At nine o'clock I parked on West Liberty Street. Just a hint of daylight remained in the western sky although the university's new mega-wattage streetlamps created a stark contrast of light and shadow. I walked a block to Halsted then headed south to Maxwell where I noticed that a chain-link fence now completely surrounded the block. A fire-damaged three-flat from the 1880s was the only building left standing. At nine-fifteen I stood in front of the gate near the bandstand and debris pile. The site was not locked. Nobody worried about junk getting stolen. Maybe it was the chaotic pattern of shadow and light, but the pile of rubble where Snooky's body once lay looked taller and pointier than I remembered. About eight feet to

271

the left of the rubble was a steel drum into which I emptied both cans of lighter fluid. Tossing the empty containers aside, I reached up to the top of the heap and put Snooky's journal on a piece of drywall. The neighborhood was quiet. The only activity came from the next block where a hot dog stand served its world famous Polish sausage and bone-in pork chop sandwiches. Kalijero barked through my earpiece, scaring the crap of me.

"Start walking around the block," he said. "Say something every ten feet."

"Where are you?"

"Don't worry. Get walking."

Trusting Kalijero seemed like a good idea, so I walked and whispered until I had circled the block, returning to the gate around nine-forty. Kalijero told me to stay put and shut up.

The time spent waiting for Voss was torture. I didn't know which raced faster, my mind or my heart. At nine-fifty, Kalijero's voice startled me again by announcing Voss's impending arrival. A strange feeling of calm now replaced my anxiety. A minute later I saw Voss's lumbering figure approach. He wore an open raincoat with one hand buried in his pocket, where I assumed he held a gun.

"A neighborhood in transition," Voss said and walked through the gate. He glanced at the debris pile then walked a complete circle around the bandstand before stopping to lean against the side of the stage. "When I was growing up," he said, "we used to call this place Jew Town."

I followed him inside the fence and stood on the opposite side of the debris pile. "Feeling nostalgic?" I asked.

"Whaddya so nervous about?" growled Voss.

"Who's nervous?"

"You're standing over there, keeping that pile of junk between us. And that's bad logistics." Voss sidestepped into the shadowed area next to the stage, then back out. "You're at a disadvantage if you can't see me."

"I get the feeling you were here earlier today, mapping out the place."

"Always plan ahead," said Voss. "But I'm just here to do a little business, that's all."

"So let's get down to business. Who killed Snooky and why?"

"Whoa! Whoa! Whoa! Where's my book?"

"Don't worry, it's around. And it's got everything you want on Kalijero."

"And Mildish, Baron, and Tate."

"Ah! So you were interested in them as well."

Voss smiled. "Hey, it's gravy. A little extra leverage on big shots is always good to have."

"They really don't know anything about Snooky's murder, do they?"

"Naaah. Them bozos don't know shit."

"For a while, I really thought Chancellor Tate was the killer," I said. "Like he panicked about what Snooky might know about him."

"Yeah, sure. That makes sense."

"Does it? He kills a guy then dumps the body outside his own office?"

"Yeah, well, somebody wanted to send a message." Voss chuckled.

"Somebody or you?"

Voss straightened up. "It sure sent a chill through all Snook's clients, no?" Voss laughed again. "C'mon, let's get this over with. Give me the book."

"Who killed Snooky?"

"Give me the book. Then we'll talk."

"You told me Snooky cried like a little bitch—"

"I made that shit up." Voss stepped forward, waving his hands. "I just wanted to get under your skin, that's all." Voss held out the envelope full of cash I had included with the note. "Here's your earnest money back. Take it." He tossed the envelope over the pile.

I said, "I'm new at this, so be patient. I'm supposed to give you the book so you can cover me with your gun and then walk out of here?"

"What gun?" Voss showed both hands. "Look, I'm not the monster you think I am. My beef with Kalijero is personal. And you know what? I don't harbor any bad feelings over you banging my head on that concrete step."

I acted like I was mulling things over, then said, "Oh, what the hell. I guess I should just learn to trust people." I pretended I had the book in my pocket, made a motion as if about to toss something to Voss, then stopped. "On second thought, I'd really like to know who killed Snooky."

Voss calmly walked around the junk pile to face me. Then he took out a semi-automatic pistol and said, "Put your hands behind your head." After I did as told, Voss approached me, grabbed my shirt, yanked it up, then tore the transmitter off my chest. "Hey, Kalijero, can you hear me? Fuck you! You got nothing!" Voss looked at me. "Give me the ear bug or I'll knock it out of your head." I handed it over then watched him stomp on both devices.

"I'm ticklish," I said as Voss started searching me with one hand while holding his gun with the other. First he checked my jacket pockets then started going over my torso. When he reached my gun, he lifted it from the shoulder holster.

"Glock forty, not bad," he said then tucked the gun into the belt of his trousers. I put my arms down. "It really doesn't matter if you have a gun or not, Landau. If I shoot you, it's clearly self-defense." Voss stepped backward into a shadow, shouted, "Bang," then walked forward back into the light. "Where's the book?"

"Tell me about Snooky's murder."

"Show me the book."

"You're just so used to things being easy, right, Voss? You came here thinking you could just get what you wanted and walk away without having to admit you killed Snooky."

"I didn't kill no one. That scumbag you wasted in the alley did the killing."

"But you were there, supervising the murder, to make sure the meth-head left money in Snooky's wallet. That prevented Tate, Mildish, and Baron from thinking it was just a robbery. You wanted them to see Snooky's corpse as a message that someone had just acquired a little accounting leverage. Always planning ahead. Someday, you would turn that leverage into cash or favors." I took Voss's smirk as a grudging acknowledgment.

"Why shouldn't I just waste you and leave?"

"Because you want Snooky's book and all the power it holds. Because if shots are fired, Kalijero and the cavalry come in, guns blazing. You're getting sloppy, Voss."

"It's dark, you lured me here." The brashness in his voice had tempered somewhat.

"Give me the truth, I give you the book, you walk out with your corrupt kingdom intact." I laughed. "I mean, why not? You know I'm not wearing a wire anymore."

Voss adjusted his grip on the gun. "You go to all this trouble just for some goddamn truth? Who cares?"

"I promised my father I'd find out what happened."

"Oh, I get it, it's some kind of Landau-blood-honor thing. Fine. But I'm telling you right now, if I don't leave this shit hole with what I want, I will fuck you up, and it will be self-defense."

"You couldn't go after Snooky directly," I said, "because he had too many friends. Other creeps, connected types like you. Together, they could probably take you out. You knew the kind of money Kalijero was bringing in at O'Hare's Tailspin. You found out he used Snooky's services. You found out about Snooky's friendship with Lisa. You manipulated her into helping you. She's a little wacky, emotionally unstable. You exploit her weakness. You find out she has her own vendetta against Tate. You told her if she could get the names and dates and account numbers, she could bring Tate down and destroy him."

Voss pretended to yawn. "Snooky cleaned Kalijero's cash. That was a no-brainer. But I gave the tattoo broad five hundred bucks anyway to verify Snooky had a Greek cop as a client. She's a smart broad, you know. She tells me about Tate using Snooky. Maybe Tate's not paying his taxes? That's against the law, isn't it? I do a little snooping. Whaddya know? Tate is connected to Mildish and Baron."

"But you still need the book and Lisa can't get it. A shit storm begins when Kalijero starts complaining about you supplying meth to the strip club."

"What? Who said that?" Voss did his best to look outraged.

"Nice try, Voss. I'm supposed to believe dealing meth is against your moral principles?"

Voss started pacing, moving in and out of light. "I ain't worried about steering a little crystal to the club—if that's what you're thinking. You know why? Because it's a hell of a revenue enhancer! We damn near doubled our profits after those dopes got their first taste of whoring around on meth. All that cop brass getting nice, fat envelopes. Fuck it. What do I care? I'm not cooking it, I just push it along."

"But it's not just the club, is it? You couldn't resist using Lisa's junkie clients. They did you favors—like murdering Snooky—and you got them meth. If one of those scumbags got killed, so what? Plenty more to choose from. But you gotta get that book because you're worried about Kalijero. So you send an army of meth-heads to tear Snooky's house apart."

Voss stopped pacing. "Okay, you're a brilliant investigator. Time to hand it over."

"After Snooky died, things changed between you and Lisa. Like you said, she's no dummy. When you realized she knew you had one of her junkie friends kill Snooky, you reminded her of how powerful you were and that a lot of circumstantial evidence stared her in the face."

"That little bitch wanted that book as bad as I did! She didn't give a damn about Snooky. She just wanted to ruin Tate."

"Bullshit! Lisa never would've helped you if she knew Snooky would get killed! But now you've got her scared and you can't get Kalijero out of your mind. You're looking for a little insurance. So you introduce Lisa to the idea of framing Tate as a meth dealer—hoping to throw the scent off your own meth-dealing ass. She gets a junkie or two to call his cell phone, his office, his house. His business card shows up on a dead scumbag."

"I'm getting bored, Landau. But hey, if you want to finish telling me what you know, that's just dandy. Or maybe you're done?"

"You're not bored, you're nervous."

"Why? Because I had some mob-lackey money-laundering piece-of-shit nobody cared about killed?"

"I could never understand people like you. Is it because you've been untouchable for so long you think you're exempt from consequences?"

Voss stepped forward, snarled, "I am the consequence!" then retreated.

"You were wrong. Somebody did give a damn about Snooky. But this meth thing. You know when you cross a line? And you make people nervous? Sometimes they get all federal on you. Wire-tappy kind of federal."

"I know, dumbass. I'm insulated from all that."

I took the glass vial from my pocket and held it up. "This is one of several vials I found at a dead junkie's flophouse. If you look close, there's a beautiful thumbprint encrusted in a milky white residue that smells like cat pee. You know, I bet this thumbprint just might belong to someone already in the database who knows what happens to repeat drug traffickers if they refuse to cut a deal—like giving up their suppliers."

"You're definitely the dumbest Landau who ever cursed this city. I told you I'm insulated. I just give orders once it comes in, direct it places to be stored—"

"All right, all right," I said. "The book is lying on top of the crap pile."

Voss walked up to me and pointed his gun at my forehead. "Just remember, Landau. Try anything and it's self-defense against the Snooky avenger."

"What can I try? You took my gun."

"Shut up and get the book."

Voss backed up a few steps. As I reached up to the top of the debris pile and grabbed the journal off the chunk of drywall with my right hand, I found the matches with my left. I held the book up. "Okay, now what?"

"Throw it to me."

I had an unobstructed path to the steel drum. The junk pile lay between Voss and the drum. If I dove behind the pile, Voss would have a small window to get a clear shot at me before I could get behind the drum. Loaded with rubbish, I figured it weighed at least fifty pounds. I slipped a finger behind one of the matches, bent it forward, and held the match head against the striking surface.

"Just in case you're wondering," Voss said while removing my .40-caliber from his belt before presenting a posture with double-fisted guns. "I'll fire your gun into the ground then shoot you with mine." Voss laughed. "You shot first, I returned fire. That's what Kalijero's report will say."

"Okay, Voss," I said. "Take the damn book and fuck off."

I held up the book, cocked my arm back, then followed through with a throwing motion before diving to my left, executing a tuck-and-roll, journal and matchbook still in hand. As I scrambled on my belly, a shot rang out. Just as I got behind the drum, a second shot cracked, followed by a flash, then intense pain from the igniting matches burning my hand. I screamed but endured the pain long enough to drop the flame into the steel drum, setting its contents ablaze with a whoosh.

Kalijero rushed in, shouting for everyone to drop their weapons. Voss tossed my .40-caliber within a few feet of me. I imagined Kalijero just inside the gate on one knee, pointing his gun at Voss's profile.

"I'm behind the steel drum," I shouted. "I'm unarmed."

"Kalijero!" Voss shouted. "Landau tried to kill me. Arrest him!"

Peering around the drum, I saw Voss standing his ground, ready to fire at whatever part of me was exposed or, perhaps, thinking about approaching me for a kill shot.

"Drop your weapon, Voss!" Kalijero shouted. "Then we'll talk about it."

"Goddamn it, Kalijero! Cuff that little shit and bring him to me."

"Voss! Put your gun away and relax. What the hell is wrong with you?"

"You put a wire on Landau, you piece of shit! I'm supposed to trust you?"

"Hey, that was Hauser's call. You know you got enemies, so what? You won this round, they got nothing."

Voss stood in place, cursing and making noises as if in pain. I thought any moment he would begin stomping his feet or throw himself on the ground kicking his legs. Finally he said, "You're damn right you got nothing—you piece of shit!"

"Walk away," Kalijero said. "Live to fight another day."

"No. You're going to arrest this prick for trying to kill me or you can watch me shoot him in self-defense. Or should I make a few calls to the brass enjoying their extra income from that little business you started? Those fat envelopes are a tough habit to kick."

"Hey, Voss, you still want your book?" I held the journal up near the flames at the top of the drum.

"Stay put, Voss," Kalijero said. "I swear to God I'll shoot. Landau is an unarmed civilian."

"Go ahead and arrest me, Jimmy," I shouted.

"You heard him, Kalijero. What're you waiting for?"

"It's okay, Jimmy. I mean it's better than getting shot and it's better than you losing your pension. But first there's something I want to show you." I reached into the breast pocket of my sport coat, took out a pen, then held it up. "See this, Voss? It's a damn good pen but it's also a damn good voice recorder." I unscrewed the pen and held up the top half. "See that? I can plug that sucker into a USB port and download everything that was said from the moment you walked in here. Isn't that cool?"

His outrage was palpable. I thought the streetlights momentarily dimmed as Voss's body shook, trembled, and twitched like he had a convulsive disease.

Voss's face now resembled a central processing unit trying to calculate a realization that didn't involve going to prison or getting shot or both. As was often the case with aging, unscrupulous cops, they got fat, careless, and complacent. In addition, Voss committed the sin of ignoring technological advances. I imagined his grimmest calculation included an understanding that many who had supported his corrupt lifestyle would now gladly facilitate his downfall to save their own asses. Perhaps that was the computation processed just before I saw Voss lift his gun hand and take a step toward me. I dropped the journal into the fire and ducked behind the drum. Three shots were fired and I was aware of feeling no pain resembling a bullet strike. Looking up, I saw Kalijero standing in firing position. Voss lay on the ground, dead I hoped, although his groaning quickly told me otherwise.

"Landau, you hit?" Kalijero said. Apparently, I had not been aware of my own groaning.

"No, it's just my sore ribs and burned hand," I said, getting to my feet. Kalijero called for medical then we both walked over to Voss. He lay on his left side in obvious pain, having been shot in the right hip. I examined his upper body but saw no wound. I looked at Kalijero. "You missed? From ten feet?"

Still staring at Voss, he said, "I only fired once."

"What? You let that bastard shoot at me twice?"

Kalijero looked at me. "He squeezed off another shot as he fell! He might as well have shot at the moon! And stop complaining. You're welcome, you ungrateful prick."

"I'm ungrateful? You just saw all your problems go up in flames with Snooky's book. You should be on your knees licking the mud off my shoes."

Kalijero looked at the steel drum then back to me. I assumed a variety of sentiments ran through his brain, relief being the dominant emotion.

Although I didn't really expect Kalijero to offer me an open display of gratitude, I got the feeling his sudden loss for words said a lot.

60

Kalijero allowed me to observe the department's technology specialist download the audio file. Voss's raspy, high-pitched voice came across to everyone's satisfaction. Even Hauser cracked a smile. Along with state and federal charges of distribution and trafficking of methamphetamine, state prosecutors included a first-degree murder charge. Contrary to their reputation of invoking a code of silence, the police quickly furnished all essential documents and in-house records related to Voss's conduct in the Internal Affairs Division, including recently discovered complaints filed by both officers and citizens. When the investigation moved beyond meth into the day-to-day operations of O'Hare's Tailspin, nonexistent evidence of money trails persuaded prosecutors to delay filing charges against other police personnel rumored to be involved in prostitution, pimping, and pandering—although the early retirements of the deputy chief and superintendent of police did not go unnoticed.

Witnesses at Officer Voss's highly publicized trial included meth addicts, strippers, prostitutes, aldermen, state legislators, and Lisa Audrey Moreau—wearing a navy blazer over a white blouse, knee-length khaki skirt, and tan oxford shoes. To the delight of reporters and the dismay of the judge, Lisa employed powerful dramatization recalling her experiences with Voss, deftly intertwining her personal life with testimony regarding Voss's obsession with acquiring Snooky's accounting journal. Lisa also acknowledged what she called her "casual participation" with Voss's attempt to frame Tate as a meth dealer by supplying Voss with her ex-stepfather's business cards and having some of her meth-addicted clients call Tate's phone. Lisa demonstrated her storytelling abilities, skillfully describing her fear of Voss while adeptly illustrating her resentment of Tate as the man who cast her out of the house for being a troubled child and the man who was a rotten husband to her mother. Under questioning on the stand, Lisa also reluctantly cleared her stepfather of suggestions he behaved inappropriately with children, stating she had started the rumor purely in an attempt to ruin Tate's reputation. She tearfully admitted she had used her half-sister, Audrey Prenevost, to spread the scurrilous charge, instilling false memories into her consciousness.

Although Voss spent three months immobilized in a cast, he could be thankful for Kalijero's bullet missing any main arteries and for the Illinois governor's moratorium on the death penalty. While Lisa became a public curiosity, Voss received a life sentence.

* * *

I visited Frownie shortly after Voss's arrest. When I reminded him that I had purposely left him out of the loop, he reminded me that he was determined to die before I did. I pretended not to notice his voice choking up or the tear he blinked away. He was really asking that I give up investigating murders. Once again I left his house saying only that I couldn't be sure where my career was headed. I think he understood.

My father, too, had been kept in the dark of the final showdown. I assumed Frownie told him all the details though because when I called him he at first acted somewhat indifferent, as if I was telling him about a plot to a movie I had just seen. It didn't take long before Dad struggled to finish sentences as emotion cracked his stoic façade and plunged him into a passionate lecture on why I needed to find another profession, or at least give up murder investigations. I made no promises, and didn't remind him that he had started up this business by hiring me.

After I changed the subject to Dad's health, the conversation reverted back to the father I had been more accustomed to, one that insisted his prostate cancer was nothing more than a nuisance, that he felt fine despite how crappy he looked, and that I should stop worrying about him and think about getting some money in the bank. Later that day we met for lunch at a joint that served his favorite Vienna hot dogs and had recently introduced a veggie burger. I asked Dad about some of the old Tribune articles describing Great-Granddad's exploits, then listened to him reminisce about how smart Great-Granddad was and how well Great-Granddad worked the system. Somehow, the nostalgia took on a broader scope with Dad reminding me that movies only cost a dime in those days, and that for a nickel you could get an extra helping of chocolate sauce on your ice cream. Before saying goodbye, I suggested we have lunch again next week and Dad agreed.

* * *

"This does not look like the birthplace of Chicago Blues," may have been the last thought of accountant Charles "Snooky" Snook before someone fired two bullets into his head and dumped his body on a pile of debris at the intersection of Maxwell and Halsted. Why Maxwell Street had been chosen as the location where the successful CPA and "hoodlum's bookkeeper" would meet his violent end, would not become immediately clear . . ."

Ellis Knight had his story. The Partisan ran a special edition devoted to a tale of murder, politics, and big-city corruption told through the eyes of the characters who played out the drama. The article was a sensation, the subject of radio talk shows, and briefly the attention of the national media. Knight's follow-up article, detailing Lisa Moreau's journey through the criminal justice system received only moderate attention. With the help of a sympathetic public and pressure from unnamed politicians, she was handed a suspended sentence and three years' probation.

A third article by Knight chronicling the lack of prosecution of any politician, administrator, or construction magnate—went largely unnoticed.

61

Gazing at Lake Michigan, Susie and I sat on the steps of the stone amphitheater at Diversey Harbor, eating pita pocket sandwiches.

"You barely winced," Susie said.

"What do you mean?"

"When you sat down. Hasn't it been about three months since you hurt your ribs?"

She was right. It had also been three months since she suggested I contemplate whether I wanted her to know me better. We had spoken often during those three months, mostly about the trial, but we hadn't met on a date—until that afternoon.

I said, "You haven't asked why it took so long for me to ask you out."

Susie took a bite of her sandwich and chewed awhile on my statement before saying, "I could've asked you out, too."

I thought she was kidding, but as she continued chewing and keeping her gaze over the lake, I remembered we lived in the twenty-first century. "Well," I said, "how long did you expect me to wait for your call?"

Susie gave me a wry look and we both laughed. "Seriously, Jules, I'm not some naïve waif who assumed an impromptu kiss the night before you left for L.A. meant our relationship was destined to be something more than friendship."

"Impromptu? How do you know I hadn't spent all day planning out a strategy for that kiss?" We both laughed again, this time louder.

We ate in silence awhile, then I said, "You really helped me, yet you've asked very few questions—about the investigation." Susie nodded but said nothing. "No longer curious?"

"Well, maybe you'll tell me one day, if you want," she said. "But for now, why don't we keep it simple and just focus on getting to know each other? Start with your people. Tell me where you came from."

I wasn't sure if I had ever received such a request. Susie wasn't asking what I wanted from life or what I hoped to be one day, but where I came from. So I started telling the story of the Landaus. She listened, asked questions. A bunch of times, we laughed our heads off. The hour passed quickly, then she had to get back to her shop. We said goodbye. Only later that evening, while Punim and I relaxed on the recliner, did I realize how wonderfully comfortable it had felt just sitting on those concrete steps, talking to Susie, letting her get to know me.

###

Like his character Jules Landau, Marc Krulewitch, the author of *Maxwell Street Blues, Windy City Blues, Gold Coast Blues,* and *Doubt in the 2nd Degree,* is descended from an infamous Chicagoan. He grew up in Highland Park, Illinois, and now lives with his wife in Colorado.

Thank you for reading my book. If you enjoyed it, won't you please take a moment to leave me a review at your favorite retailer?